The Two Hotel Francforts

The Two Hotel

Francforts

A Novel

DAVID LEAVITT

B L O O M S B U R Y

New York · London · New Delhi · Sydney

Lyrics from "World Weary" copyright © NC Aventales AG 1928
by permission of Alan Brodie Representation Ltd
www.alanbrodie.com

Published by Bloomsbury USA, New York

All papers used by Bloomsbury USA are natural, recyclable products made
from wood grown in well-managed forests. The manufacturing processes
conform to the environmental regulations of the country of origin.

LIBRARY OF CONGRESS CATALOGING-IN-PUBLICATION DATA

Leavitt, David, 1961–
The two Hotel Francforts : a novel / David Leavitt. — First U.S. edition.
pages cm
ISBN 978-1-59691-042-3 (hc : alk. paper)
1. Man-woman relationships—Fiction. 2. Marital conflict—Fiction.
3. Life change events—Fiction. 4. Portugal—Fiction.
I. Title.
PS3562.E2618T86 2013
813'.54—dc23
2013015952

First U.S. Edition 2013

1 3 5 7 9 10 8 6 4 2

Typeset by Westchester Book Group
Printed and bound in the U.S.A. by Thomson-Shore Inc., Dexter, Michigan

In memory of my father, Harold Leavitt

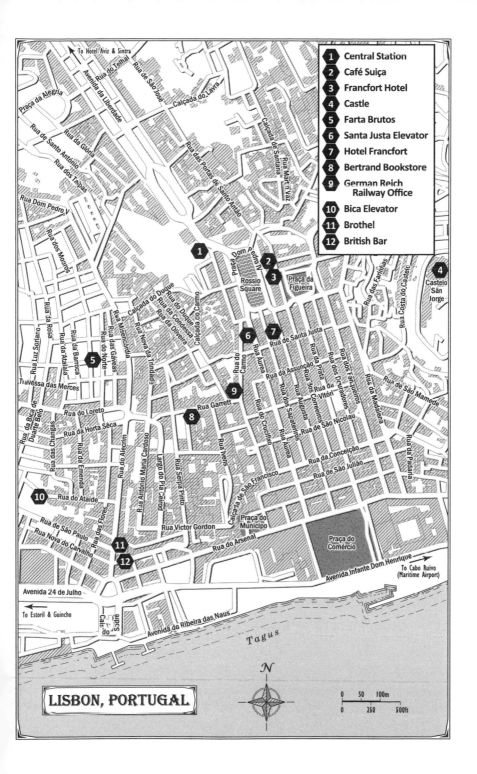

LISBON, PORTUGAL

1	Central Station
2	Café Suiça
3	Francfort Hotel
4	Castle
5	Farta Brutos
6	Santa Justa Elevator
7	Hotel Francfort
8	Bertrand Bookstore
9	German Reich Railway Office
10	Bica Elevator
11	Brothel
12	British Bar

To Hotel Aviz & Sintra

Rua do Telhal
Rua de São José
Calçada do Lavra
Avenida da Liberdade
Praça da Alegria
Rua da Glória
Rua de Santo António
Rua do Santo António
Rua dos Fabas
Rua Dom Pedro V
Rua dos Mouros
Rua da Rosa
Rua Luz Soriano
Rua da Barroca
Rua da Atalaia
Travessa das Merces
Rua da Bica de Duarte Belo
Rua do Loreto
Rua das Chagas
Rua da Horta Sêca
Rua da Emenda
Rua de São Paulo
Rua Nova do Carvalho
Avenida 24 de Julho
To Estoril & Guincho
Cais do Sodré

Calçada de Santana
Rua Marti Vaz
Rua das Portas de Santo Antão
Calçada do Duque
Rua do Duque
Rua da Condessa
Rua Nova da Trindade
Rua das Gáveas
Rua do Norte
Rua Misericórdia
Calçada do Carmo
Calçada do Carmo
Rua do Carmo
Rua Garrett
Rua do Alecrim
Rua António Maria Cardoso
Rua das Flores
Largo do Picadeiro
Rua Serpa Pinto
Rua Ivens
Rua Victor Gordon
Praça do Município
Rua do Arsenal
Calçada de São Francisco

Praça Dom Pedro IV
Rossio Square
Praça da Figueira
Rua das Fanilhas
Rua Costa do Castelo
Castelo São Jorge
Rua de Santa Justa
Rua Aurea
Rua da Assunção
Rua da Prata
Rua dos Correeiros
Rua dos Douradores
Rua dos Fanqueiros
Rua da Vitóri
Rua Augusta
Rua dos Sapateiros
Rua de São Nicolau
Rua Aurea
Rua do Crucifixo
Rua da Conceição
Rua de São Julião
Praça do Comércio
Avenida Infante Dom Henrique
To Cabo Ruivo (Maritime Airport)
Rua de São Mamede
Rua da Madalena
Rua da Padaria

Avenida da Ribeira das Naus
Tagus

N

0 50 100m
0 250 500ft

Anywhere

1

We met the Frelengs in Lisbon, at the Café Suiça. This was in June 1940, when we were all in Lisbon waiting for the ship that was coming to rescue us and take us to New York. By us I mean, of course, us Americans, expatriates of long standing mostly, for whom the prospect of returning home was a bitter one. Now it seems churlish to speak of our plight, which was as nothing compared with that of the real refugees—the Europeans, the Jews, the European Jews. Yet at the time we were too worried about what we were losing to care about those who were losing more.

Julia and I had been in Lisbon almost a week. I am from Indianapolis; she grew up on Central Park West but had dreamed, all through her youth, of a flat in Paris. Well, I made that dream come true for her—to a degree. That is to say, we had the flat. We had the furniture. Yet she was never satisfied, my Julia. I always supposed I was the piece that didn't fit.

In any case, that summer, Hitler's invasion of France had

compelled us to abandon our Paris establishment and fly headlong to Lisbon, there to await the SS *Manhattan*, which the State Department had commandeered and dispatched to retrieve stranded Americans. At the time, only four steamships—the *Excalibur*, the *Excambion*, the *Exeter*, and the *Exochorda*—were making the regular crossing to New York. They were so named, it was joked, because they carried *ex*-Europeans into *ex*ile. Each had a capacity of something like 125 passengers, as opposed to the *Manhattan*'s 1,200, and, like the Clipper flights that took off each week from the Tagus, you couldn't get a booking on one for love or money unless you were a diplomat or a VIP.

And so we had about a week to kill in Lisbon until the *Manhattan* arrived, which was fine by me, since we had had quite a time of it up until then, dodging shellfire and mortar fire all the way across France, then running the gantlet of the Spanish border crossing and contending with the Spanish customs agents, who in their interrogation tactics were determined to prove themselves more Nazi than the Nazis. And Lisbon was a city at peace, which meant that everything that was scarce in France and Spain was plentiful there: meat, cigarettes, gin. The only trouble was overcrowding. Hotel rooms were nearly impossible to come by. People were staying up all night at the casino in Estoril, gambling, and sleeping all day on the beach. Yet we were lucky—we had a room, and a comfortable one at that. Yes, it was all right with me.

Not with Julia, though. She loathed Portugal. She loathed the shouting of the fishwives and the smell of the salted cod. She loathed the children who chased her with lottery tickets. She loathed the rich refugees who had rooms at better hotels than ours and the poor refugees who had no rooms at all and the mysterious woman on our floor who spent most of every day leaning out her door into the dark corridor, smoking—"like Messalina waiting for Silius," Julia said. But what she loathed most—what she loathed more than any of these things—was the prospect of going home.

Oh, how she didn't want to go home! It had been this way since the beginning of the war. First she had tried to convince me to stay in Paris; then, when the bombs started dropping on Paris, to resettle in the South of France; then, when Mussolini started making noises about invading the South of France, to sail to England, which the Neutrality Act forbade us from doing (for which she would not forgive Roosevelt). And now she wanted to stay on in Portugal. Portugal! I should mention—I *can* mention, since Julia is dead now and cannot stop me—that my wife was Jewish, a fact she preferred to keep under wraps. And it is true, in Portugal there was no anti-Semitism to speak of, quite simply because there were no Jews. The Inquisition had taken care of that little problem. And so she had decided that this country in which she was so disinclined to spend a few weeks would be a perfectly agreeable place to sit out the rest of the war. For she had sworn, when we had settled in Paris fifteen years before, that she would never go home again as long as she lived. Well, she never did.

So that was how we came to be at the Suiça that morning—the Suiça, the café that, of all the cafés in Lisbon, we foreigners had chosen to colonize. We were sitting outdoors, having breakfast and watching the traffic go round the oval of the Rossio, and it was this notion of settling in Portugal that Julia was going on about, as I drank my coffee and ate a second of those delicious little flan-filled tartlets in which the Suiça specializes, and she laid out a hand of solitaire, which she played incessantly, using a special set of miniature cards. *Slap-slap* went the cards; *natter-natter* went her voice, as for the hundredth time she related her mad scheme to rent an apartment or a villa in Estoril; and as I explained to her, for the hundredth time, that it was no good, because at any moment Hitler might forge an alliance with Franco, in which case Portugal would be swallowed up by the Axis. And how funny to think that when all was said and done, she was right and I was wrong! For we would have been perfectly safe in Portugal. Well, it is too late for her to lord that over me now.

It was then that the pigeons swooped—so many of them, flying so low, that I had to duck. In ducking, I knocked her cards off the table. "It's all right, I'll get them," I said to Julia, and was bending to do so when my glasses fell off my face. A passing waiter, in his effort to keep his trayful of coffee cups from spilling, kicked the glasses down the pavement, right into Edward Freleng's path. It was he who stepped on them.

"Oh, damn," he said, picking up what was left of the frames. "Whose are these?"

"They're mine," I said, from the ground, where I was still trying to collect the cards: no mean feat, since a breeze had just come up—or perhaps the pigeons had churned it up—and scattered them the length of the sidewalk.

"Let me help you with that," Edward said, and got down on his knees next to me.

"Thanks," I said. Seeing that the task was more than we could manage, several of the male patrons at the café, as well as several of the waiters, got down on their knees with us. Like commandos, we scrambled to gather up the cards, chasing down the ones that the breeze had batted out of reach, while Julia watched with a sort of paralyzed detachment. Of course, I understood—perhaps I alone understood—how much was at stake. For if four or five of the cards went missing, it would be unfortunate. But if just one went missing, it would be a catastrophe.

And miraculously, all of the cards were found—at which all of the men who had participated in the operation burst into spontaneous applause.

"Thanks," I said to Edward—again.

"Why are you thanking me?" he said. "I'm the one who stepped on your glasses."

"It wasn't your fault."

"No, it was the pigeons," Iris Freleng said, from two tables away.

"Some fool must have tried to feed them," Edward said. "They're ruthless, these birds. Piranhas of the air, the locals call them."

"Do they?"

"They might as well. The word's Portuguese."

"Are they damaged?" Iris asked.

"Not much," Julia said. "A few of the corners are bent."

"I meant your husband's glasses. Even so, I'm glad to hear it. I've never seen cards that small."

"They're special solitaire cards," I said. "My wife is something of a connoisseur where solitaire is concerned."

"I am not a connoisseur," Julia said.

"The versions she plays require two decks, which is why the cards have to be so small. Otherwise you'd need a dining table to spread them out on."

"How interesting," Iris said. "Myself, I've never gone in for cards."

"I am *not* a connoisseur," Julia repeated, fitting the cards back into their box, on the alligator-skin surface of which the word PATIENCE was picked out in gold.

"Of course, we'll pay to have them replaced," Edward said. "The glasses."

"It's all right," I said. "I have a spare pair at the hotel."

"That's lucky," he said. "I mean, that you have a hotel."

Then Iris suggested we join them at their table. After all the trouble Edward had caused, she said, the least they could do was buy us coffee.

"Or a drink," Edward added.

I looked at Julia. Her expression was blank. "Very kind of you," I said. But when I got up to make the short journey between the tables, I tripped.

"Steady on," Edward said, catching me by the arm.

We all sat down together. We exchanged names. We looked one another over. From what I could tell, the Frelengs were roughly our age—the early forties. Iris wore her hair in a snood. She had a British accent, while Edward had the sort of uninflected American accent to which no regional identifiers attach themselves. His voice was soft and hard at once, like the noise of car tires on wet gravel.

They asked us where we were coming from and we told them Paris. And they?

"Oh, we've lived all over the place," Iris said. "Nice, Bordighera, Biarritz. Then a few years ago we took a cottage in Pyla. That's a little fishing village, just outside Arcachon."

"Being so close to the Spanish border, we figured we could wait until the last minute to leave," Edward said. "But when the last minute came, we only had five hours to pack and get out."

"On top of which," Iris said, "my passport—wouldn't you know it?—was due to expire that day. That very day! The one that had my American visa in it. And so when we got to Bordeaux, first we had to go to the British consulate for the new passport, and then to the American consulate for the new visa, and all that before the Spanish consulate and the Portuguese consulate."

"We were in Bordeaux, too," Julia said. "At the Splendide, the manager was renting the armchairs in the lobby by the half hour."

"The Red Cross shelter wouldn't accept dogs."

Suddenly Julia screamed and leaped to her feet.

"What's wrong?" I asked, leaping up too.

"Something's licking my leg."

"Don't worry, it's only Daisy," Iris said, and hoisted a wire fox terrier up from under the table. "You love the taste of moisturizing cream, don't you, Daisy?"

"It scared me half to death," Julia said. "Does it bite?"

"She's fifteen," Edward said. "Her biting days are past, I think."

A delayed consciousness that she had just made a spectacle of herself stole over Julia, who sat down again hurriedly.

"You must excuse my wife," I said. "She's not used to dogs."

"You mean you didn't have dogs growing up?" Iris said.

"We had a poodle, but it was more my brother's."

"The remarkable thing about dogs," Edward said, "is that when you get them they're babies, and then before you know it they're the same age as you are, and then they're old. It's like watching your children grow up to become your grandparents."

"Daisy was a beauty in her time," Iris said. "She could have been a champion if she hadn't had a gay tail."

"What's a gay tail?" I asked.

"It means that the tail curves too much," Edward said.

"Poor thing." Iris arranged the dog in a sitting position on her lap. "You thought you were going to spend your dotage in a cottage by the sea, didn't you? Well, so did we."

Tears filled Iris's eyes.

"Now it's my turn to excuse *my* wife," Edward said. "This whole business has been harder on her than she likes to let on. Not that it hasn't been hard on everyone. You, for instance—"

"Us?" I said. "Oh, we've been lucky."

"And just how is that, pray tell?" Julia said.

"Well, we've made it this far without getting killed, haven't we? A ship's coming to rescue us. And when you think what some of these poor devils wouldn't give to have a ticket on that ship—"

"I'm sorry, but I don't see why their having to leave their homes is any worse than our having to leave our homes," Julia said.

"Oh, but it is," Iris said. "Because we've got somewhere to flee *to*, haven't we? Whereas all they have to look forward to is exile—that is, if they find a country willing to accept them."

"But it's exile for us, too," Julia said. "France was our home, too."

"All we are is interlopers," Iris said. "Tourists who stayed on for a few years or a few decades."

"That's a bit harsh, isn't it?" Edward said. "Why, that old lady we met the other day, Mrs. Thorpe—she's lived in Cannes fifty years. She doesn't have any people in the States, no money, nowhere to go."

"At least it's better than a concentration camp," Iris said—at which Julia started a little. "No, the truth is, Daisy's the only real European here. Why, do you know what people keep coming up to ask me? If she's a schnauzer! Imagine that, mistaking you for a Hun dog!"

"Though of English stock, Daisy was born in Toulouse," Edward said. "The product of a morganatic marriage between a British champion and a French peasant girl."

"Champion Harrowhill Hunters Moon," Iris said.

Daisy had now put her front paws up on the table. Very delicately, she pulled a roll off a plate and nibbled at it. "That reminds me," Iris said. "We've got that appointment with the vet at eleven. It's nothing serious," she added, to Julia, who was sitting as far back in her chair as possible, "only her feces haven't been terribly solid and I'm thinking she might have worms. There's a certain kind that look like grains of rice. Then again, she's been eating rice."

Julia went very pale.

"But, darling," Edward said, "don't you think we ought to first help Mr. Winters back to his hotel, so he can fetch his spare glasses?"

"Oh, of course," Iris said. "How rude of me."

"Please don't worry," I said. "I'll be fine."

"Nonsense," Julia said. "You're blind as a bat without your glasses."

"Where are you staying?" Edward said.

"The Francfort," Julia and I said in unison.

"But how funny," Iris said. "So are we."

"You must be at the other one," Edward said. "Otherwise we would have seen you."

"The other one?"

"There are two—the Hotel Francfort, which is over by the Elevator, and the Francfort Hotel, which is right here, next to the café."

"We're at the one by the Elevator," I said.

"That's the nicer one. You know, it's become a running joke among the foreigners. 'Just think, here we are fleeing the Germans, and we end up at a hotel called Francfort.' "

Iris looked at her watch. "Tell you what, Eddie," she said, "why don't *you* walk Mr. Winters back to his hotel—"

"The blind leading the blind, right?"

"—and perhaps Mrs. Winters can come with me to the vet?"

"Me?"

"You don't mind, do you? I'd so appreciate it. If nothing else, the company. If I'm to be honest, I'm sick to death of spending all my time with Eddie. No offense, darling."

"None taken."

"But I'm terrible with dogs," Julia said. She looked to me for rescue.

"Sounds like a good idea to me," I said.

"I'll get the check," Edward said.

"How could you?" Julia mouthed at me. But I pretended not to see. I was blind as a bat, wasn't I?

2

We put Iris, Julia, and Daisy into a taxi. Julia got in first. Then Iris handed her the dog. Until that moment, I hadn't noticed how tall Iris was, especially compared with Julia, who was only five foot one. Just to fit into the taxi, Iris had to fold herself up like a penknife.

Holding out his arm to stop traffic, Edward led me across the street. I was almost giddy with relief and gratitude—to him, and also to Iris, who had just done me the great favor of taking Julia off my hands for a while. For the past weeks had been arduous, and Julia—well, the kindest thing to say would be that she had done little to make them less so. Just getting her to eat was an effort. At home she never ate much, and now she was eating virtually nothing. Nor did she care for our room at the Francfort, though it was paradise compared with some of the places we had slept during our trip: squalid hotels, barns, one night on the floor of a rural French post office, several nights in the car. I don't want to suggest that Julia was incapable of coping with adversity. On the contrary, I have no doubt but that, had the journey been one she was keen to be making, she would have gladly put up with all manner of discomfort. But the journey was not one she was keen to be making, and so each bed, each dinner, each toilet was an ordeal.

"Do you think they'll have lunch?" I asked Edward. "Our wives, I mean?" I was hoping that Iris might succeed where I had failed, get Julia to eat a square meal for once and, in so doing, buy me a few more hours of freedom.

"I can't see why not," Edward said. He took my arm, as if I really was a blind man. "Now, I don't know how familiar you are with the city—"

"Not very."

"Then I'll play tour guide for a bit. The neighborhood we're in is Baixa. The neighborhood in the hills ahead of us is the Bairro Alto. The neighborhood in the hills behind us is the Alfama. That's where the castle is. White peacocks roam the grounds. Now we're crossing the Rossio. The Rossio isn't its official name, of course. Its official name is Praça Dom something-or-other. That big statue way up there on the pedestal, that's Dom something-or-other himself. Oh, and here's an interesting bit of local color. Can you make out the paving stones? They're laid in a pattern of waves. The effect is supposed to be nautical, suggesting Portugal's dominion over the seas. Well, in the last century, when the English expats colonized Lisbon, they called the Rossio 'Rolling Motion Square,' because when they crossed it after a night of drinking they got seasick. Careful!"

I had nearly fallen; would have fallen if he hadn't caught me.

"You seem to know the city so well," I said. "Have you been here before?"

"My first time. I got in seventy-two hours ago. Which makes me an old Lisbon hand."

"An older hand than I am after a week." Again I tripped, landing against his side.

"You can't see anything, can you?"

"Oh, I can see the outlines of things. Colors, shapes. Over there's a big yellow worm. And next to it's a bouncing ball. And tops spinning."

"The worm is a tram. The ball is a dog. The tops are children." He tightened his grip on my arm. "Now that I think about it, I wonder if it wouldn't be in my best interest to make sure you *don't* get your other glasses."

"Why's that?"

"Because without them, you're my prisoner. You're completely in my power."

He punched me lightly on the biceps. I laughed. I couldn't help it.

"What's so funny?"

"I don't know . . . I suppose it's just how strange the world looks."

"And how does it look?"

"As if a wind's blowing everything. Even the solid things. The writing on the signs—it's like skywriting that's starting to break apart."

"And me? How do I look?"

"Oh, you I can see just fine. I'm nearsighted, not farsighted."

"Yes, but how?"

Suddenly he stopped me in my tracks. He took me by the chin and turned me to face him. Close up, his features came into a focus that was all the sharper for the vagueness of the background. A zigzag scar ran the length of his chin. The nose flared, the small green eyes blinked once . . . twice . . .

"You look," I said, "—well, fine."

Apparently this answer was more droll than I had intended, for he laughed and patted me on the back. We resumed our walk. "A curious word, 'nearsighted,' " he said. "I mean, to say someone's nearsighted—isn't it like saying of an armless man that he has two legs? Or to call someone who doesn't eat fish a meat eater? Why, if we talked that way all the time, how would we ever say anything to each other, any of us? But we *do* talk that way all the time."

I had no idea how to reply to this—which, I suppose, was illustrative of his point—so I said nothing. We had now reached the opposite side of the Rossio, the one on which the swankier cafés— the Brasiliera, the Chave d'Ouro, the Nicola—were situated. Edward still had his hand on my arm. He was not so much leading me as pulling me, the way one might a dog on a leash. Not that I minded. Indeed, it was a pleasure, after so many weeks shouldering the burden of Julia, to be able to lean on someone else's shoulder. And Edward's shoulder was—how to put it?—reliable. In part this was because he was tall. I am five foot eight—seven inches taller than my wife, but seven inches shorter than Edward, whose stature was particularly noteworthy in Portugal, where few of the men exceed five-five or five-six. Yet there was more to it than just that. He had the quality that certain dogs do, of seeming always to have a destination in mind, even when they don't.

He asked me what I did for a living and I told him. (I worked for General Motors then. I managed the Buick sales division in France—or did, until the Germans came.)

"So you're gainfully employed," he said. "That's refreshing. I can't remember the last time I met someone who was gainfully employed, other than waiters and hotel managers. Needless to say, I'm not gainfully employed."

"No?"

He shook his head. "I've never had a job in my life. Wait, that's not true. The summer I turned sixteen, I worked in a shop. I sold yerba del sol tea, homemade preserves, and books on occultism. I never got paid, though. They still owe me seven dollars."

"Where was this?"

"In California, in the Theosophist community where my mother lives. Or perhaps I should say the Theosophy community that lives on my mother."

I didn't know what Theosophy was. "And where will you go once you're back in the States?"

"Oh, New York. I mean, where else is there?"

"Are you from New York?"

"I've lived in New York. I'm not really from anywhere. My father was Hungarian, but by the time I was born, he'd long since left Hungary. As for my mother—well, technically she's Polish, though she grew up in England. Which meant that they could only ever communicate in second languages. And given that my mother speaks excellent English but not very good French, and that my father spoke excellent French but not very good English—well, is it any wonder that until I was five I didn't utter a word?"

"But your English is perfect."

"That was luck. I had a great-aunt who lived in New York. She took me under her wing. Thanks to her, I got an education."

"Where?"

"Harvard, then Heidelberg—briefly—then Cambridge for the Ph.D.—the one I never finished. That was where I met Iris—at Cambridge. What about you?"

"Oh, just a little college in Indiana. Wabash College. You've probably never heard of it."

"I have, actually. I just can't put my finger on where."

We were now approaching the Francfort—our Francfort. I'm told the hotel closed a few years ago. It was on Rua Santa Justa, at the foot of the famous Santa Justa Elevator, from the turreted roof of which you could get a splendid view of the city, the docks, the distant hills in the shadows of which, on clear nights, Estoril and Sintra glinted. The Francfort had a revolving door. I have always loved revolving doors, the mirror and whirl of them, how, when you pass through one, for a brief moment you're sealed in, coffined, a hostage in a wedge of glass . . . And now I was in one compartment of the revolving door and Edward was in the one behind it, pressing me forward at such a speed that I tumbled out the other side as if I were drunk . . . About the lobby's tiled floor, islets of furniture were dispersed, each with its own reef of rug. The curtains were drawn against the sun. In the artificial gloom, women's earrings winked like coins; the pinpoint gleam of cigarettes might have been torchlight.

"Look at this!" Edward said. "A proper hotel lobby! Our Francfort doesn't have a lobby, only a mean little reception. Oh, and you've got a winter garden, too."

"Not much use in the summer, a winter garden," I said, as if it were something to be ashamed of. "Well, thanks for getting me back in one piece. I think I can manage from here."

"Nonsense, I'm not having you break your neck going down a dark corridor. Wait a second."

Then he strode off to the front desk, where for about five minutes he chatted with Senhor Costa, the hotel manager, in a French too idiomatic and swift for me to follow. For though I had lived in France for fifteen years, working for an American company as I did, I had never really mastered the language. Neither had Julia. This was for both of us a source of embarrassment.

When he returned, he held the key to our room. "Sorry about that. I was just asking him to take my name in case a room happened to open up . . . Oh, a lift! What we wouldn't give for a lift, especially now that we're on the top floor."

"Yes, but it's a very old lift," I said as we stepped inside. "It breaks down all the time."

"*Shh.*" Edward touched a finger to his lips. "You mustn't say things like that or they'll hear you." At which the lift, as if to prove his point, shuddered and heaved, lurched upward, trod air, as it were, for a few long seconds before hauling itself, with a great groan of effort, to the second-floor landing. "See what I mean? It's the same with cars. You mustn't praise them or they'll break down. Of course, being in the car business, you must know that."

"I don't make a habit of talking to my cars."

"Wise of you. Their conversation isn't much."

Again he took my arm. Down the corridor he led me—he and Messalina nodded to each other like old acquaintances—to my door, into which he fitted the key as if it were his own. Sunlight spilled through the cleft. "I say, this is nice," he said, taking in our little room with its narrow bedstead, its intricate tiled floor, its single chair over the back of which Julia had flung one of her slips. Pots and jars, the unguents and emollients on which my wife relied to maintain her youth, lay scattered over the surface of the vanity. "Oh, and don't tell me you've got a bathroom!"

"I'm afraid we have, yes."

"Don't be afraid, be glad. May I?" He nudged open the door. Underwear hung drying from a cord that Julia had rigged up over the tub.

"I'm sorry things are in such a state," I said. But Edward wasn't listening. First he tried the cold tap, then the hot tap. Then he lifted the plug from the drain. Then he touched his fingers to one of the pairs of Julia's panties.

"Silk," he said, caressing the material. "With handmade lace. Very nice."

I was flabbergasted. Was this a compliment? And if so, who was being complimented?

"Julia has always been very particular about her things," I said.

"She has a tiny waist," he said, reaching his hand through one of the leg holes. "Iris's figure is more zaftig. Rubenesque—if Rubens had ever painted Scottish lasses. Of course, she'd never wear this kind of thing. She only ever wears plain white cotton knickers. Schoolgirl knickers." He smiled at me. "Do you like that sort of thing? You know, a grown woman in little girl's pants?"

"I don't know. I haven't really thought about it."

"Oh, come on. You must have thought about it." He stepped closer. "Schoolgirl knickers on a woman with curves. The effect can be quite eye-catching."

"Excuse me." I left the bathroom and walked to the window, which I opened.

"Are you all right?"

"Fine. I just needed some air."

Now he was standing behind me, his hands on my shoulders. "Ah, that's a good smell. A real Lisbon smell. Linens drying, fish guts, coal smoke . . . And what's that? Listen."

Aside from the wail of a shutter that had come unmoored, the only sound was a pianist—a child, I guessed—practicing a Brahms intermezzo.

"Oh, him," I said. "He's been playing that same piece since we got here, only he can't seem to get past this one chord. Just a sec, here it comes." And indeed the pianist, having made it through the first few bars, reached the troublesome chord; flubbed it; started again. "Every day it's the same. It gets rather maddening after a while."

"At least it's not traffic. Our room overlooks an outdoor market. If we close the window, we suffocate from the heat. But if we open it, we can't sleep for the noise. Which is to say nothing of the stench."

"Odd thing, the two hotels having the same name."

"Isn't it? I asked around about that. The story is, they used to have the same owner. And when he died, he left one hotel to one son and the other to the other, but the brothers got rivalrous and tried to outdo each other in renovations, until finally they both went bankrupt and had to sell. And though it's been years since the hotels have had any affiliation, the quarrel lives on, as if of its own volition. The problem is, no one outside of Lisbon realizes that there are actually *two* Hotel Francforts—or should that be Hotels Francfort?"

"I'm not sure."

"Let's say Hotel Francforts. And since no one outside of Lisbon realizes there are two, half the time letters addressed to guests at the one arrive at the other, where, as often as not, they're thrown into the trash."

"Really?"

"I've seen it happen. It's a disaster for the refugees, who are always waiting for something vital to come in the mail. May I?" He pulled the chair out from under the vanity and sat. I turned toward him. His legs were spread just wide enough that his trousers bunched at the crotch.

"Sit down," he said.

There was nowhere to sit but on the bed, so I sat on the bed. He put his hands behind his head, in the process sliding down in his chair a little. Now his legs, crossed at the ankles, stretched to the point where our shoes—the tips of our shoes—touched.

"Pete," he said. "May I ask you a question?"

"Of course."

"Did I offend you earlier, talking about your wife's underwear like that?"

"Offend me? No."

"Still, I shocked you." He drew in his knees and leaned forward. "You really must forgive me. Years of hotel life have made me uncouth."

"I thought you had a house."

"We do—now. Before, though, during the years of pilgrimage, as I call them, we lived in hotels. Dozens of them. And every night, after dinner, the ladies would repair to the lounge. And every night, after dinner, the gentlemen would repair to the smoking room, for cigars and dirty stories. Continental resorts are old-fashioned in that way. Of course, you're innocent of all that." He nudged my shoe with his.

"No, I'm not."

"It's okay. I find it refreshing."

"But I'm not innocent. How could I be? All my life I've worked in auto showrooms. Car salesmen aren't exactly shrinking violets. You hear a lot of racy stories."

"Really? Tell me one."

"I can't think of any just now."

"All right, then. Sell me a car. I'd love to buy a car from you."

"I can sell you *my* car. She's a beaut—a 1939 Buick Limited six-passenger Touring Sedan, hardly ever driven, with just the miles between Paris and Lisbon on the odometer."

"You drove to Lisbon? What was that like?"

"On the road to Bordeaux, the traffic went at a crawl. There were farmers with donkey carts, and peasants pushing their mothers in strollers, and horses loaded up with every imaginable sort of junk—chamber pots, milking stools, crates of chickens. And in the midst of it all, the Packards and the Hispano Suizas, honking their horns to speed things up. And then every few hours a military convoy would show up, trying to go the opposite direction, toward Paris, but since the road had no shoulder, everything would just end up in a hopeless tangle . . . And I thought, France is doomed."

"My God."

"And Julia refused to go out into the fields. All the other women did, even the ones in limousines—they had no qualms about hitching up their furs and squatting. But not Julia."

"We came by train," Edward said. "On the Sud Express, we were stuck nine hours outside of Salamanca, with the lights out and the rain bucketing down. It rained all the way to the Portuguese frontier. The sun only came out when we crossed. I mean it came out literally as we were stepping across the frontier. How's that for cheap symbolism?" Suddenly he snapped his fingers. "Now I remember where I've heard of Wabash. 'The Wabash Cannonball.' How does it go? Past the lakes of something-something, where the something-somethings fall . . ."

"No changes to be taken on the Wabash Cannonball."

"A train, wasn't it?"

"There are all sorts of stories about it. For instance, that it had seven hundred cars. And the engine was so fast that you arrived before you left."

"Funny you should say that," he said, "because when I was a boy, whenever I'd go to visit my mother in California, I'd perform this funny sort of ritual. I'd walk the length of the train, front to back, going backward as the train went forward, to the caboose. And then in the other direction, to the engine. I had to do it. It was like not stepping on a crack . . . Well, I'd forgotten all about that until just a few days ago, on the Sud Express, I found myself doing the same thing. Only the train was moving so slowly that I could match my pace to its pace. I could walk backward at exactly the speed that it was going forward. So that in every one of the windows, the scene was the same. A muddy field, a goat . . . Now, if *that* train had had seven hundred cars . . ." He uncrossed his legs, then recrossed them in the other direction, in the process stretching them out a little. Now our feet scissored each other.

Neither of us moved. The loose shutter slapped its wall. The pianist hit the inevitable wrong chord.

"Oh, your glasses," Edward said. "You still haven't got your glasses."

But I had forgotten all about my glasses.

3

It took me ten minutes to find the glasses. While Edward stood by, bemused, I rifled through our trunk, my suitcase, Julia's suitcase, the gas-mask holder in which we kept our money and papers, before finally locating them in my Dopp kit: an old pair, tortoiseshell, the lenses a little scratched.

No sooner had I put them on than I was nauseated. "Are you okay?" Edward asked, holding out his hand to steady me.

Now his eyelashes were sharp as needles, his scar as raw as if it were fresh.

"I'm fine," I said. "I just need to get my bearings. The prescription is a little weaker than on the other pair."

"I've never worn glasses. May I try them?"

I handed them to him—and was relieved to see his body melting back into imprecision.

He put them on and reeled theatrically.

"My God, I can't see a thing."

"That's because your vision's good."

"Twenty-fifteen. Better than perfect. I often wonder why they don't make glasses for people who see *too* well. I mean, to see so clearly that it hurts—isn't that a kind of impairment? A kind of . . . delusion?" He took the glasses off, wiped them with his shirttail, and returned them to me. "Well, I've enjoyed this little comedy of errors. I thank you for it."

"Shouldn't I be thanking you?"

"Why? Because I broke your glasses?"

"No . . . Because you brought me back."

"Oh, it was the least I could do." He walked to the door, turned the handle, and pivoted. "By the way, you wouldn't care to have dinner with us tonight, would you? You and your wife?"

His tone, to my ear, was noncommittal, and, wanting to sound noncommittal in kind, I said that it would depend on Julia. She might be too tired.

"We'll play it by ear then. Or eye, as the case may be. And now you know where to find me."

"At the other Francfort."

"This is the other Francfort. Or maybe they're both the other Francfort. Well, goodbye."

We shook hands and he left. I stayed by the door until I could no longer hear his footsteps. Now that I was getting used to wearing glasses again, I was startled by how much the room resembled a seraglio. It wasn't just the jars and pots on the vanity, it was Julia's gowns, her negligees, her very smell—of cigarettes and face powder and Jicky by Guerlain. Yet Edward's smell was there, too, astringent and canine. To put her off the scent, I threw open the window. The loose shutter had been secured, the pianist had given up for the time being. Down on the street an old woman sat on a stool, peeling potatoes.

In the bathroom, I took off my clothes. What I saw in the mirror did not impress me: standard-issue Anglo-Saxon face, cheeks potatoish in their stolidity. But for the pomegranate-red nipples, the chest was as undifferentiated as a field. My belt had pressed a pinkish trail into the abdomen, as if a tractor had just passed over it . . . A Midwestern body. A Great Plain. And how varied, by comparison, was the landscape just of Edward's face! The scar in particular fascinated me. Hadn't he mentioned Heidelberg? Somewhere I'd read that at German universities the students engaged in sword fights as a rite of passage. Facial wounds were badges of honor, which they washed lovingly with rancid water. Was this, then, the story of Edward's scar? Whatever it was, I wanted to read it. I wanted to read Edward.

It was getting on for lunchtime. It occurred to me that I was ravenous, so I got dressed and went down to the hotel restaurant. On the way, I left my key at the front desk in case Julia should come back. Only a few tables were taken, for Lisbon is a town in which people eat late. I ordered an omelette. It arrived prepared in the Spanish style, with chunks of potato. I devoured it. Then I had a flan, three apricots, and a banana. Then I drank two *garotos*, those little Portuguese steamed coffees with milk, followed by two glasses of *aguardente*, which is the Portuguese equivalent of an eau-de-vie. Then I went back to the lobby. The key to our room was no longer on the peg. My stomach lurched. I reminded myself that I really had to eat more slowly. My digestion was not what it had once been.

Not wanting to risk the elevator again, I walked the two flights of stairs to our floor. I knocked.

"Who is it?" Julia called from the other side.

"It's me."

The door clicked open. She didn't kiss me or even greet me. Instead she returned to the vanity, on the surface of which she dealt herself a hand of solitaire. From the ashtray she picked up a half-smoked cigarette; took a puff; put it down again.

"When did you get back?" I said.

"Twenty minutes ago," she said.

"And how was it?"

"What?"

"Your outing. Did you have a good time?"

She turned and glared at me. "A good time? Are you joking? After riding miles and miles in a taxi to some godforsaken slum . . . And that filthy dog, with its disgusting breath . . . And then the hour's wait in the broiling heat to see the vet, with that sample of its droppings *steaming* there between us . . . And you ask if I had a good time?"

"I'm sorry. I didn't realize—"

"But the worst part, the part that really got my goat—you know she's English. I mean, she has an English passport. And so in Bordeaux they could have boarded that ship if they'd wanted to—the one Churchill sent over to rescue the marooned Brits. They could have boarded that ship, in which case they'd be in London right now. Today. But they didn't. And why? Because of the dog."

"Really?"

"Yes! That's it! The only reason! They don't have any great yen to go to New York. She *told* me that—New York or London, it's all the same to them. They're nomads, she says. Yet they gave up the chance to sail to England, they put themselves through the hideous ordeal of getting all those visas and crossing Spain and coming here, and all because if they went to England, the dog would have to be quarantined. A fifteen-year-old dog! What do you think of that?"

"Well—that they must really love that dog."

"Of course, I understand that for some women a dog can be a child substitute. Yet when you consider the circumstances—"

"But Julia, it's not as if their not going to England means that we could have. You know perfectly well we couldn't. They wouldn't have let us on board."

"So you insist. You wouldn't even try. How do you know they wouldn't have?"

"They know the law as well as we do."

"Even if we'd offered the captain money?"

"An English captain? Please."

Her game having reached a stalemate, she gathered up her cards. "It just seems so unfair, that they should pass up a chance I'd kill for. And for the most ridiculous of reasons."

"Ridiculous to you, maybe."

"I challenge you to find a single person in Lisbon who wouldn't agree that not going to England for the sake of a fifteen-year-old dog is ridiculous."

I didn't answer that. I opened the window, which she had closed.

"This room is filthy," I said. "It stinks."

"The maid hasn't been. The maids here are worthless—all they do is make the bed and change the towels, and that only when they feel like it. They don't even pick up your clothes."

"And you can't pick up your own clothes?"

"Why should I? Why should I? We're only here for another week. Ten days at the outside. I despise this hotel. I despise this city."

"Yet just this morning you were going on about wanting to stay here."

"Oh, I'd rather stay here than go back to New York, if it comes to it. Not that I have any choice in the matter. It seems I'm my husband's slave."

"You're not my slave. You can do whatever the hell you want."

"So what are you suggesting, that I stay on my own?"

"Don't be silly."

"No, I think that is what you're suggesting. And you know what?

I think it's a fine idea. In fact, I can't see any reason not to start packing right away, especially since you seem to find my personal habits so intolerable."

"I never said that."

"Well, don't you worry. Soon I'll be gone and you can keep the room just as tidy as you like."

"Julia, please—"

"Excuse me." She stood, pushed me out of the way, took her suitcase from the armoire, and began throwing into it all the clothes that were strewn about the room, the pots and jars, the solitaire cards, even the underwear hanging over the bath, though it wasn't yet dry.

"Julia, this is madness. You can't stay here on your own. How will you live?"

"I'll get a job."

"But you don't have papers. You can't work without papers. And anyway, it's not safe."

"It seems perfectly safe to me."

"For now, yes. But how long will that last? You've got to see, it could get terribly dangerous, even for us. Especially if we enter the war. In addition to which there's the fact that you're—"

"What? Go on. Say it."

"All right. Jewish."

"And how are they supposed to find that out? It's your name on the passport. Winters isn't a Jewish name."

"Yes, but Julia, in Germany they're making people *prove* they're not Jewish. It could come to that here, too, if Portugal ends up on the other side. Please, darling." I stopped her hand, with which she was rummaging in the armoire. "Please be realistic."

Whatever she was holding, she dropped. I let her hand go. She sat down on the edge of the bed and began to weep. "It's not *fair.*

When I went to Paris, I told my family I was never coming back to New York, and I meant it. And now they'll have the chance they've been waiting for all these years—to laugh at me. To say 'I told you so.'"

"But you don't even have to see them."

"Are you joking? They'll be on the pier waiting for us. The minute we step off the gangplank, there they'll be."

"But how will they know we're coming?"

"My mother will know. She knows everything I do."

I sat down next to her and put my arm around her hot, narrow shoulder blades. "I won't let that happen," I said. "I've told you from the beginning, Julia, I'll take care of you. I'll protect you. Why, we don't even have to stay a single night in New York, if you want. We can take a taxi right from the pier to Grand Central. Catch the train to Chicago. Maybe visit my brother Harry—"

"He's never liked me. He disapproved of your marrying me."

"That was ages ago. He's missed us."

"I wouldn't be comfortable there. I'm not comfortable anywhere except Europe. When we set sail from New York, I swore I'd be buried here—you remember—and I meant it."

"And you will be, Julia. You will." She glanced up at me. "Oh, I don't mean it like that. What I mean is, when the war's over, we'll come back. We'll start up where we left off. Because as the crow flies, New York's not really far, is it? Literally as the crow flies, now that there are these Clipper flights."

"I wish there were no flights at all. No ships, no flying boats, no way to get across the Atlantic."

I kissed her cheek. "That's how you feel today," I said. "Trust me, once we've put these last weeks behind us, things will look brighter."

"We'll see."

She got up then. She went into the bathroom. I could hear water running in the sink.

"Oh, I meant to ask you," I said through the half-open door, "what did you think of her—aside from the dog?"

"Who? Iris? She's mad—but then again, those people usually are."

"Those people?"

"Writers. Didn't he tell you? They're Xavier Legrand. You know, the detective novels. They wrote the first one as a lark and then, just to see, sent it to a publisher in the States. They pretended that the author was a neighbor of theirs, a retired French police commissioner, and that they were his translators. Well, for the first three books they managed to fool everybody, but then a *French* publisher started sniffing around, wanting to bring out the originals. Which of course was out of the question, since there were no originals—the books were written in English—so they had to make a clean breast of it. But no one seemed to mind, and now it's an open secret that Xavier Legrand is really this expatriate couple. They've done quite well, too. Not that they need the money."

"They've got money?"

"Of course, she didn't say so. Those sort of people never *say* so—and yet it's the way they don't say so that tells you."

She came out drying her face. That we were not "that sort of people"; that I had to work; that without my job we couldn't have afforded to live in France—it had always been a sore point for her. My background is solidly middle class—my father ran a smelting works—which made me, in many ways, an improbable match for her. What she really needed was a man like Edward, a man with money to burn, money he didn't have to earn. Yet when I met her, there was no such man in the offing, or at least none who was willing to give her what she was holding out for, which was an apartment in Paris. I don't mean to poor-mouth. We lived more than comfortably, Julia and I. Never once in the course of our marriage did I have to deny her anything she wanted. But we weren't rich. Almost everything I earned, we spent. What savings we had were in francs, which in the wake of the German takeover had lost most of their value. Indeed, had it not been for the three hundred-dollar bills (a gift from my brother Harry) that, in a moment of cautionary foresight, I had stowed away in my sock drawer, I don't know how we would have survived in Lisbon. Probably Julia would have had to sell her jewelry.

Eventually she sat down again at the vanity. She reshuffled her cards.

"He asked if we'd like to have dinner with them tonight," I said after a moment. "Edward, I mean."

"Oh? And what did you tell him?"

"That it would depend on you. On whether you felt up to it." I took a breath, let a few seconds pass. "What do you think?"

"Why not? One has to eat."

"You mean you'll go?"

"Why do you sound surprised? Whatever else you might say about them, they're not bores. And what's the alternative? Another dreary dinner here at the hotel? No, thanks."

"All right, I'll call them to let them know we're on. Or better yet, I'll drop by their hotel and leave a note. Yes, it might be better to leave a note."

"What do you think I should wear?"

"Why not go out and buy yourself a new dress?"

"In Lisbon? Please." But I could tell from her tone that she was entertaining the possibility.

"Well, I'm off," I said. "I'll be back in half an hour or so. Also"—I was now standing in the doorway—"do bear in mind, darling, that England's not a safe bet. After all, there's rationing. Any day, bombs could start dropping."

"And any day U-boats could land off Long Island," Julia said.

"You're right," I said. "Any day U-boats could land off Long Island."

4

⌒

Had you met Julia that summer, the summer of 1940, you would probably have thought her a sedate woman, elegant and underfed and austere. She was forty-three but looked thirty-five, with taut pale skin and bobbed brown hair and huge eyes like those of a nocturnal marsupial. She dressed conservatively. Lanvin or Chanel, not Schiaparelli. Tweed or cotton or black silk, not sea-foam green chiffon. Nothing about her appearance suggested eroticism or pique or vulnerability. But she was full of surprises.

We had met . . . but here is the thing: I can't for the life of me remember exactly where we met, only that the occasion was a reception following some sort of public lecture or recital or poetry reading. For in New York, in the twenties, public lectures and recitals and poetry readings were largely the province of the restless and the lost—both unions of which I was a card-carrying member. I was then twenty-five and working at an Oldsmobile dealership on Broadway, a job I had acquired through my brother Harry, who, though two years my junior, was already rising through the ranks at General Motors. Like many youngest children, Harry considered it his duty to take care of his elder siblings, both of whom he regarded as wastrels. Well, our brother George—he really was a wastrel. He still is. I was merely aimless. Following my graduation from Wabash, I had moved back in with our parents, whose marriage was on the skids. My father had another woman, and my mother knew it. Most nights she drank herself into a stupor at the kitchen table. One afternoon my father summoned me into his study and said, "It doesn't matter if you hate me so long as you take care of your mother." As if that wasn't guaranteed to drive me out of the house! So I wrote to Harry, who arranged the job for me in New York. I think he understood that it would do me a world of good to get out of Indianapolis and start earning my own money. As for our mother, well, he took on that duty, too. Youngest children are like that. It was a sacrifice for which, in later years, he would take every opportunity to punish me.

And so I found myself in New York, selling cars, and in fact being somewhere other than Indianapolis did do me a world of good, and in fact it was a great thing to discover that I had the capacity to earn my own money. Yet I was still aimless, I had few friends, which was why, most evenings, I would go to the aforementioned public lectures and recitals and poetry readings. And at one of these I met Julia, who was also a regular at such events, but for different reasons. Though from a wealthy family, she had very little cash at her disposal. She lived with her widowed mother, who kept her on a tight leash.

Some background here. Julia's people were Bavarian Jews. Her maiden name was Loewi. Back in the 1850s, her grandfather and two of his brothers had emigrated from Fürth to New York, where they founded a fabric-covered-button manufactory. From fabric-covered buttons they moved into hops, from hops into commodities.

In New York, I have since learned, the German Jews go to great lengths to distance themselves from their Yiddish-speaking cousins, most of whom arrived in the early part of the century, in flight from poverty and pogroms. Well, by then the German Jews—Julia's Jews, if you will—were well established. On Central Park West they had their own Fifth Avenue. They even had their own club, the Harmonie Club, right smack-dab in the heart of Manhattan and, more tellingly, right across the street from the Metropolitan Club, its gentile twin, from which it differed only in its conspicuous lack of Christmas decorations in December. A Polish Jew had about as much chance of getting into the Harmonie Club as any Jew had of getting into the Metropolitan Club—and this was understood to be in the order of things. For how else was an immigrant population to prove its entrenchment but by exercising the power to exclude? As a girl, Julia attended German Jewish cotillions. Her brothers rowed in German Jewish regattas on the Hudson. And though there were always other cotillions, other regattas, from which they were barred, and knew themselves to be barred, nonetheless *their* cotillions, *their* regattas were reported right alongside these others on the society page of the *New York Times*. Examples of rebellion or anomaly in the family history were rare. One of Julia's uncles, a lawyer just out of Harvard, shot himself in the head in his office on a winter morning in 1903. It was assumed that he was a secret homosexual. Another settled in Haiti, tried to organize a coup against President Hyppolite, and was summarily deported, after which he devoted most of the rest of his life to lawsuits against the U.S. government. Finally there was Aunt Rosalie. Before the war, she and her husband, Uncle Edgar, had sailed to France. They were en route to Vienna, where Edgar, who suffered from diabetes, was to consult a specialist, but halfway across the Atlantic he fell into a coma and died. He was buried at sea. Subsequently it was assumed that Rosalie would return home in mourning. Instead she took a villa in Cannes and married a Swedish tennis instructor. Given the course Julia's life was to take, you might think she would have looked upon her aunt with admiration, but in fact she despised and feared her. Well, perhaps we all despise and fear those relations whose existence proves that we are not, as we would like to believe, originals.

Like Harry, Julia was the youngest child. I myself am an eldest child. By nature I am gluttonous, impetuous, indifferent to worldly success—the polar opposite of Harry, who is methodical, abstemious, and enterprising, as well as stoically, humorlessly self-sacrificing. To hear him tell it, everything he has ever done in his life has not just been for someone else's sake but has required him to deprive himself of a pleasure small or great (though, to be honest, the only thing in which he really takes pleasure, so far as I can see, is self-deprivation). This is often how it is with the last-born child. He knows himself to be the product of middle age and its disillusionment, and that this is why there are so few photographs of him as a baby, and why as a child he was left so much to his own devices or, worse, at the mercy of his siblings, who tortured him. The last-born child must learn to fend for himself. He has no choice. And Julia's case was worse, because to the burden of being the youngest was added that of being a daughter in a world that favored sons. Hence the single-mindedness, the bleakness of prospect, the tenacity that were the signal features of her character.

Of course, when I first met her I saw none of this. Rather, what I saw was a creature at once fleet and nervous, like those tiny deer you sometimes startle in the woods in the Florida Keys. The very night we met, she asked me to take her back to my room—and it was a revelation. All my life, I saw, I had been looking, in the absence of any pressing desire or goal, for a purposefulness outside myself on which I might, as it were, ride piggyback. It could have been a religion, it could have been a political party, it could have been a collection of musical instruments made from shoeshine boxes. Instead it was Julia. I adored her, I wanted her, and if I didn't yet know her—well, what of it? Do you really need to know something to know that it enchants you? (Probably you do. Good luck, though, in convincing a young person of this.) Of course, there were signs I should have heeded. She lied to me about her age. She said she was twenty-four when really she was twenty-nine—three years older than I was. Also she had no friends, or at least none to whom she ever introduced me. As for her family, she said that she despised them and was living with her mother only until she could afford to flee. They were crass—whereas she valued art; had taken lessons in painting and pottery and singing; had tried her hand at writing a novel. But none of the paintings satisfied her, her pots kept falling off the wheel, and she gave up the singing when her teacher told her she had to quit smoking. As for the novel, she could not stop rewriting the first chapter. At the end of a year she had generated nine hundred pages, all of them first chapters.

Now she had an idée fixe, and it was to live in Paris. Only in Paris, she believed, could the artistic impulse that New York had frustrated take root and bloom. I asked her how many times she had been to Paris, and she said that she had never been there once. A trip with two of her sisters had been planned for the summer of 1914, but the war had interrupted. (She never forgave the war for it.) Luckily, she happened to have a French governess at the time, a prematurely elderly young woman who in the evenings would read aloud to her from the Comtesse de Ségur's *Les Malheurs de Sophie*, that work by which, for mysterious reasons, so many little girls of the period were entranced. It was from Sophie, Julia said, that she gleaned her earliest notions of a French self, as well as her earliest conviction that she was destined to reside in Paris—a conviction that only grew as she grew, and moved from the misadventures of Sophie to those of Colette's Claudine, of which her governess disapproved strenuously and which were, for that reason, all the more enticing. Now I have before me Julia's copy of *Claudine in Paris*. The pages are brittle and puffy, for she had a habit of reading in the bath. Many passages are underlined, including this one:

"We were sitting at a little table, against a pillar. To my right, under a panel daubed tempestuously with naked Bacchantes, a mirror assured me that I had no ink on my cheek, that my hat was on straight and that my eyes were dancing above a mouth red with thirst, perhaps a little fever. Renaud, sitting opposite me, had shaky hands and moist temples.

"A little moan of covetousness escaped me, aroused by the trail of scent left by a passing dish of shrimps."

Today I wonder which was stronger in Julia—the longing for Renaud or for the shrimps. The shrimps, I suspect. For if she'd wanted a Frenchman, I really believe she could have found one. She might have had to wait a bit, but she could have found one. The trouble was, a Frenchman would have asked more of her and given less in return. He might have cheated on her. He might have interfered with the rapture of the shrimps. I do not want to suggest that Julia was venal; only that, like most youngest children, she was highly pragmatic. What she needed was a husband who was sufficiently in her thrall that he would do all he could to make her happy, but sufficiently lazy that he could be counted on for loyalty. And that bill I fitted perfectly.

So we got engaged, and she sprang on me the idea of moving to Paris, and I was not at all averse to it. On the contrary, her passionate desire provoked an equally passionate desire in me—the desire to satisfy her desire. For I had never in my life encountered a will so tenacious or a longing so intense as Julia's. Perhaps gurus inspire in their disciples a feeling similar to this, the feeling that a woman of determination can incite in a man whose capacity for ardor, though great, has no specific ambition or goal on which to spend itself. Accordingly, I wrote to Harry to ask if he might find me a job in the Paris office of General Motors, or in a Paris auto showroom. Quite reasonably, he responded with suspicion. Was a woman involved? he wanted to know. I replied that one was, at which he took the first train from Detroit to New York to investigate. The dinner the three of us had together was not, as you can imagine, a great success. Julia and Harry must have recognized the youngest child in each other, for they regarded each other with immediate suspicion. He asked her a lot of questions that I would never have been bold or rude enough to ask her myself, and, in the course of asking them, compelled her to divulge two facts that she had so far managed to keep from me. First, she was Jewish. Second, she was divorced. That she was Jewish came as no surprise. I had guessed as much. That she was divorced, I will admit, was a bit of a blow. After we sent Harry off in a taxi, we had a teary scene. She told me that she had not wanted to tell me that she was Jewish in case I should have religious qualms and that she had not wanted to tell me about her first husband in case I should think less of her for being a divorcée. It had all been long ago, when she was very young. His name was Valentine Breslau. They had not loved each other. The union had been imposed on them by their parents, who wished to solidify a business alliance between the families. Valentine had promised to take her to Paris for their honeymoon. Instead he took her to the Poconos. He made "loathsome" demands of her, and when she refused to satisfy them, he turned to prostitutes. For six months she put up with his brutishness, until finally she could take no more and left him, returning to her parents. He pleaded with her to come back. She refused. Her parents pleaded with her to go back.

She turned a deaf ear. Her father was a "beast" about the matter, she said, worried more about the business partnership that the divorce threatened to capsize than his own daughter's welfare. Shortly thereafter, he had a heart attack and died. Telling me this, Julia burst into a fit of weeping. I took her in my arms and promised that I would make everything all right, even with her mother. Her mother, Julia was convinced, had psychic powers. She could read Julia's mind. By way of example, Julia told this story. One afternoon, shortly after the divorce, she and Mrs. Loewi had a fierce argument, at the end of which Julia left the parental apartment, vowing never to return. For a few hours she rode around town in a taxi. Then she decided to check in to a hotel. Now, the hotel in question, she assured me, was not a famous one, and God knows, there are thousands of hotels in New York. Yet somehow the manager was expecting her, knew her name, and told her that he had no rooms. Horrified, she fled to another hotel—and here too the manager was expecting her, knew her name, and told her that he had no rooms.

This episode Julia interpreted as follows: her mother, having foreseen which hotels she was going to try—having foreseen this even before Julia had tried them—had telephoned to warn the managers that her daughter was on the way, and that she was not about to pay her bill.

I laughed. I suggested this was silly.

Julia was not amused.

"Perhaps she employs spies," I said.

"She doesn't need to," Julia said.

I decided that I would go to see her mother myself. I would tell Mrs. Loewi that I intended to marry her daughter no matter what. Even without the family's blessing, I would marry her. Even if they disowned her, I would marry her. I did not tell Julia about this plan. I knew she would try to stop me. At the Loewi apartment, an elderly manservant showed me into the dining room. Though the room overlooked Central Park, the curtains were drawn, as if to prove that a view was something the family could afford to ignore. The table was long, with ornate and uncomfortable chairs. Mrs. Loewi was waiting for me. She struck me as an exceedingly old-fashioned lady, with manners that dated, like her clothes, from the last century. She sat at the head of the table. I sat directly to her right. We drank tea. All through my speech, she kept her plump hands folded in front of her. Her face was impassive. At last I stopped speaking. A few seconds passed, and then she said this one clear sentence: "I beg you to reconsider." That was all. Her voice was higher than I had expected, less forceful, more girlish. I waited for something more. Nothing came. I was taken aback. I had expected demurrals, threats, at the very least the offer of a bribe that I could gallantly refuse—instead of which, here was this one brief advisory, uttered dispassionately, as if from a sense of duty. Eventually I stood. She stood. Upright, she was even shorter than Julia, though stouter. She might have come up to my elbow. She led me to the door, where she shook my hand. For the first and only time, I looked into her eyes. And what did I see there? Compassion. Relief. A smidgen of cunning.

In the vestibule, I called for the elevator. On the way down, the attendant gave me what I considered an impertinent look. In the lobby the doorman, having ushered me into the revolving door, pushed it so hard that I stumbled out the other side. I would have fallen had a passerby not caught me. I was sure it was deliberate. I did not, however, go back in and punch the doorman in the jaw. Instead I hurried away. I headed south, toward my own apartment, where Julia awaited me.

It was then, for the first and only time, that I doubted my soon-to-be wife. I doubted her so much it frightened me—I mean the *doubt* frightened me, not the thought that was its impetus: that she might be a liar and a fraud. For it's never the facts, is it? It's always the doubt . . . And so we disregard every warning sign, no matter how blatant, rather than let anything interfere with our getting what we want—which makes us all liars and frauds . . .

Then I got to the apartment—and there she stood, my Julia, vivid in her wrath and dread, braced for the worst. For somehow or other— maybe from the doorman or the manservant—she had found out what I'd been up to. "What lies did she tell you about me?" she asked. By way of reply, I shut her mouth with my lips. I assured her that it didn't matter, that all would be well. By now Harry had fina- gled the position in Paris for me—not with much confidence, he made clear. He didn't trust Julia. He said she rubbed him the wrong way. Nor should I imagine that the job in Paris would be a cake- walk. I was on probation. My boss there would report directly to Harry on my progress. Harry had "cashed in quite a few chips" to get me this job, he warned me, and if I failed, it would be he who suffered the consequences. My baby brother's fate was in my hands— just as my fate was in his. "And it's not as if I wouldn't like to take off and live in Paris," he added, "but someone has to keep an eye on poor Mama." A few days later, Julia and I were married at a registry office. The next morning we sailed to France on the *Aquitania*. It was from aboard ship that she sent the famous telegram to her family in which she vowed never again to set foot on American soil.

I wish I could say that Paris lived up to Julia's expectations. Alas, however, it did not—and perhaps it never does, for those who have expectations of the place. I myself had no expectations of the place, so I was happy there. I liked my job. The cars interested me, as did the peculiarities of running an American office in a European city, a subject about which, I joked, I could write a book, and might. Crois- sants in the morning, steak au poivre at lunch, a glass of Cointreau after work, before heading home to Julia, my Julia, beautiful and ardent and rippling with disquiet. In the end she had not fulfilled her artistic destiny. Rather she had grown into a woman of fashion, idle and a little vain, who spent her days strolling through boutiques, and reading *Vogue*, and consulting with interior decorators in a ceaseless effort to bring our apartment in line with the fantasies of her youth. Not once in all the years of our marriage did she so much as look at another man, I can assure you, though plenty looked at her. If anything she was a bit of a prig. An inordinate amount of her time she devoted to playing solitaire. Now I see that her energy was all for the ascent. She could only write first chapters. The middle, the vast middle, defeated her. Nor was her family, even at this great distance, ever all that far from her. She was constantly encountering them in cafés and restaurants and on the streets. We might be sitting at a table at the Café de la Paix on a sunny Sunday afternoon. I would look up from the menu and suddenly she would be gone. Evaporated. When she returned a few minutes later, she would be wearing dark glasses. "That's Aunt Sophie over there," she'd whisper. Or "That's Cousin Hugo." Or "That's Aunt Louise, she must be here on holiday"—which would be my cue to ask for the bill, whether we had eaten or not . . . I have no idea how many of these phantasms were in fact the people Julia thought they were. Nonetheless I always accommodated her. And how could I not? For at the sight of them she went genuinely pale, and afterward, in the taxi, her heart beat so loudly in her chest that I could feel it . . . I wanted to make her happy—making her happy was my vocation, and more often than not I succeeded. Or so I believed. Of course, I was a fool. Smug in my satedness, manfully satisfied that I was satisfying her every desire, I failed to see what was obvious even to her: those desires were vapor; their fulfillment was vapor—until a morning came when I woke and found that the burden of her care was crushing the life out of me. I had become my brother.

5

Before dinner I went to Bertrand, the bookstore on Rua Garrett. I wanted to see if they had any copies of Xavier Legrand's books, and indeed they did. The one I bought was called *The Noble Way Out*. According to the jacket, it told the story of a French politician who, on the eve of his arrest for the murder of his blackmailer, is found dead in his office, an apparent suicide. The case looks to be open and shut, as they say, until the novel's hero, Inspector Voss of the Paris *sûreté*, arrives on the scene and raises doubts not just as to whether the politician killed himself but as to whether he killed his blackmailer. So the good inspector now has two murders, not one, on his hands.

I brought the book with me to the Suíça that evening. I was thinking I might ask Edward to sign it. As soon as I saw him, however, I had second thoughts and buttoned the jacket pocket in which the book was stowed. The Frelengs had already staked out a table on the sidewalk. As we approached, Edward stood and waved. Since our last meeting, he had shaved—there were two small nicks on his cheek—while Iris had taken off her snood and pinned her hair loosely atop her head. I had for some reason assumed that her hair was brown. In fact it was a lustrous red. She had on a peasant skirt and a crocheted blouse that gave her a sort of Edwardian poetess air. So far as I could tell, she wore no makeup, which I worried might make Julia self-conscious. Despite her initial reluctance, Julia had finally given in to impulse and bought herself a new black dress. She was wearing her pearls. She was wearing the one pair of shoes she had held aside during the long trip from Paris in case some occasion should arise that required pristine shoes. Her skin gleamed with lotion, as if polished.

No sooner had we sat down than Daisy, who was lying at Edward's feet, hauled herself up with a grunt, stumbled over to Julia, and began licking her ankle.

"Daisy, please," Edward said.

"You'll have to forgive her," Iris said. "She licks everything these days. Shoes, blankets, dirty socks."

"It's true," Edward said. "Even when she goes up the stairs, she licks each one before she steps on it, I suppose to make sure it's real."

"Daisy, that's enough, now, leave Julia alone," Iris said.

"It's quite all right," Julia said, reaching down to pat Daisy's head—and to push her away.

"We've never been to Pyla," I said. "What's it like?"

"Just a typical little fishing village," Edward said. "With a few hotels that, toward the end, were full of Belgians."

"For them it was the place to flee *to*," Iris said.

"And your house?" Julia asked.

"Rustic. Always a fire going in the winter."

"It was for Daisy's sake that we moved there in the first place," Edward said. "You see, she spent her youth living in hotels, with no place to run except up and down corridors, being chased by maids. And so we felt that in her old age she deserved to do the things she was bred to do—root hedgehogs out of their holes, roll around on the carcasses of dead fish."

"Daisy has a particular fondness for dead fish," Iris said. "Every afternoon Eddie would take her for a walk on the beach, and if there was a dead fish in sight, you could bet she'd head straight for it."

"Really."

"Also we had a marvelous cook, Celeste, who'd make all sorts of special dishes for her, only to come to me afterward with her nose out of joint and say, 'Madame, j'ai préparé pour le chien un ragout de boeuf, eh bien, il va dans le jardin manger les crottes de chat. Comme si c'était des bonbons!'"

"Might I hold her on my lap?" I asked.

"What a good idea," Julia said.

I lifted the dog off the ground—which gave Julia a chance to pull her legs back under her chair. Now Daisy's face was just a few inches from mine. Her eyes were clouded, her teeth a brownish yellow. With little in the way of fuss, she turned around twice, curled into a ball, and went to sleep.

As surreptitiously as she could, Julia dipped her napkin in her water glass and touched it to the ankle Daisy had been licking.

"And you," Iris said. "Where in Paris did you live?"

Julia winced at the past tense. "In the sixteenth," she said. "On Rue de la Pompe."

"Oh, I know that area. So . . . bourgeois. What was your apartment like?"

"Well, you know, typically Parisian. *Parquet, moulures, cheminée,* as they say."

"We just had it redone," I said.

"The original decor was Empire," Julia said. "Elegant but heavy.

But then I met this marvelous decorator, a genius really, and now we hardly recognize the place."

"Oh yes? What did he do?"

"First he took down the wallpaper and whitewashed the walls. Then he sanded the paneling until it was practically raw. Then, where the big Aubusson used to be, he laid a plain wool carpet, and in front of the fireplace he put a white leather sofa and a couple of boxy armchairs with parchment sides, and a shagreen table—"

"What's shagreen?" Edward asked.

"Fish leather," I said.

"Sharkskin," Julia corrected. "And a few Louis XV pieces to round things out. And nothing on the walls. Nothing at all. That's his signature."

"And a screen to hide the piano," I said. "I don't know what he has against pianos."

"Maybe his mother made him play Brahms," Edward said, and winked.

"And the work was so extensive we had to move into a hotel for two months," Julia said. "And it was only last November that it was finished." With the dry end of her napkin, she dabbed at her eyes.

"It was photographed," I said. "You can see the pictures in *Vogue*. American *Vogue*. The February issue."

"The March issue."

"Really!" Iris said. "It must have been heartbreaking to leave."

"Oh, it was," Julia said.

"Do you have someone minding the place?" Edward asked.

"Our concierge," Julia said.

"If she's still in Paris," I said. "My guess is that she'll have left by now."

"Of course she hasn't left Paris," Julia said. "Not everyone has left Paris. Some of the French feel it's their patriotic duty to stay."

"And your decorator?"

"I hope for his sake he's left Paris," I said, "given that he's Jewish and—" I was about to say "queer," then changed my mind. "We haven't seen him here in Lisbon, though, which makes me worry he never made it out."

"Jean has friends in Marseille," Julia said. "He's probably gone to stay with them."

"Or he might be in Portugal but stuck off in *résidence forcée,*" Edward said. "This newspaper fellow—the *Chicago Tribune*, I think—was just telling us about that."

According to the newspaper fellow, Edward went on, the Portuguese political police had, as of two days ago, stopped the regular train service from Vilar Formoso, on the Spanish border, to Lisbon. Now only British and American citizens were being let through to the capital, the only exceptions to this rule being those who could show both valid visas for non-European countries *and* tickets on ships due to sail for Africa or the Americas. "Of which there might be five."

"And the others?"

"That's where the *résidence forcée* comes in. Basically these are beach resorts and spa towns, places where there are plenty of hotels that would normally be full but aren't, because of the war. Well, that's where they're being shipped—the refugees. And they're not allowed to leave."

"*Résidence forcée,*" Iris said derisively. "It's just a fancy name for a concentration camp."

"If you think about it, it's a stroke of genius on Salazar's part," Edward said. "Because if he were to actually put them in concentration camps, he'd have to foot the bill. Whereas this way *they* have to foot the bill."

"But if they aren't allowed into Lisbon, how are they supposed to get to the consulate to get their visas so they *can* leave?"

"Exactly. That's the trouble. And there are so many more of them than will actually get visas—"

"Sir, you are correct," said an elderly, bald-headed man sitting at the next table. "I myself was today refused a visa. My wife also."

"Oh yes?" Edward said.

The old man nodded. He was very thin and wore a good suit that clearly had not been cleaned in many weeks. With him was a woman of small stature and regal bearing. She had immense diamonds on her ears, a fur coat slung over the back of her chair.

"Sir, we come from Antwerp," the old man said. "By profession I am, how do you say, *comptable.* Though born in Latvia, my wife and I have lived in Belgium twenty years. Fifteen years we are naturalized Belgian citizens. Our children are Belgian, our sons enlisted in the Belgian army. Well, when the bombs came, we had no choice but to go. From the frontier we drive to Paris, from Paris to Bordeaux, like everyone, with a mattress tied to the roof—yet what good, sir, is a mattress? Everywhere, along the road, what do we see but cars with shattered windows, full of bodies, and on their roofs, mattresses, perfectly sound? You could have slept on those mattresses.

"Then in Bordeaux, at last, we obtain visas. We cross the border into Spain, we cross Spain, thinking, all the way, Lisbon, our hope. Lisbon, yes, port of freedom. And then finally we arrive, and what do we find? Freedom? Bah! A mirage! A lie! The American consul, he says, 'Well, Fischbein, and now I need five copies each of visa application, two copies of birth certificate, a certified copy of tax, and the same for Madame.' 'But sir,' I say, 'when the Germans came, we had two hours, we did not think to bring tax.' 'Ah, well, I am sorry, Fischbein,' he says. 'Oh, and you must also bring a paper from your bank that you have sufficient funds, and letters from two sponsors in United States.' 'But it is impossible,' I say. 'The bank is taken over by Germans, our account is seized, my business is seized.' 'Ah, well, I regret it, I do,' he says, 'but it is out of my hands, this is the law of the United States.' 'Well,' I say, 'yes, the law of peace, but now is a time of war—you must change the law.' 'But sir,' he says, 'there are quotas for each country, for Belgium the quota is 492.' Four hundred ninety-two, yes, when for England the quota is 34,007."

"Where did you get those figures?" Edward asked.

"I have calculated myself." From his jacket pocket, he fished out a piece of onionskin stationery bearing the logo of the Suiça. "Look, sir, according to your own State Department, the immigration quota for each European country is to take the ratio of naturalized American citizens born in that country as measured by census of 1920 and calculate to 150,000. And so I calculate—"

Suddenly Madame Fischbein threw up her hands. "Abel, why do you waste your time?" she cried. "Can you not see what is in front of your own eyes? They do not want us, no one wants us, we are *les ordures*, the best we can hope is that they shall put us on a refuse barge and ship us to, God knows where, Terre de Feu."

"But it is not right."

"Since when does right matter?" She turned to Edward. "Sir, I must apologize for my husband. He cannot tolerate reality, he lives in a dream. Not a pleasant dream, a dream of figures, numbers, all day doing his arithmetic, again and again, it is a kind of madness. How much quota here, how much quota there. You will forgive us. Abel, we must go."

Majestically, Madame Fischbein rose. She had on vast amounts of jewelry: three or four strands of pearls around her neck, half a dozen bracelets on each wrist, gold rings on every finger.

"Poor things," Iris said after they had gone. "She must be wearing all the jewelry she owns."

"It was probably all they could escape with," I said.

"So in ancient times, the dead were buried with coins under their tongues," Edward said, "so they might pay Charon their passage across the Styx."

6

The reader might have observed that to the conversation recorded above, my wife contributed not a word. I can assure you, however, that she was listening. I could tell by the way she ran her pearls through her fingers, like worry beads.

Of all the ironclad arguments I had made against her staying in Europe, the one she had the hardest time refuting was that she was Jewish. On this point she had always been touchy—and not because she was anti-Semitic. That is to say, she bore no secret or explicit hatred toward her race, or toward herself for being a member of it. And yet I do think she saw her Jewishness as a burden that she would have paid a good price to be rid of. This is often the case with those aspects of our identity that matter nothing to us personally but a great deal to those with whom we must conduct business in order to live in this world. It might have been different if she had possessed anything in the way of religious feeling, or had any personal experience of anti-Semitic persecution beyond knowing that her parents, had they tried to rent an apartment on Fifth Avenue, would have been turned away rudely. But her parents never did try to rent an apartment on Fifth Avenue—and this is the crucial point. It was not the Loewi way to make trouble. It was the Loewi way to navigate around trouble, or ignore it, or both.

Paris, of course, was a different story. There was no way you could live in Paris in those years without being conscious of the deep and abiding hatred that so many of the French felt toward their own Jews and, more strongly, toward foreign Jews. Following the Dreyfus Affair, this hatred had gone underground for a time, only to reemerge, cautiously at first, in the wake of Hitler's rise to power. You felt it more as an insidious and shadowy threat than as an outright danger. Starting in the mid-thirties, our concierge, Madame Foucheaux, of whom we were otherwise so fond, and whom we would have trusted with our lives, was often to be seen sitting in her little glass cage off the foyer, reading *Je Suis Partout* and *Gringoire* by the waxy yellow light of a ceiling lamp. Her son Jean-Paul, who lived with her, subscribed to both publications, giving the old lady the back issues when he was through with them. Though Jean-Paul was an out-and-out Fascist, he was never less than exceedingly polite to us, always taking off his cap to Julia and helping her with her packages. From this I deduced that he had no idea she was Jewish. That said, we had several neighbors in the building who *were* obviously Jewish, and whom Jean-Paul refused so much as to acknowledge publicly. On the door of one of these neighbors, an Austrian doctor and his wife, swastikas and defamatory slurs were scrawled on three separate occasions in 1938. None of us doubted for a minute who was responsible for this vandalism— not even, I suspect, poor Madame Foucheaux, who shook her head and wept. Yet no one said or did anything, and when eventually the couple moved out, and Jean-Paul, passing us in the hall, took off his cap to Julia as usual and muttered something to the effect of "Good riddance," she either did not understand his words or pretended not to understand them.

I think it frustrated my wife intensely that she could not just cast off her Jewishness as she had her New York life, or as she might a dress that had gone out of fashion. In this she resembled the many bourgeois French Jews who, because they regarded themselves as French first and Jewish second, made the mistake of assuming that France would regard them the same way. France did not, however—nor, for that matter, did our own United States. Later I learned that when Julia's decorator, Jean, arrived in New York from Buenos Aires at the end of 1940, the immigration officer crossed out "French" on the passenger manifest and penciled in "Hebrew" above it. Thank God Julia never had to undergo such a thing. It would have been the death of her.

Rarely, if ever, did she speak of her relatives in Germany. I don't know how much she knew about them. Given how close-knit her family was, I cannot believe that she had no awareness of them, or felt no concern about their plight. If she did, however, she never let on—I think because to speak of her relations in Germany would have been to acknowledge the Nazi threat in a way that might undercut her arguments for staying in Europe. It is really astounding to me, the human capacity for self-delusion, of which I myself am as guilty as anyone, and as much when what is at stake is something to be lost as something to be gained. And perhaps this capacity is a good thing, a necessary thing, a talent we must cultivate to survive—until the moment arrives when it kills us. In any case I knew my wife well, and so I knew that her silence during our conversation with the Fischbeins was a silence of attention and dread, and that merely to sit through that conversation without bolting or screaming she had had to muster all the reserves of good manners that her governess had drilled into her in her youth, and that this effort had cost her.

And then Edward stretched his arms into the air, and said we should be going, and asked for the bill. In that manner typical of American men, we jousted over it. He won, which is indicative of how much he took me off guard, for in bill battles I am usually no slouch. "I'm taking you to a wonderful little restaurant I've discovered," he said as we headed out across the Rossio. "It's called Farta Brutos. Really, that's what it's called."

"Does it mean what it sounds like it means?" I asked.

"A literal translation would be something like 'well-satisfied brute,'" he said. "Think Bluto from *Popeye*."

"The food isn't exactly refined," Iris said. "But oh, is it authentic!"

"That sounds lovely," Julia said, in a voice that betrayed her distress. Cambrinus, the restaurant favored by the wealthiest refugees, was more to her taste. When we had gone there a few nights earlier, Cartier was at the next table.

"I'm glad you feel that way," Edward said. "Myself, I have no patience for tourist traps." Then he put his arm around Julia's shoulders. She flinched. Their pace quickened, until they were about ten feet ahead of Iris and me. Nor could I race to catch up with them without abandoning Iris, who had charge of Daisy and was obliged to stop every few seconds while she sniffed at moist spots on the pavement.

"Your wife is so pretty," Iris said. "So . . . petite. When I was a girl, I would have given anything to be that size. I shot up early, you see. By the time I was fifteen I was already five foot eleven. The girls at my school—souls of kindness, they were—called me Storky. To compensate, I developed a stoop, and now I have a permanent curvature of the spine to thank them for."

"But that's terrible."

"Oh, there are worse things than a stoop. Besides, when I'm with Edward I don't feel it so much. With other men—perhaps it's that my self-consciousness makes them feel self-conscious. Emasculated. You, for instance."

"Me? I don't feel emasculated."

"Then why haven't you put your arm around me the way Edward has around Julia? Admit it. It's because you find me daunting. Well, don't worry. I don't really want you to put your arm around me."

"All right."

"This whole business of couples switching partners when they walk—I find it tiresome. Look how he towers over her! I imagine he's charming her. He has a way with women. Why, do you know what he said to me the first night we spent together? He said, 'I'd like to paint you in the posture of Parmigianino's *Madonna with the Long Neck.*'"

"Really."

"I ask you, how could I resist him after that? No one had ever compared me to a painting before. So I married him."

The gulf between Iris and me and Edward and Julia had now widened. Across the divide, Edward's laughter tumbled. Julia was walking stiffly. What was he saying to her?

We were on our way to the Santa Justa Elevator, which, though it was located within spitting distance of our hotel and was considered one of Lisbon's great attractions, neither Julia nor I had yet ridden—yet another of the many things we hadn't done in our week in the city that the Frelengs, in their seventy-two hours, had. The first time I saw the Elevator, I thought it was a medieval tower. It had a crenellated roof. It even appeared to lean—an illusion, I soon learned, brought about by the city's sheer verticality, the way the old buildings list, clinging to their perches. Almost nothing in

Lisbon is level, yet the hills are steep, which explains the necessity of the so-called *elevadores*, most of which are actually funiculars, shooting like arteries through the veining of narrow streets that crawl up the hillsides. In fact, the Santa Justa Elevator is the only one of these that is an elevator proper. The metal sheath through which its cars ascend soars up 150 feet in the air. "It will come as no surprise," Edward said when our little group had recoalesced, "that the architect who built it studied with Eiffel."

"Speaking of Eiffel," Iris said, "did you hear what happened when Hitler marched on Paris? He wanted to ride the elevator to the top of the Eiffel Tower, but the operators cut the electrical cords."

"Good for them," I said.

"And he only stayed one night. I suppose Paris was too rich for his taste."

We stepped into the foremost of the cars. It was paneled in polished oak and had been manufactured, a brass plaque informed us, by R. Waygood & Co., Engineers of London. "Further evidence of the enduring bond between England and Portugal," Edward said, pirouetting to escape the tangle of Daisy's leash. "The oldest unbroken alliance in Europe—which is probably the only reason they're letting the British through to Lisbon instead of sending them off into *résidence forcée*."

"And the Americans?" Julia said.

"America's neutral, so no harm, no foul."

"Speaking of England"—*speaking of*, I had discovered, was one of Iris's favorite locutions, since it allowed her to change subject at will—"did you hear that the Duke of Kent is in town? He's to be the guest of honor at the inauguration of Salazar's Exposition, where there will also be delegations from France *and* Germany."

"Leave it to Salazar to get those three eating out of the same trough," Edward said.

"Something else we haven't been to," I said. "The Exposition."

"The Exposition of the Portuguese World," Edward said, adopting his tour-guide voice, "celebrating the nation's double centenary—Portugal having been founded in 1140 and attained liberation from Spain in 1640."

"I've heard it's splendid," Julia said. "They say an entire Angolan village has been shipped over for the occasion."

"Isn't that horrible?" Iris said. "Those poor people, on display behind ropes. Like animals at a zoo." She glanced at Daisy, who had gone to sleep on the elevator floor. "Anyway, as I was saying, it's because the Duke of Kent's in town that the Duke of Windsor isn't. He and the Duchess have to cool their heels in Madrid until George leaves. They're furious about it, but there's nothing they can do, since it would be a breach of protocol for the brothers to be in the same country."

"How do you know all this?"

"I eavesdrop. It's part of our method. I pick up the gossip, out of which I forge a plot. Then Eddie collects the facts so we can be sure it's accurate."

"What was it Oscar Wilde said?" Edward said. " 'Anyone can write accurately.' "

" 'Anyone can *play* accurately.' He was talking about the piano."

"What my wife is saying is that she's the brains of the operation, while I do the drudge work. Make sure she's got her facts straight, which she usually hasn't. Correct her spelling, which is usually egregious."

"So you're writing a novel set in Lisbon?" Julia said. "How interesting. I wonder if we'll end up being characters in it."

"Don't put ideas in her head," Edward said.

"The premise—still very rough—is a suicide in a Lisbon hotel," Iris said. "An *apparent* suicide. I got the idea because that was how we got our room. You see, we'd been shown the door at a dozen other places, and so when we tried the Francfort, it was a shot in the dark. And then, to our astonishment, the manager told us that just that morning a room had become available, its previous occupant— these were his exact words—'having had to leave suddenly in the night.' Now I ask you, how likely is it that anyone, at this moment in time, would leave a Lisbon hotel suddenly in the night?"

"She spent a whole day scouring the room for evidence," Edward said. "Cracks in the ceiling in case he'd hung himself. Blood on the tiles."

"Did you find any?" Julia asked.

"Alas, no," Iris said. "But what do facts matter?"

"How are you going to get your detective to Lisbon?" I asked.

"He's Jewish. He'll come to Lisbon for the same reason we did."

"You're Jewish?"

"I'm not. Eddie is."

"Julia knows that," Edward said. "In fact, we've just been talking about it. Our grandmothers come from the same part of Bavaria. We think we might be cousins."

Julia frowned. Now I understood why she had been so stiff when Edward had his arm around her.

All through this conversation, the elevator's conductor—an old man in an ill-fitting uniform—had been standing on the curb, smoking. Now he stubbed out his cigarette and got into the car with us. We were the only passengers. Nonetheless he waited until nine o'clock precisely—church bells confirmed the hour—to close the gate and switch on the motor. The elevator creaked, purred, and began its ascent.

There is a feeling that you get, or at least that I get, when an elevator lifts off: a queasiness, almost a weightlessness, as if the ground has dropped away under your feet; a feeling, now that I think about it, not unlike that of passing through a revolving door. If the women hadn't been there, I would have put my hand on Edward's shoulder. But the women were there, and so I had only the woodwork to steady myself against as, outside the glass, the roof of our own Hotel Francfort sank below the dusk sky and a pair of ladies' underpants, unloosed from a clothesline, billowed before drifting down toward the street.

Then we were at the top. We got out. To our left, a narrow spiral staircase rose.

"View finest at sunset," Edward said. "Let's go."

He picked Daisy up and headed up the stairs. Iris and Julia followed. I took up the rear so I could catch Julia if she got dizzy.

The first thought I had when we got to the roof was that the railings were entirely too low to keep someone from falling.

The second was that I had never in my life seen such a view.

"Isn't it extraordinary?" Edward said, coming to stand next to me. "Three hundred and sixty degrees. Look, there are the castle ramparts. You couldn't see them when you didn't have your glasses, Pete. And the river—it might be wider than the Mississippi. And there's the Rossio. It's only from up here that you really get the nautical effect—how the waves seem to roll."

"Please, Eddie," Iris said, "you're making me queasy." She had her hand on her stomach.

"My poor wife suffers from vertigo *and* seasickness," Edward said.

"It's true," Iris said. "That's why, of all the methods of committing suicide, jumping is the hardest for me to imagine. The courage it must take—"

"It was how Jean's father killed himself," Julia said.

"Who?" Iris said.

"Jean. Our decorator. His father jumped out the window of their apartment on Avenue Mozart. This was in 1915. He was German, you see, and though he'd lived in France for years, he'd never bothered to change his citizenship. And so when the war came, he was declared an enemy alien, though he had two sons fighting on the front. Fighting for France. And then within a month of each other the sons were killed. So he jumped out the window." She said all of this matter-of-factly.

"You never told me this," I said.

"I only thought of it now because of what you just said"—she looked at Iris—"that you wondered how anyone could muster the courage. Well, he did."

As if she was suddenly cold, Julia rubbed her bare arms.

"I'm sure it says a lot about a person, the way he'd choose to kill himself," Edward said. "If it was up to me, I'd put a pistol in my mouth. Spectacular yet painless. How about you, Pete?"

"Me? I wouldn't. I've never even thought about it."

"Oh, come on. You must have. Everyone has."

I shook my head.

"It's true," Julia said. "He is hopelessly committed to life." Her tone was almost bitter.

I turned toward the river. Even though it had been years since I left the Midwest, coasts still humbled and appalled me. The first time I saw the Atlantic, I was twenty. I wanted to run screaming. I'm told people from the Northeast feel the same thing when they step off a train in Kansas or Nebraska for the first time. The endlessness of the plains, the vastness of the sky—it's a kind of horror to them.

Then something strange happened. Pigeons began circling the Elevator. Without warning, one of them dove at Edward's head. He ducked, and Daisy suddenly leaped up, barking and lunging. "Whoa, steady girl," Edward said, scooping her up into his arms. Yet she didn't stop barking. She didn't stop lunging.

"What on earth has got into her?" Iris said.

"It's these pigeons," Edward said. "I told you, they're infernal."

"But it's not like her. She's a terrier. She's always been oblivious to birds."

"Hadn't we better go down?" I said. "It's getting dark."

"Isn't it amazing," Julia said, "how in the summer the sun takes forever to start setting, but then when it does, it sets so fast?"

It was true. In minutes the sky had gone from yellow to blue to purple, like a bruise. "Pete's right," Edward said. "If we don't go soon, we'll have to lick the steps, like Daisy."

For some reason we descended in reverse order—me first, then the women, then Edward taking up the rear. From the platform, an ironwork bridge thrust out into the shadows. We crossed it, Iris clutching my arm, defiantly not looking at the pedestrians making their way along Rua do Carmo, 150 feet below.

"I remember someone telling me once that when you fling yourself off a roof, you should make sure to dive, not jump," she said. "That way your head hits the ground first and you die instantly." She laughed. "My, what a grim turn the conversation has taken! We were all so lighthearted earlier."

"I know," Edward said. "You'd think the world was ending or something."

7

With a self-assurance that was beginning to seem predictable, Edward led us through a warren of cobbled streets so narrow that the old women leaning out of their windows could almost kiss. How he had discovered Farta Brutos in the first place was what I wanted to know. It had no sign. Nor did the streets at the corner of which it was situated appear to have names. Each sloped upward at such a precipitous angle that the restaurant itself was sunk a few feet below the sidewalk. The door was so low that I had to bend down to get through it. In a sort of antechamber, a raucous group of young men was eating at a circular table. "That's something else that you don't see in Paris anymore," Iris said to me. "Young men."

Soon the owner—elderly and pot-bellied, with suspiciously luxuriant black hair—stepped over to greet us. Seeing Edward, he cried out with joy. They shook all four hands. They embraced. They kissed each other on the cheek.

"Look at him," Iris said, nudging me in the ribs. "You'd think he was a regular. Yet we've only ever been here once. And it's like this everywhere we go."

The owner ushered us down a few more steps into the dining room proper. It was only slightly bigger than the antechamber. It had five tables, all but one occupied by Portuguese men, smoking and shouting. "Lucky I reserved," Edward said, taking a seat at the one empty table. I tried to pull out a chair for Julia, but there wasn't space. She had to slide in sideways. The chairs themselves were low and narrow, with rigid backs. Through the windows you could see the shoes of the people passing by outside.

"What do you think?" Edward said. "Definitely not the sort of place you'd run into the Duke of Kent."

"Probably he doesn't have the stomach for it," Iris said as a waiter deposited carafes of wine and water, a basket of rolls, and a ramekin containing what appeared to be fish paste onto the table.

"Is there a menu in English?" Julia said.

"Oh, you don't bother with a menu here," Edward said. "You leave it to Armando to choose for you."

"Lovely."

Edward poured the wine, which was amber in color and rather pale. "*Vinho verde.* A specialty of the north, made from unripe grapes. And now I'd like to propose a toast. To us. The four seasons."

"Four seasons?"

"Yes, since all of them are represented here tonight. Mr. Winters, with his summery wife, Julia. Then me—Freleng is almost *frühling*, isn't it? And the autumn-blooming Iris."

"But irises bloom in spring."

"Not all of them do," Julia said. "A few bloom in autumn."

"Do they?" Iris said. "I didn't know. As Eddie will tell you, I'm an idiot when it comes to gardening."

We toasted, and for a moment Iris's small, wet, very blue eyes met mine. There was in them a vulnerability at odds with her sardonic tone. Or was the sardonic tone merely defensive, a child's fists beating against intolerable knowledge?

Soon Armando returned, bearing a tureen of thick, brownish-red soup, which he ladled out for us. To Daisy he gave a bowl of water and a kidney. Tasting the soup, I could not help but wonder if a kidney had also been involved in its preparation—that or some pig's blood, for it had a distinctly metallic flavor. Offal holds no fear for me. I dug in with gusto. So did Edward. Julia, on the other hand, took one sniff and cringed, while Iris—such was her enthusiasm for the *vinho verde* that she appeared hardly to notice the soup, which in any case was soon cleared away, to be replaced by a steaming casserole of duck and rice atop which slivers of chorizo sausage lay curled.

"This is the specialty of the house," Edward said. "It's prepared like an Italian risotto, then put in the oven so the rice gets crisp."

He dolloped some onto my plate. How different this was from French food! "In French cooking," I said to Edward, "either you get the purity of a particular ingredient—for instance, mâche in a salad—or you get a flavor that defies you to identify any of the ingredients. Here you get both."

"Exactly. The rank pungency of the duck meat, the acridity of the chorizo, the . . . How would you characterize the rice?"

"Rice doesn't have a taste so much as a texture. It's something for the palate to resist."

"Listen to them," Iris said to Julia. "Why can't men talk sensibly? It's only food."

"And then the collective flavor of each forkful," Edward said, "which almost brings tears to the eyes, because there's something so, well, nostalgic about it, yet it's entirely new . . . I mean, you can tell that, for someone, this is the food of childhood. Nor does it matter that it's not your own childhood. The past—some collective notion of the past—comes alive in your mouth."

"Been reading Proust lately, have you?" Iris said.

"I think I could live here," Edward said, "if I could learn the language. The language—that would be the challenge."

"It sounds like Russian to me," Julia said.

"Of course, it's easier to read than to speak," I said. "When I look at the newspapers, I recognize maybe half the words."

"Speaking of Portuguese," Iris said, "do you know what the locals have taken to calling our own Suiça? Bompernasse."

"*Bom* what?"

"Bompernasse. It's a pun. Montparnasse combined with *bom perna*, which is Portuguese for 'nice legs.' "

"Because of all the barelegged Frenchwomen who sit outside in the afternoon, smoking," Edward said, "which is something no self-respecting Portuguese woman would do. In fact it would be a scandal for a Portuguese woman even to go into a café."

"Such a backward country in some ways," Julia said.

"But Julia, I thought you wanted to wait out the war here," I said.

"That doesn't mean I consider it the ideal place to live," Julia said. "I mean, it's not Paris."

"Is Paris your favorite place on earth?" Iris said.

"Of course. Isn't it yours?"

"Oh, I wouldn't say anywhere was my favorite place. Now, Eddie—he really can feel at home anywhere. Close your eyes, spin the globe, send him wherever your finger lands, and I guarantee you, within a month he'll be mayor."

"But isn't feeling at home anywhere really the same as feeling at home nowhere?"

"No, in fact it isn't," Edward said, "though that's a common misperception. In fact, the person who feels at home nowhere is in

an entirely different category from the person who feels at home
everywhere. Iris is that person."

"It's true," Iris said. "I don't even understand what people mean
when they say they feel 'at home.' "

"Well, isn't it—I don't know—a sense of belonging?"

"So I'm told. But 'belonging,' 'home'—they're just words to me.
And don't bother trying to explain them—it would be like trying to
convey the notion of sight to a blind man."

"But surely you must have a feeling for the place you grew up."

"You assume that I grew up in a place. I didn't. I was born in
Malaysia. My mother died in childbirth, my father when I was four.
I hardly remember him—or the amah who nursed me. I was five
when I was sent back to England, and though I had some relations
there, they didn't have much interest in me, so from then on it was
just school after school . . . until I met Eddie."

"Little Orphan Iris," Edward said.

"I think it's probably why I have a dog," Iris said. "A dog is a
constant. You can rely on a dog in a way you can't rely on a place. Of
course, when we left Pyla we could have left Daisy behind. Our
friends told us we were mad, that getting to New York would be difficult enough without having to worry about an old dog. Well, I put
my foot down. I'd have stayed in Pyla myself, brazened out the occupation, rather than abandon Daisy to some French peasant who
for all I knew would shoot her the moment we were out of sight." She
was teary-eyed again. "And then in Irun, at the Spanish customs,
the officer insisted that Daisy was commercial merchandise and we
had to pay duty on her. I said, 'She's fifteen years old. How much do
you think you could get for her?' But I had the feeling he'd take his
chances rather than lose the argument, so we paid the duty."

A waiter cleared away our plates and laid three immense bowls
on the table. The first contained a watery custard, the second pears

purpled in wine, the third a thick orange porridge. "Raw egg yolks and sugar," Edward said, helping himself. "Extremely sweet."

"Too sweet for my taste," Julia said.

"Do you think we could give some of the egg stuff to Daisy?" Iris asked. "They say eggs are good for dogs. They lend luster to the coat."

"If you don't think it'll bring on diarrhea," Edward said. "Diarrhea is the last thing we need."

Julia shuddered. I served myself some of the custard and looked across the table.

For the second time all evening, Edward's eyes met mine.

For the second time, he winked.

8

After dinner we walked back to the Rossio. The streets were loud with the plaintive wail of fado singers.

"Call me a snob, but I just don't get the appeal of the fado," Iris said.

"They're such sad songs," Julia said.

"The fado is meant to be sad," Edward said. "It is the ultimate expression of that most Portuguese of emotions, *saudade*, which might best be defined as the perpetual longing for a perpetually elusive . . . no, not satiation. Rather, that which will never be."

"Perhaps, what will never be on the menu at Farta Brutos?" I suggested.

"Yes!" Edward said.

"If you ask me, it's just caterwauling," Iris said. "Daisy can't bear it, can you?"

Daisy was busy smelling some pigeon droppings on the pavement.

"Not here, Daisy," Edward said, tugging at her leash. "We don't want to stop here."

I looked at him questioningly. With his shoulder he indicated the window display we had stopped in front of. Castles, Meistersingers, elves. Friendly old Munich, hearty old Heidelberg. Gay, carefree waltzing in Vienna.

"The German Reich Railway Office," he said.

"As recently as December, they were advertising in *Vogue*," Julia said. "Sixty percent off with special travel marks."

A young man wearing a homburg stepped up to us. "You are planning a trip, Madame?" he asked Julia.

"What?" Julia said. "Oh, no. I mean, not to Germany."

"But you are Americans. Why not go on holiday in Germany?"

"Actually, we're not American," Iris said. "We're Tasmanian."

"Tasmanian?"

She nodded. "Have you been to Tasmania? It's lovely. Famous for its animals, most notably the Tasmanian devil." She pointed to Daisy. "Of course, this one's tame—more or less. Still, I wouldn't get too close."

The young man tipped his hat and fled. Edward burst out laughing.

"What was that all about?" I said.

"A German informer," Edward said. "They're all over the city. Usually they pretend to be English, hoping to pick up some information."

"You could tell because he had a big behind," Iris said.

"What?" Julia covered her mouth with her hand.

"It's my wife's theory," Edward said, "that informers can always be recognized by their big behinds."

"It's not a theory. It's something I was told. By someone who knows."

"But why should they have big behinds?" Julia asked.

"Maybe it's all the sitting they do," I said.

"Or the double life," Edward said. "It could be the double life, the double life itself, that brings on the big behind. Pete here, for instance—he doesn't have a big behind. And I'll bet he's never led a double life. Am I right, Pete?"

"About the behind or the life?"

"Let me have a look," Iris said, stepping behind me. "My God, it's true! There's just this . . . flat plane. You'd think he had no buttocks at all."

"Of course I have buttocks. Only these trousers—"

"But Pete, you don't." Almost in spite of herself, Julia burst into laughter. "I mean, you do, only there's just . . . not much to them."

"Reductio ad absurdum," Edward said, "a man with a clear conscience."

"Whereas you, my darling," Iris said, "have a distinctly protuberant behind. Not fat, just . . . protuberant. You could bounce a dime off it," she added to Julia.

"With all that implies," Edward said.

By now we had passed under the bridge we had crossed earlier, the one that connected the Elevator to the Bairro Alto. Above the Rossio, a neon stopwatch told the time, the words OMEGA O MELHOR pulsing beneath it.

"For a poor country, they certainly seem to have plenty of money for electricity," Julia said.

"It's too much," I said. "It gives me a headache."

"Would you rather go back to the blackout?"

"In some ways." The truth is, I have always preferred darkness to light, silence to noise.

Outside the Francfort Hotel, I reached to shake Edward's hand, but he didn't take it. "Anyone care for a nightcap?" he said.

"Count me out," Iris said. "I've hardly slept since we got here, and I have a feeling that tonight I just might. Julia's tired, too. Aren't you, Julia?"

"Actually—"

"Let them go," Iris said, touching her arm. "Men need time to themselves. Especially when they've been cooped up with their wives for weeks and weeks."

"Oh, all right. I am a bit tired. But you go, Pete."

"How about it, Pete?" Edward said.

"I'm game if you are," I said.

Once we had dropped off our wives at their respective Francforts, an unexpected shyness overtook us. We walked without speaking. On the sidewalks of Baixa, old men were playing cards by the light of gas lamps around which flies swarmed. Boys kicked soccer balls—this at an hour when any self-respecting Anglo-Saxon child would already have been in bed for hours.

Soon we passed my car, my Buick, dried sprays of Spanish mud on the fenders.

We stopped.

"That's my car," I said.

"Really?" Edward said. "Do you have the keys?"

I did, as a matter of fact. Out of habit, I still put them in my pocket every time I went out—not just the car keys, but the keys to our apartment in Paris, to my office, to the *chambre de bonne* to which Julia's decorator had relegated our old furniture.

"Let's take her for a spin," Edward said. "Let's go to Estoril."

"But I don't know the way."

"It's simple. Head to the river and turn right."

We got in. The car's interior smelled of naphthalene, cigarettes, some vile coffee I'd spilled somewhere in Spain. When Julia and I had first gotten to Lisbon, I'd parked the Buick and tried to forget it. For ten gruesome days, it had been all the home we had—a few nights it had been our bed—and so the mere sight of it was enough to conjure the drone of German planes, the uninflected voices of those Spanish customs officers, the jolt of poorly paved roads. But now it was Edward, not Julia, who was sitting across from me, and the pleasure I had once taken in the car revived. His rangy legs spread out before him, he opened and shut the glove compartment, pulled out the ash drawer, lowered and raised the sunshade.

I switched on the ignition and edged out into the street, barely wide enough to accommodate such a mammoth vehicle.

"Do you drive?" I asked Edward.

"Me? No. Iris does, though. *And* sails. *And* rides." He unrolled the passenger window, out of which he thrust his long arm.

"She seems quite a capable woman, Iris," I said.

"She is like Salazar," Edward said. "Prime minister, foreign minister, minister of the interior, minister of finance. She is the cabinet."

"And what does that make you?"

"A lowly peon. Obeisant. The functionary who keeps his job by making sure never to have an opinion, then shoots himself at his retirement party . . . Seriously, though, my wife is a marvel. Far more intelligent than I am, though of course she doesn't believe it. It's because her education was so piecemeal, she never got the basics—you know, how to do long division, how to punctuate a sentence properly. Latin and Greek. God! Whereas I did Latin and Greek for eons. I'm supereducated, hypereducated. Yet compared to her, I'm stupid."

"If you're stupid, I'm a cretin. I'm no smarter than—than this ashtray."

"But you *do* something. You have a job. You sell cars."

"And you write books."

"Stupid books. Did Iris tell Julia how we got started on them? It was a bet. Alec Tyndall, this fellow we met in Le Touquet—his wife was reading Agatha Christie. Well, one night he and I got drunk and he bet me a hundred pounds that he could write a detective novel before I could. And I took him up on it."

"I assume you won."

"Yes. But I wouldn't let him pay me. I couldn't. By then we were getting royalty checks."

"Royalty checks are something to be proud of."

"No, they are not something to be proud of. The *Tractatus Logico-Philosophicus* is something to be proud of. The Incompleteness Theorem is something to be proud of."

I didn't know what the Incompleteness Theorem was. I wondered if it had anything to do with Theosophy.

"In the world I live in, men aren't measured by their brains," I said. "They're measured by what they earn."

"Then in your world I'm nothing, because I've never earned a dime in my life."

"But the novels must make money."

"Chalk those up to Iris. Like I said, she's the brains of the operation." He fiddled with the door lock, pulling it up and pressing it down. "Here's where we turn, by the way."

I turned. We were driving alongside the river. To our left the hulls of ships loomed, their surfaces mottled in the moonlight. A breeze came up, filling the Buick with maritime smells—brine, burning rubber, fish guts—that I inhaled with relish, hoping they would eradicate the naphthalene, the cigarettes, the coffee, all the tired, residual odors of our slow exodus.

"I like this car," Edward said. "I really do. Here's an idea. Let's pretend I'm a customer, a stranger. Make your pitch. Sell me a car."

"When it comes to luxury, you won't find anything to compare with the Limited," I said. "She's got a whopping 140-inch wheelbase and a fifty-six-inch front seat. That's just a trifle less wide than a full-size Davenport—and no less comfortable, because the seats are built on a foundation of Foamtex rubber over Marshall springs and upholstered in smart Bedford cord. You could be relaxing at your favorite club."

"My favorite club! I love that. Go on."

"The rear armrest retracts into the seatback and has a built-in ash receptacle, while the doors are equipped with capacious side pockets, attractively shirred and ideal for holding magazines, road maps, and small parcels. Window and ventipane controls are designed for sure grip and easy operation and have richly colored plastic knobs that harmonize with the interior trim. Now let's have a look at the dashboard. See the electric clock mounted in the glove-compartment door? Stays accurate within three seconds a year. Plus you've got an automatic electric cigar lighter and multiple ash receivers. Not only that, this particular model features Buick's exclusive retractable Sunshine Turret Top—ideal for warm afternoons. But don't think that just because the Limited is spacious, she's slow, because she comes equipped with our 141-horsepower Dynaflash oil-cushioned, valve-in-head, straight-eight engine. You can go from ten to sixty miles per hour in eighteen seconds flat. And our exclusive BuiCoil spring rests guarantee a smooth ride even on the roughest road. Now, hold on to your seat and watch the clock." I shifted gears, pressed my foot to the accelerator.

"Whoa," Edward said, putting a hand on the dashboard.

We hit sixty. "How many seconds was that?"

"Fourteen. I'm sold. I'm ready to write the check."

"You can write it, but I won't take it."

"Why not?"

"The same reason you wouldn't take that fellow's money—the one you made the bet with . . . No, I'm afraid I'll just have to sell her at a loss. Well, easy come, easy go . . . Do you know what I heard yesterday? The last time the *Excambion* set sail, some Polish grandee was hawking his Rolls-Royce on the pier—as the ship was getting ready to weigh anchor. Literally as it was weighing anchor."

"But why sell at a loss when I'll give you market value?"

"And what do you propose to do with a car when you can't even drive?"

"I'll leave it here. To pick up when I come back."

"So you think you'll come back?"

"Why not?"

I brooded over this for a moment. "Julia seems to think that if we leave, it's for good. She's putting in for staying here, in Portugal."

"It might not be the worst idea. Portugal's neutral, after all. I know, people say it won't last. Still, I wouldn't underestimate Salazar. He's shrewd. He knows how to play both sides against the middle."

"Then why are people like the Fischbeins so desperate to get out?"

"Because they've got no status. No standing. And look what they've come out of. War. Real war. They'd like to put an ocean between themselves and that. We had it easy, comparatively speaking."

I couldn't disagree with this. In Paris, the war had at first seemed little more than a costume party. In anticipation of air raids, Julia had bought herself a Charles Creed *alerte-plaid* poncho and an haute-couture gas-mask holder in red tweed with gold studs from Lanvin. According to *Vogue*, an haute-couture gas-mask holder was now a necessity no sophisticated Parisienne should be without.

Things got worse in the spring. A few bombs fell. Nonetheless, the attitude of the newspapers remained phlegmatic. Then one afternoon, on my way home from work, I happened to notice smoke rising from behind the foreign ministry. I wondered if it was another bomb. It turned out that the functionaries were throwing bales of documents out the windows, onto a bonfire.

That evening, under cover of darkness, the government fled the capital—first for Tours, then Bordeaux—and the next evening, our

Buick packed to the hilt, Julia and I followed suit. In the gas-mask holder, which had never held a gas mask, we put everything we didn't want the customs agents to find.

"Look," Edward said, pointing out the window. "It's the Exposition!"

I looked. The Exposition was floodlit like an aerodrome. Everything about it was titanic: the pavilions, the statues, the fountains shooting sprays of water sixty feet in the air. "This is what happens when modernism comes under the spell of Fascism," Edward said. "The avant-garde becomes the vehicle for the promotion of the very forces it should seek to subvert. A modernist vernacular is hijacked for the purposes of promulgating the values of an idyllic past, a past that never was. A sort of politically enforced nostalgia . . . Is that perhaps the definition of Fascism?"

"I couldn't say."

"And to think that this time next year it'll all be torn down."

"Really?"

"Of course. It's just a stage set. Otherwise how could they have knocked it up so fast? You know, you've really got to hand it to Salazar. He's got that show-must-go-on spirit. I mean, the war couldn't have come at a worse time for him."

"At least the hotels are full."

"Oh, but they were supposed to be full. With tourists, not refugees."

This was correct. Earlier I had asked Senhor Costa how many of the guests at the Francfort were in Lisbon for the Exposition. "Perhaps ten," he had said—under his breath, as if it was shameful. "As for the rest—what passports I have seen, sir! Bulgarian, Hungarian, Polish, Russian, Japanese, Soviet, Luxembourger, Nansen. All come to Lisbon, and why? To leave Lisbon."

What was odd—what no one at first understood—was why Salazar had let so many refugees in in the first place. Edward's opinion was that it was all thanks to the Portuguese consul in Bordeaux. "Do you remember the scene at the consulate?" he asked. "The consul was signing visas all night, signing every visa that crossed his desk. When Iris and I were there, he had a rabbi helping him, an old-style rabbi, wearing a prayer shawl. The rabbi would stamp the passport, then the consul would sign it. No questions asked. Like an assembly line."

Though I didn't remember the rabbi, I did remember the consul: a fat man with a beard, spooning stew into his mouth with one hand and signing with the other. It was true, he wasn't turning anyone away. It was also true that when Julia and I finally left with our visas, at around eleven at night, the consulate was still open and showed no signs of closing. By contrast, the Spanish consulate closed every afternoon on the stroke of five, no matter how long the line snaking up its stairwell.

"The point is, by signing all these visas, the consul was flagrantly violating his orders, which were not to issue a single visa without getting clearance from Lisbon. He had a conscience—for which he'll pay dearly. And in the meantime Salazar's stuck with a hundred thousand refugees."

"Can't he send them back?"

"Back where? Spain won't have them. France won't have them. Did I tell you about the couple Iris and I met on the International Bridge? The wife was Dutch, the husband Belgian. It turned out they'd made it through the French border patrol and crossed into Spain, only to be told by the Spaniards that there was something wrong with the wife's visa—they couldn't read the date or something—and she had to go back to France and get a new one. So then she walked back to the French side of the bridge, where the French guards told her that she couldn't enter France because she didn't have a French entry visa. So then she trooped back to the Spanish side, only to be told . . . Well, you get the picture. For all I know, she's still on the bridge."

Julia and I had also crossed the International Bridge. There were two lanes for cars—one for ordinary cars, such as ours, which moved at a crawl, and the other for vehicles with diplomatic plates, of which perhaps ten passed during the five hours we spent on that bridge. Getting through Spanish customs took another five hours, at the end of which an officer mapped out a route to the Portuguese frontier. If we diverged from this route, we were warned, we could be arrested.

Spain might have been the worst part of the trip. Julia refused to eat anything. Such was her fussiness about the sanitary facilities that she developed an acute case of constipation. For hours at a time she played solitaire—she had rigged up a sort of board that she could hold on her lap—or gazed at the photographs of our apartment in *Vogue*, from which she sometimes read aloud: "It was the wish of the lady of the house, an American long resident in Europe, to maintain the flat's Parisian charm while reducing its Parisian crowdedness. Less of everything—Colette instead of Proust! Matisse instead of Ingres!—but still distinctly *à la française*." She had only one copy, and it was getting dog-eared.

Now, in the Buick, I looked at Edward. I wanted to reassure myself that it was actually he, not Julia, who was in the passenger seat. Like a dog, he had his face out the window. "Look, we're in Estoril!" he said. "There's the Atlantic!" He pointed at a hotel, from the roof of which the name ATLÂNTICO pulsed out in neon. "And that's the Palace!" Again, the name, PALÁCIO, was written on the roof—which led me to wonder if he'd even actually been to Estoril. It was an impression he liked to give, that anywhere he went was a place he'd been before.

We parked the car. From the steps of the casino, an English-style park rolled toward the ocean. We walked up an avenue lined with palm trees to the entrance. "Feel that breeze," Edward said. "So much cooler than Lisbon. Doesn't it remind you of the Riviera? You know, that slightly convalescent air, and all these hotels that look vaguely like hospitals. And then the train tracks dividing the beach from the town. Only it's not the Mediterranean on the other side, it's the Atlantic. That's a big difference. I could never abide Mediterranean resorts, the water like a tepid bath. Whereas an ocean is wilder than a sea. Listen, even from here you can hear the waves."

I listened—and heard the engines of limousines, the wail of dance music, the chattering of café-goers. Certain words are the same in every European language. Visa. Passport. Hotel.

We arrived at the casino. As at Macy's, commissionaires with epaulets on their shoulders held open the doors. Past the gaming tables and the poker parlors and the cinema and the Wonder Bar Edward led me to a vast rotunda where Europeans in evening dress were dancing. He pulled a table out from the wall, indicated that I should sit, then, when I had, pushed the table back in so that it pinned me.

"I feel like a child being tucked into bed," I said.

"Just call me Nanny," he said. Overhead, an immense chandelier shivered. The orchestra was playing Noël Coward's "World Weary," the singer pronouncing the lyrics phonetically:

When I'm feeling weary and blue, I'm only too
glad to be left alone,
dreaming of a place in the sun when day is done
far from a telephone . . .

"Hardly ever see the sky," Edward sang along, "buildings seem to grow so high."

Give me somewhere peaceful and grand
Where all the land slumbers in monotone . . .

A waiter appeared. "Absinthe," Edward ordered. "It's legal here," he added after the waiter had left.

"I know. I've never tried it."

"Really? The kiss of the green fairy is bitter." Under the table I could feel the pressure of his leg against mine. "I actually learned quite a bit about absinthe when we were writing the second of the Legrand novels. Iris's idea was that the victim should be an absinthe hound. Since he can't get the stuff in Paris, he has it smuggled in from Spain. Well, his wife hates him, so she decides to do away with him by putting cyanide in his absinthe. Her gambit is that the coroner will declare the cause of death to be absinthe poisoning—which he does."

I'm world weary, world weary,
Living in a great big town . . .

"And is there actually such a thing as absinthe poisoning?"

"Only to the extent that there's such a thing as alcohol poisoning. The thujone itself is relatively harmless."

The waiter returned, bearing on his tray the elaborate implementa of absinthe. These included a carafe of water and two tiny glasses, each of which he filled a quarter of the way with the viscous green liqueur. Then he balanced a leaf-shaped perforated spoon atop each glass. Then he put a sugar cube atop each spoon. It was Edward who poured the water from the carafe through the sugar cubes—at which the absinthe clouded. "To sweeten, a little, the green fairy's kiss."

We toasted wordlessly. In flavor the absinthe reminded me of some strong licorice my mother used to keep by her bedside—to mask, I suppose, the bourbon on her breath.

I'm world weary, world weary,
Tired of all these jumping jacks . . .

Suddenly a woman stumbled out of the crowd. "Eddie, is that you?"

"Oh, God," Edward said. "Hello, George."

The woman leaned over for a kiss, so that her breasts hung like bladders. A diamond-studded cross dangled between them. She was in her sixties, with freckled skin and untidy gray-black hair.

"George, this is Pete."

"Georgina Kendall, pleased to meet you," the woman said, holding out a hand that seemed to be all swollen knuckles. "I'm here with Lucy. You remember Lucy? From the train?"

He nodded.

"Eddie and I met on the Sud Express, when it was stuck outside Salamanca," Georgina said to me.

"In war, trains never run on time," Edward said aphoristically.

"Tell me about it! Anyway, we got to be great friends, the four of us—Lucy and me and Eddie and Aster. How is Aster, by the way? And that charming little schnauzer."

"Both fine. Are you staying here in Estoril?"

"Yes, we're at the Palace, and it's costing me a fortune—Lucy has a weakness for the tables—but I'm hoping the material I'm collecting for my book will earn us back her losses and then some. You see, I'm a writer"—this to me—"and I'm working on a memoir. Not a diary—a memoir. I mean, I'm writing it as if I'm already back home, sitting in my study, recalling all I've been through. It's to be called *Flight from France*. Now, you may ask why I'm doing it that way, and I'll tell you. It's because I know the market. This time next year, I guarantee, the bookshops will be swamped with memoirs of foreigners escaping France, and I'm not about to let anyone pip me at the post."

"But isn't that a bit tricky?" Edward said. "You'll have to falsify your perspective. Pretend that you're looking back when really you're right in the thick of things."

"Illusion, as you know perfectly well, Eddie, is the writer's stock in trade. Anyway, no one likes to read diaries. They're so boring. 'June thirtieth. Woke up, had breakfast. June thirty-first. Woke up, had breakfast.'"

"June thirty-first?"

"Well, you know what I mean."

"But what if something totally unexpected happens? What if Portugal joins the Allies? Or Franco teams up with Hitler? It'll ruin your ending."

"Now you're making fun of me."

"No, I'm not. I'm challenging you. I'm calling your bluff."

"Dear Eddie," Georgina said as she turned to me, "he seems to think writers ought to behave like newspaper reporters. He doesn't understand that for us time doesn't exist. Consider Proust." She smiled, showing her small, uneven teeth. "Well, I must be off. Give Aster my best. And the dog."

As she disappeared into the crowd, I pressed my leg harder against Edward's. Suddenly I wanted to hurt him. I wanted to make him cry uncle.

He didn't even blink. "Now that, my boy," he said, "is a hack. *Hackus literarius.* In case you've never seen a live specimen."

"I've never even heard of her."

"Better that you haven't. She's a charlatan. Just another of these rich American women who've been idling around in Nice since the Napoleonic Wars. Nice, or maybe Saint-Tropez."

"Strange, this notion of writing about what's happening as if it's already happened."

"Fear of the future, that's what it is. She thinks that if she can make the present the past, the future can't hurt her."

"And you? Aren't you afraid of the future?"

"What's to be afraid of? The future doesn't exist. It's the past that frightens me."

"Why?"

"Because it can't be undone, and it can never be known." Under the table he changed position, so that his legs were squeezing mine. "That's the trouble, you see, these days we all spend so much time worrying about the future that the present moment slips right out of our hands. And so all we have left is retrospection and anticipation, retrospection and anticipation. In which case what's left to recall but past anticipation? What's left to anticipate but future retrospection?"

"I know what you mean," I said. "It's like my brother Harry. The last time I saw him and his wife, they spent the whole of breakfast arguing about where to have lunch."

"Exactly."

"And the whole of lunch arguing about where to have dinner."

"Yes!"

"And the whole of dinner going over what they'd had for breakfast *and* lunch."

"That's it! That's the thing to avoid."

"But how can you avoid it when everywhere you turn, you have to make plans, learn from your mistakes, strategize?"

"Right, how can you? How the hell can you?" He leaned in closer. "Are you feeling it now?"

"What? Your leg?"

"No, I know you're feeling that. The absinthe."

"I'm not sure. What am I supposed to feel?"

"You're supposed to hallucinate."

"I might be hallucinating. I'll need to check."

I looked out at the crowd.

"What do you see?"

"People dancing. Oh, there are the Fischbeins. Do you see them?"

"I do. I do see them. So either we're having the same hallucination or they're really there."

If the Fischbeins were there, they didn't recognize us. Monsieur Fischbein wore a tuxedo a size too big for him, Madame Fischbein a green taffeta evening gown. Against her freckled wattle, her pearls gleamed. Her fur coat was again slung over the back of her chair.

"They are as bad as the Germans," Monsieur Fischbein was telling some unseen auditor. "They say to us we need one paper, we bring. Then they say to us we need another paper, we tell them we cannot bring. Then they say to us they are sorry, we should try another country. But where, I ask you? Terre de Feu?"

It seemed it was always Terre de Feu.

"We will go back to Antwerp," Madame Fischbein said. "Whatever the Germans do, it cannot be worse than this."

With a fatalistic flourish, the old couple took to the dance floor. Around and around they waltzed, to the tune of "When I Grow Too Old to Dream," Madame leaning her forehead against Monsieur's bony shoulder. "Look at them," Edward said. "Gather ye rosebuds while ye may and all that. It's the end of Europe, that's why they're dancing, and of course Lisbon is the end of Europe, too. The fingertip of Europe. And everything that Europe is and means is pressed into that fingertip. Too much of it. It's a cistern full to overflowing—and each time a ship sails, the water level goes down a little. But not nearly enough. And in the meantime the floodgates remain open."

"Hold on a minute. According to what you just said, Lisbon is a cistern—"

"Right."

"So the refugees are water—"

"Correct."

"But that means that when they get on the ship—the ship is carrying water as its cargo. Carrying as its cargo the very element on which it sails."

"What, you're saying my metaphor *doesn't hold water?*"

We both burst out laughing.

"Now are you feeling it?"

"I believe I am."

"Shall we have some more?"

"Let's."

He refilled our glasses. How long had I known him then? Twelve hours? Fourteen? It's true: in war, trains never run on time. And now this one, like the Wabash Cannonball, was about to arrive at its destination—only it hadn't yet left. Or had it left the moment he'd stepped on my glasses?

Half an hour later, he asked for the bill. "Don't even try," he said when I took out my wallet.

I stood, and was surprised that my legs still worked.

"Where to?"

"The beach. Not the one here in Estoril—it's crawling with police. We'll go down the coast, to Guincho."

We got into the car. For a moment I entertained the possibility that I ought not to be driving in such a condition. I entertained it and dismissed it. For I felt none of the symptoms of inebriation, not giddiness nor agitation nor sleepiness. Rather, what I felt— have you ever driven on a wet road in winter? Do you know that moment when suddenly the car seems to lift right off the surface of the earth? That was what I felt.

I had no idea what time it was. There were timepieces everywhere—on my wrist, on the dashboard—yet I didn't look at any of them. After Cascais, the road grew narrower and more windy, far too windy to accommodate such a gargantuan vehicle— and still I navigated them effortlessly, as if the laws of nature had ceased to apply, as if the car had suddenly acquired an unsuspected elasticity, allowing it to bend like an accordion. Even when a bicy- clist appeared in my headlights, I didn't flinch. I simply veered around him. In retrospect, I understand that it was all the absinthe, and that this is one of the many reasons why absinthe is dangerous. Now I wonder that we didn't kill someone, or get killed ourselves.

Then we got to Guincho, where two or three other cars were parked on the road's shoulder. Through a grove of umbrella pines, Edward led me out onto dunes that descended to a crescent-shaped beach. Here and there, shadowy hummocks rose where couples slept or made love under blankets. The moon was high. "Now do you see what I mean about the difference between the Atlantic and the Med- iterranean?" he said, taking off his shoes. White-tipped breakers slapped the shore. He rolled up his cuffs and waded into the surf. As I followed, I tried to fit my footprints into his, so that there would be only one set.

The water stung my ankles. "It's cold," I said, stepping back, but Edward wasn't listening.

"Where the land ends and the sea begins," he said. "That's Camões, the great Lusitanian poet. He wrote that about Cabo da Roca, at the

westernmost point in all of Europe. It's just a little ways to the
north. Look." He put his hands on my shoulders, pointing me in the
direction of some murky cliffs. "Can you see it?"

"I don't know. But I'll tell people that I did."

"Yes. Let's tell people that we did."

He did not move his hands.

"Pete—"

"What?"

"May I say something?"

"Of course."

"I have never in my life been so happy as I am at this moment."

His voice was so solemn I nearly laughed.

"Do you think I'm mad or evil to say that?" he went on. "I mean,
here we are in Portugal—Portugal, for God's sake—and all around
us, all you can see is suffering and fear, suffering and panic. And
then when you consider that the people here, they're the lucky ones,
just because they managed to get this far . . . What right do I have
to be happy? Yet I am. I'm not ashamed of it, either."

"Maybe it's because you're safe."

"Yes. There's a sense of relief you can't help but feel—at knowing you've been thrown clear of danger. And yet the panic and fear
of others, the panic and suffering of others . . . It's still there
And we're feeding on it, aren't we? We might as well admit we're
feeding on it. It should really only belong to them, this weird vitality,
this sense that you can do things you wouldn't normally let yourself
do . . . We have no right to it, yet we're sharing in it . . . And that's
not the only reason I'm happy. That's not even the principal reason
I'm happy. It's because of you."

"Me?"

"Isn't that obvious?"

"But why? I'm so ordinary. And you've done so much in your life, gone to Harvard and Cambridge, known so many interesting people—"

He covered my mouth with his hand. "Quiet. You don't know anything about me. You don't know—anything."

He was now standing so close that I wondered if he was going to kiss me. Instead he took off his jacket. With one swift motion he yanked his shirt and tie over his head.

"Let's swim," he said.

"Swim?"

"Come on!" Already he had his trousers and shorts off. White buttocks blazing, he ran into the water, where he got on his knees as if in prayer. A wave crested over him. It withdrew and he was gone.

"Edward!" I called.

A few seconds later, another wave hurled him back onto the sand. "That was glorious!" he said, pushing his hair back. "Come on!"

I didn't hesitate. I pulled off my clothes as he had, without ceremony. I took off my glasses. The patch of darkness toward which I swam might have been a rock or a sea monster. All I had to navigate by was Edward's voice. "Warmer," he said. "Colder . . . Warmer . . ."

Suddenly we collided. The hair on his chest was slick as seaweed. I could feel the contours of his pectoral muscles. I could feel his erection.

Behind us a wave was building. I tried to draw away, but Edward wouldn't let me go. "The thing to do is to go under it," he said. "Hold on to me."

Then he pulled me down until we were sitting on the sandy bottom. The wave broke over us. I felt it as the faintest trembling.

We rose again. I was laughing. He took my head in his hands, and now he did kiss me. Another wave broke, pulling us apart from each other, sending us tumbling.

"Edward!" I called, but he didn't answer. I turned and saw a bigger wave approaching and, remembering what he had said, I dove down, cleaving myself to the ocean floor.

This time I felt the wave as a rumbling—what I imagined an earthquake would feel like.

"Pete!" I heard him calling as I broke the surface.

"I'm here!" I answered.

Separately we stumbled out of the water. The tide had carried us thirty feet or so up the shoreline. To reach our clothes we had to backtrack. "A pity we didn't bring towels," he said, drying his face with his shirt.

I put on my glasses. The salt water had marked them. As in a cartoon of drunkenness, I saw spots

"Where are you going?" I asked Edward, who had picked up his pile of clothes and was moving in the direction of the dunes.

Again he didn't answer. Maybe he hadn't heard me. I picked up my own clothes and followed him, until we reached the perimeter of the pine trees. Tufts of beach grass burst sporadically from the sand. Edward put his clothes down and stepped toward me.

Very delicately, he took the glasses from my face, folded them, and rested them atop his pile of clothes.

"Why did you do that?" I said.

And he said, "So that you can truthfully say you never saw what was coming."

Somewhere

9

It was five in the morning when I got back to Lisbon. Though the sky was still dark, the stars were gone. You could feel the imminence of sunrise. The entrance to the Francfort was locked. I had to ring the bell three times before the porter, vexed to have been wakened, let me in. The lobby had a hushed, churchlike air. An OUT OF SERVICE sign now hung on the elevator, so I took the stairs to the second floor, where I knocked timorously on the door to our room. No reply. I knocked a little louder. Still no reply. It was while I was pondering the dilemma of how to knock loudly enough to wake Julia, yet softly enough not to wake our neighbors, that I heard a groan and a stumble. Wraithlike in her pajamas, Julia let me in. The room was impossibly shadowy, as rooms where others have been sleeping so often seem to those who have been out all night.

"I had a terrible headache, so I took a Seconal," Julia said. "What time is it?"

"Never mind. Go back to sleep."

She staggered to the bed and was at once snoring. I went into the bathroom and got undressed. In my jacket pocket I found the copy of *The Noble Way Out* that I had bought at Bertrand, still in its brown-paper wrapping. I put it on top of the toilet, then took off my shoes. They were full of sand. My socks, too, were full of sand. When I pulled down my pants, sand spilled onto the floor. With a brush, I tried to sweep it all up—to no avail, since every time I bent over, more sand fell from me. The grains were clustered in the hair on my chest and legs. They seemed to be moving, like lice. I got into the bath, where I rinsed and rinsed with tepid water, and yet it seemed that there was always some further crevice or cleft in which the sand hid. Soon the drain was blocked. The tub wouldn't empty. I dried off and dressed. Clearly Julia was down for the count, so I headed downstairs, where I told the porter to let her know that I would be at the Suiça. In the interval, the sun had risen. Save for the occasional businessman reading his newspaper as he walked, the occasional market woman carrying a basket of fish on her head, the streets were empty. At the Suiça, yawning busboys were just taking the chairs off the tables. The coffee that the waiter brought me was the first of the day, with grounds at the bottom of the cup. On the sidewalk, pigeons strutted, their feathers the color of pencil-eraser smudges.

I tried to clarify in my head the events of the previous night. The trouble was, everything was clouded in an absinthe haze, in which the actual could not easily be distinguished from the hallucinatory. Perhaps instinct itself is a sort of green fairy, the bitter taste of which we temper with excuses: I was drunk. It was late. The world was ending. Of course, such excuses are paper thin. Even as we make them, we don't believe them. They are part of the ritual, along with the carafe and the sugar cube and the perforated spoon.

Toward dawn, the green mist cleared a little. We were walking back to the car, the cuffs of our pants rolled up, our shoes in our hands. There was still some moonlight, which gave me a chance to reflect upon how big Edward's feet were—at least twice as big as Julia's. On each meaty knuckle, a tuft of stiff, pale hair stood out. For a man who is habituated to sleeping with women, the body of another man is always a bewilderment, not in its strangeness but in its familiarity—the strangeness of its familiarity. Touching Edward on the beach, in the dark, I might have been touching myself—and so I assumed that what I would want done to me he would want done to him. And sometimes he did. But sometimes he did not.

Hard, hairy sternum where there should have been pillowy breasts; stomach going soft but still firm under the surface fat; testicles like prunes, and the organ itself, gay like Daisy's tail, circumcised, and so requiring more than its own lubrications to function—a bit of a problem, that, since on the beach we had nothing to hand, as it were, except what we could make in our mouths. And we kept getting sand in our mouths . . . All this came back to me as I sat outside the Suiça, and the sun resumed its posture of perennial bored sovereignty, like a lifeguard on his high chair, and the pigeons gathered, on the lookout for any new customers who, out of gratitude at finding themselves, after so many months, in a city with bread to spare, might give them some crumbs . . . Either I was in the throes of the strangest dream I'd ever dreamed or everything I'd known until now—my entire life—was the dream, and Edward the warm bed in which I had at last awakened from it.

Then I saw Julia crossing the Rossio on the diagonal. She was wearing high heels, and between these and the black-and-white polka-dot dress she had chosen, I thought how much she looked like a pigeon; whereas Iris was like a great awkward waterbird, a pelican or, as her classmates had observed early on, a stork. Julia had her black hair tied back with a white ribbon. "I meant to wash it this morning, but I couldn't," she said as she sat down. "What the hell happened in the bathroom? It looks as if a sandstorm hit."

"That's my fault, I'm afraid. I was on the beach last night."

"The beach! I thought you were just going out for a drink."

"We were. But then on the spur of the moment we decided to go to Estoril."

"At that hour? How did you get there?"

"We took the car."

"Our car?"

"Why not? What else is it for?"

She pushed a stray hair out of her eyes. "I hope you found some-place to park it when you got back."

"Actually, I left it at the station in Estoril. Don't worry, I'll pick it up this afternoon. We'd had quite a bit to drink, so we came back in a taxi."

"I see." A pause like the trembling ash on the end of a cigarette. "Quite a night, was it?"

"Do you disapprove?"

"Not at all. In fact, I'm rather pleased. You're usually such a stick-in-the-mud, it's good to know you're capable of having an adventure. Even if it isn't with me."

The formation of habits is something else that travel accelerates. After a week, the waiter at the Suiça knew us well enough that we didn't have to order. For Julia he brought a cup of black coffee, for me another *garoto*, as well a plate of those flan-filled tartlets I loved so much.

"Anyway, was it fun?" She was stirring nothing into her coffee. "Did you have fun?"

"I suppose."

"It's curious, in Paris you never had many male friends."

"Well, other than the guys at work, who was I supposed to pal around with? Your decorator?"

"What, you couldn't have been friends with Jean just because he's a fairy?"

"His being a fairy had nothing to do with it. We just didn't have much in common. And I didn't have a whole lot of time, Julia. You seem to have forgotten that. I had a job. On the weekends I was tired. The last thing I wanted to do was to, I don't know, play tennis with your decorator."

"But here in Lisbon it's a different story, is that what you're saying?"

"Well, I've got time. For the first time since I can remember. Unlike these poor souls who have to wait all day in lines in front of consulates. And so, yes, I did enjoy myself last night. I did."

"You act as if I'm trying to take that away from you. I'm not."

I wiped my glasses—and remembered how Edward had lifted them from my face.

"You don't like him, do you?" I said.

"Edward?" Julia lit a cigarette reflectively. "Well . . . I wouldn't say I *dis*like him. He's just a bit of a know-it-all. If anything, I find him dull."

"And Iris?"

"Oh, I like *her*. She's interesting. I mean, she's done such interesting things. What puzzles me is how she ended up with *him*. Yet you often find that with women who grew up as orphans, they gravitate toward men who need mothering. It's the same with the dog. A way of giving back what they didn't get themselves as children."

"I wonder why they never had children of their own."

"Oh, but they did. They do. A daughter. Retarded or something. She's in an institution—in California, I think."

I put my glasses back on.

"I'm surprised he didn't say anything about it," Julia continued, "given what great pals you two have become."

I too was surprised. Then again, had the daughter been mine, would I have mentioned her to Edward?

We were quiet. Julia took out her solitaire cards.

"Do you think you and he are really cousins?" I asked after a moment.

"Of course not," she said. "Just because we have relations in the same city . . . It's ridiculous."

"Still, you *could* be cousins."

She looked me evenly in the eye. "We are *not* cousins, and I'll thank you not to bring the matter up again."

She swept the cards together and dealt.

"He's from an entirely different social class. *My* grandfather was a banker."

"What was Edward's grandfather?"

"I have no idea."

"Still, his money had to come from somewhere."

"His money? I assumed it was her money." Suddenly she was looking over my head. "Oh my God, there they are. Act like you haven't seen them."

"Why?"

"Because if we wave or make a fuss, they'll feel obliged to sit with us, and they mayn't want to. I don't want her to think we're pests."

Like a child caught spying, Julia cast her eyes downward, at her cards. Not knowing where else to look, I looked straight ahead. Iris was kneeling on the ground, trying, from what I could make out, to dislodge something from Daisy's paw. I couldn't tell if she'd spotted us.

After a few minutes, Julia's game gave out. She put away the cards and stood. "Come on," she said.

I didn't need to ask for the bill. I knew exactly how much we owed. We walked past the Frelengs' table—and Edward smiled up at us. "Hello there," he said.

"Oh, hello," Julia said, as if surprised.

Then I said hello. Then Iris said hello.

Then there was a moment when we might have sat down, or they might have asked us to sit down.

It passed.

"Well, lovely to see you," Julia said. "Come on, darling."

"Goodbye," I said.

Edward's smile was almost mournful. With his index finger he stroked a postcard that lay on the table. It was of the beach at Guincho.

10

Back at the hotel, Julia went into the bathroom. She left the door ajar. In the early years of our marriage, she would never have left the door ajar. I wouldn't have, either. Only over time does the impulse toward modesty fall away in a marriage, leaving in its wake a laxness, an ease of intimacy, that is at once comfortable and terrible. Thus, in their old age my parents had no qualms whatsoever about using the toilet in front of each other—this though it had been eons since they had slept in the same bed. Oh, it is a strange business . . .

A few minutes later she emerged. In her hand was the book I had bought earlier.

"When did you get this?" she asked.

"Yesterday. I was going to ask them to sign it, but I forgot."

"Thank heavens for that. Pete, promise me something. Promise me you will not ask them to sign it."

"Why?"

"Because it would be gauche. You've got to trust me on this. I know more about these things than you do."

Her notions of what constituted propriety had always puzzled me. "All right. I won't ask them to sign it."

"Have you started reading it?"

"Not yet."

"I might give it a look." She took off her shoes and lay down on the bed. " 'Monsieur Hellier's body had been found in his office,' " she read aloud. " 'He had shot himself in the mouth, and the blood had spilled onto a rare first edition of Balzac's *Illusions Perdues*.' "

"A lively opening."

"Though not especially original."

I took her word for this. I had little experience of mystery novels.

After lunch I took the train to Estoril to pick up the car. To my relief Julia didn't offer to come with me. She was deeply immersed in *The Noble Way Out*.

Edward was waiting for me when I got there, leaning against the chassis in perfect contrapposto. Daisy lay at his feet.

I embraced him. Apparently I was trembling. "Easy, easy," he said.

"I hoped you'd be here," I said. "I hoped so, but I wasn't sure. I thought about it on the train, and I couldn't see why you would be."

"Well, I am, so that's that. When do you have to be back?"

"I don't know. Dinnertime?"

"Good, that gives us hours."

In the backseat of the Buick, Daisy rotated twice, as was her habit, and went to sleep. I put my left hand on Edward's leg. For the duration of the trip he held it there firmly, returning it to me only when my not crashing into another car necessitated it.

"Are you tired?"

"Exhausted. You?"

"The same. I wish we could spend the whole night together—and not have to get up in the morning. But of course in a situation like ours, one always has to get up in the morning."

This was the first time he had used that word—"situation"—in regard to us. He spoke it in the voice of a man who had been in situations before.

We were passing the Exposition. In the noon light, the pavilions, so impressive at night, looked gimcrack, provisional. Or was it the city that was provisional, the Exposition that had endured for eight hundred years?

Perhaps I wasn't driving at all. Perhaps the car was standing still, while unseen laborers moved huge stage sets around me.

To test the theory, I took my hands off the wheel. The car weaved and Daisy woke with a start. I grabbed the wheel back.

"Steady," Edward said.

"I'm sorry. I'm a little lightheaded today."

"That's to be expected. You haven't slept. You've been through an upheaval."

Which upheaval was he referring to? The war? The drive to Lisbon? Meeting him?

"I'm not really feeling upheaved," I said. "Is that a word?"

"If it isn't, it should be."

"No, what I'm feeling—it's more an eerie sort of calm. Like what I felt when we crossed into Portugal. As if all the trouble was behind us, not ahead of us. Is that crazy?"

"I'd really like to learn how to drive. Maybe you can teach me when we get back. Where did you say you were from?"

I wasn't sure that I had said. "Indianapolis."

"That's Indiana, right? Well, of course. The Midwest's unknown territory to me. Maybe we could drive there together—to Indianapolis—and you could teach me on the way. And then we could go on to California. You could meet my mother."

"And your daughter?" I almost said—but didn't. For while we were talking, Lisbon had caught up with us. Soon the piers gave way to the familiar listing buildings, their facades painted fanciful shades of blue and pink and green. Morning glories blossomed on rusty iron balconies. "Park here," Edward said when Cais do Sodré— the station from which the Estoril trains departed—came into view.

"It might be hard to find a place," I said—and at that moment I found one.

"The parking god has always looked on me with favor," he said.

We got out of the car. Edward put Daisy on the leash and headed off. I followed. Like Daisy, he walked with decision, as if he knew exactly where he was going. The question was whether he did know exactly where he was going—as Daisy did not.

Taxis were circling the Praça Duque de Terceira, apparently for the sheer pleasure of it. Some of them were motorcycles; the passengers rode in the sidecars. We cut across the traffic to Rua do Alecrim, which ascends from the Tagus to the Bairro Alto at such a steep incline that at its base the street takes the form of a sloped bridge below which Rua Nova do Carvalho runs like a river. Smaller staircase bridges connect the bridge to the houses on either side. We climbed one of these. The door had no sign. Edward rang the bell.

After a moment a girl with a port-wine stain on her cheek answered. She wore a French maid's uniform that might have come from a theatrical costumery. She kissed Edward, then stepped aside to let us in.

We were standing in a tiny, rectangular entrance hall. In front of us an enormous staircase rose, as vertiginous as Rua do Alecrim itself.

Up we went, the maid first, then me, then Edward with Daisy. Never in my life had I climbed a staircase that long that was not broken up by landings, that neither doubled back on itself nor coiled around an elevator shaft.

What would happen if I fell? Would he catch me? Or would I knock him down, so that we landed at the base in a broken heap?

To keep the sensation of vertigo at bay, I trained my attention on the maid's back. She had a white apron tied around her waist, just under the bust. I counted the steps until we reached the top.

We entered a sort of reception room. The curtains were drawn. In the dim light the walls were the color of bruised figs. Dispersed about the room were sofas and chairs upholstered in muddy velvet with bullion fringe, upon which girls and women, some wearing cocktail dresses and some wearing silk slips and one wearing only a pair of silk drawers, lounged in attitudes of display. Most held glasses of what looked like champagne. A few smoked. A few rested their heads on each other's laps.

There was an odor of ammonia and licorice. On the gramophone, a fado was being sung.

Noticing Daisy, two of the girls beckoned her. She went to them without hesitation. The susurrant words they uttered as they caressed her could have been the ones they used with their clients. With their long nails they scratched her nape, pulled at the scruff of her neck. She put her ears back. From a standing position she collapsed into a squat, from the squat into a sprawl, her hind legs spread behind her.

An elderly woman, stout and even shorter than Julia's mother, stepped out from the shadows. She wore more jewelry than Madame Fischbein. Standing on tiptoe, she kissed Edward on both cheeks, as the maid had.

"This is Señora Inés," Edward said, at which she smiled and held out a hand swollen with rings.

"Enchanté," I said, wincing from her grasp: the rings cut into my flesh.

She had a walleye. The left one. The dilemma of choosing which eye to meet—the moving eye or the still eye—revived the sensation of vertigo.

"Señora Inés is from Barcelona. All these girls are. She collects *les poupées.*" He indicated a shelf from which a dozen or so porcelain baby dolls glared at us sinisterly.

"Ah, oui," Señora Inés said. "Sont mes petits."

"Garçons?"

"Bien sur, garçons. Ici on a trop de femmes."

"Isn't it remarkable," Edward said to me under his breath, "the sentimentality into which even the most hardened prostitute will lapse in her dotage?"

One of the girls—the one wearing only drawers—stood and approached him. She was thirty-five or forty, with visible ribs and the sort of pot belly that gaunt women acquire with age. She touched his shoulder and whispered something in his ear. He laughed. A colleague, younger and plumper, came up to me and folded her arms around my neck. She opened her mouth to show her tongue, very pink and flecked with tiny bubbles.

I looked to Edward. He was kissing the prostitute in the silk drawers. This confused me. What were we doing here? I wanted to ask. Were we to go off separately, each with a prostitute? Or together, with two prostitutes? Had I misunderstood everything?

No. He turned to Señora Inés, who uttered some sharp words in Spanish. The girls undraped themselves and returned to their posts.

"Can't blame them for trying," Edward said. "Come on."

The maid led us up another staircase, narrower than the first though not as long. It gave onto a vestibule off of which several doors opened. She turned a key in one of these.

I stepped through. The room was larger than ours at the Francfort, though it had a lower ceiling. A portrait of the Virgin Mary hung over the bed, which was impeccably made, with a frayed silk coverlet.

Across from it stood an armoire and a dressing table with a basin and ewer. The lamps had pink shades, fringed and singed.

After tipping the maid, Edward shut and locked the door. He slipped the key into his breast pocket and let Daisy off her leash. No sooner was she free than she circumambulated the room, stopping only to lick at a stain on the tiled floor.

"Don't, Daisy," Edward said. "It's probably something vile." He walked to the window and opened it. "Look."

I looked. To our left I could see the ramp of Rua do Alecrim and the staircase bridge. Below us was a drop of several more floors to Rua Nova do Carvalho. "Isn't it strange?" Edward said. "It's because the floor on which we entered, though it looks like it, isn't the ground floor. Rather, it's the third floor. The ground floor is way below—do you see?—on that street that runs under the bridge—the bridge of Rua do Alecrim."

"How did you find this place?"

"I have my ways." He drew me away from the window. "Anyway, I hope it will do. Believe me, I racked my brains to think of something better, but given the shortage of hotel rooms—"

"But when? Where do you find the time?"

"There are more hours in the day than you might think." He took off my glasses, which he folded and slipped into his pocket. "Of course, at first she asked a ridiculous price—the price we would have paid for two hours *with* a girl. I had to haggle her down." He pulled off my jacket and threw it on the bed. I tried to take his off in kind, but he pushed my hand away and loosened my collar. Again I reached for his jacket. Again he pushed my hand away. He unknotted my tie and pulled my shirt and undershirt, together, over my head. Then he bent down and unlaced my shoes. Then, when the shoes were off, he pushed me onto the bed, onto my back, undid my belt, and yanked my trousers and shorts down and off in one swift gesture. The bundle of clothes he shoved into the armoire, which he locked, dropping the key into the same pocket that held the room key and my glasses.

"There," he said, surveying me. "This is better than the beach. I couldn't get a good look at you on the beach." As he spoke, he ran his hands down the length of my chest, along my legs, then up again, to where my erection bobbed. When he squeezed it, I groaned. *"Shh!"* he said, covering my mouth with one hand while with the other he clutched my testicles, just as hard.

It was when he reached his hand under my rump that I arched my back and let out the noise—something between a wail and a laugh—that woke Daisy, whose tongue I suddenly felt on my ankle.

"Quiet!" Edward said. He withdrew his hands and backed away. He looked me up and down, shook his head, and laughed, almost derisively.

"Perfect," he said.

Then he picked up Daisy and her leash, unlocked the door, and left. I could hear him relocking it on the other side. I could hear his footsteps on the stairs.

I sat up. The only sounds were birdsong and, further in the distance, the gramophone, still playing fados.

"Edward?" I called. "Edward!"

No answer. I walked to the window. After a minute or so, I saw two blurry figures, one large and one small, emerge from the front door of the house, descend the staircase bridge, and turn left, toward the river.

Never had the midday sun burned my eyes like this. It was as if the rays were boring into my head.

I closed the shutters and the window and drew the curtains. Save for the weak lamplight that leaked under the door, the room was pitch black. I had to feel my way to the bed. The sheets reeked of

Dettol and perfume and cigarettes. I pulled them to my chin. I turned on my side and put my arm under my pillow. I tried to stay absolutely still, for if I moved so much as a muscle in my neck, the pain in my head became intolerable.

Considering the circumstances, I was remarkably calm. It is often like this at moments of crisis. Understanding lags behind experience. The speculative engine takes a few minutes to kick in. Once it does, the very rhythm of its rotors has an oddly soothing effect.

I laid out the possibilities as Julia did her cards. Perhaps Edward was a spy, and had staged this elaborate deception for purposes of blackmail, to induce me to betray my country. Or perhaps he was a swindler, and when I got my clothes back I would find that my wallet and passport were missing. In either case, Iris was probably in on it with him—which meant this whole business about their being the authors of the novels was a lie. They were not Xavier Legrand. For wasn't that the mark of a good con man, that he came across as utterly credible? And really, when you thought about it, the thing was very cleverly managed. For how could I go after him, when I was naked in a locked room in a squalid brothel, my clothes stuffed into an armoire the key to which was in his pocket? And not just the key to the armoire but the key to the room? And not just the key to the room but my glasses? Oh, my glasses! And to think that if he hadn't stepped on them at the Suiça, there would never have been a "situation."

I shut my eyes. The throb in my head worsened. The Dettol smelled like burning rubber. You can put plugs in your ears to block noise, a mask over your eyes to block light. But what can you do to block a smell? Nonetheless I slept.

The next sound I heard was a rapping on the door. Female voices were shouting in Spanish. Ordinarily I am a man who is absurdly conscious of time. I have never in my life set an alarm clock. If I have to get up at a certain hour, I get up at that hour. When I awaken in the middle of the night, I always know exactly what time it is.

Now, though, I had no idea.

I almost rose—then remembered that, but for my socks, I was naked. On the far side of the door, the voices railed on.

"Je ne peux pas ouvrir la porte," I said. "Je n'ai pas la clé."

They didn't understand.

"I don't have the key. Je n'ai pas la clé."

Whispered consultation. Then silence.

The next voice was that of Señora Inés.

"Monsieur, c'est l'heure. Devez sortir."

"Je n'ai pas la clé. Monsieur—l'autre Monsieur—a pris la clé. Il est sorti."

"N'avez pas la clé?"

"Je n'ai pas la clé."

More consultation. Then footsteps. Then a master key must have been found, for in a moment the door opened. Señora Inés stepped through. She walked straight to the window, opened the curtains and the shutters, then turned to look at me, her arms crossed over her breasts. No doubt the spectacle of a naked man pulling bedcovers to his chest was one with which she was not unfamiliar. And still she wore an expression of unease.

One eye stared straight at me; the other looked a little to my left, as if to see what was outside the window.

I said, "Mes vêtements—ils sont dans l'armoire. Je n'ai pas la clé de l'armoire."

"N'avez pas la clé de l'armoire?"

"L'autre monsieur a pris tous les clés, tous les deux."

That the key to the armoire was missing apparently posed more of a difficulty than that the key to the door was missing. Señora Inés summoned the maid, who, upon entering the room, burst out laughing. Señora Inés rebuked her and she shut her mouth. Instructions were issued and the maid left. Señora Inés now crossed her arms again and peered at me with her moving eye. Was she also in on Edward's scheme? It seemed unlikely. From what I could tell, his flight had left her just as perplexed as it had me.

Eventually the maid returned. She carried half a dozen keys, each of which she tried in the lock on the armoire. The third one did the trick.

Señora Inés ordered the maid out. She took my clothes from the armoire and laid them on the bed, her attitude ruthlessly solicitous, like that of a nurse. Once the clothes were sorted, she left and shut the door. I got up and dressed. The chair on which I sat to lace my shoes was ridiculously low. To my surprise, both my wallet and my passport were in my jacket pocket, where I had left them.

Once I was put back together, I stepped out into the vestibule. I could hardly see. I had to feel my way down the stairs into the salon. In silence the prostitutes watched me, to make sure I felt the potency of their contempt.

Señora Inés stood behind the bar. "Combien?" I asked, reaching for my wallet.

She shook her head. "Monsieur Edward a déjà payé."

"Merci," I said.

Now came the most difficult challenge: the stairway. Clutching the railing, I descended like an invalid. No one offered to help me. Then again, no one could have helped me—the stairwell was too narrow for two people to go down it side by side.

As I neared the door, the light became stronger. I wondered how I would explain to Julia the loss of the second pair of glasses. At least I would not have to tell her I had been robbed of my money and my passport. Or would she welcome that news? For she was shrewd, my Julia. She would quickly calculate that between my having to wire for more money and having to obtain a new passport, we'd miss the sailing of the *Manhattan*. Why, in my avidity to win her forgiveness, I might even reconsider her wish to stay on in Portugal.

I had made it to the landing. I opened the door and stepped outside. Much to my surprise, rain was falling. The sky, so brilliantly blue the whole week, was a heavy gray.

Down the iron staircase I stumbled, onto the sidewalk. Heavy drops fell like birdshot. A blur of human traffic passed. When a space opened, I plunged into it.

I turned left, in the direction of the river. Edward was walking toward me, with Daisy.

He smiled. "Glad to see me?" he said.

"What?" I said.

"Are you glad to see me?"

I swung out and punched him in the face. He reeled and fell. Daisy barked. I pulled him up from the ground by his lapels, which I felt tearing.

"You bastard," I said, and hit him again. Again he fell, again I pulled him up. He was limp as a rag doll—and smiling.

"What kind of game are you playing?"

"No game."

I hit him a third time. By now Daisy was in a panic. She was straining at her leash, barking, nipping at my heels. "Give me my glasses," I said. He handed them over. I put them on and his face came into focus. Blood was streaming from his mouth, onto his shirt.

"Can we go back inside?" he said. "I need to put some ice on my jaw."

"You haven't answered my question."

"I might have broken a tooth."

"Jesus. All right, come on."

The maid, when she opened the door, regarded us as one might a pair of capering monkeys. Somehow I managed to get Edward up the stairs, standing behind him in case he should fall, for he was far from steady on his feet. Later I would discover that he had twisted his ankle rather badly. We reached the top, where Señora Inés awaited us. Edward asked for an ice pack, which was supplied. For a few minutes he and Señora Inés spoke in rapid French, his tone placating, hers stern at first, then affronted, then yielding.

Edward handed her some bills, which she tucked into her bust.

"We can have the room for another hour," he said.

He still had the keys. Both keys. He gave them to me and we went upstairs.

Once we were inside, I locked the door. I unleashed Daisy.

"Come here," I said and removed the bloody ice pack from his face. "Open your mouth."

He obliged. I put my finger inside it, ran it along the edges of his teeth.

"Nothing broken," I said, "but you're going to have a hell of a bruise."

"I hope so."

I pushed him down onto his back and got on top of him. I kissed him roughly, knowing the kiss would hurt.

"Don't smile," I said, "or I'll hit you again."

"Don't hit me again," he said.

Those were the words I needed to hear. I pulled his tie tight around his neck, almost choking him. And then I untied it.

11

I shouldn't have hit you."

"Yes, you should. I deserved it."

"You did, actually. Why did you leave like that?"

"Why? I don't know. I was just looking at you . . . and I thought, This is perfect. This is what I've wanted from the beginning. So I left."

"It was what you wanted, so you left?"

"Well, what was the alternative?"

"You could have stayed."

"But then the moment would have been lost. By leaving, I preserved it, so to speak. And not just for me. For you. I knew that when I saw you next, you'd want it more. And you did. Daisy, don't."

"I thought you'd planned the whole thing out in advance. That you were a spy or a con man. That you'd taken my money, my passport."

"Yes, on reflection I can see how you might have thought that."

"What else was I supposed to think?"

"Oh, any number of things. For instance, that I'd gone to have a beer at the British Bar—do you know the British Bar?—and lost track of time. Which, by the way, is extremely easy to do at the British Bar, since there's a clock there—it's quite famous—on which the numbers are written backward. So that if, say, it's quarter past five, the minute hand is on the nine and the hour hand on the seven. I think I've got that right."

"But how could I have known that? Especially when you'd locked me in, locked my clothes away?"

"I had, hadn't I? That was thrilling. Finally I had you in my power."

"Then you *did* have a reason."

"In retrospect, it looks like it. Iris would certainly say so. It's her worldview. She thinks everything is plotted. Whereas my worldview is that things happen at random, and people act on impulse, and it's only afterward, when we look back, that we see a pattern. I suppose it's a matter of which parts you shine the light on, if you get my drift. My great failing is that I can't cope with time. I want to combat the degradation that memory suffers at the hands of time. And the effort is futile, isn't it, because—have you noticed?—it's always the memories you comb through the most avidly that fade the fastest, that are eclipsed the fastest by—what to call it?—a sort of memory-fiction. Like a dream. Whereas the things we forget totally, the things that sneak up on us in the middle of the night, after thirty years—they're so uncannily fresh. Daisy, please!"

"What time is it?"

"The question, of all questions, that I loathe the most. Ten to seven."

"God, what will Julia think?"

"It'll depend on what you tell her."

"We should get going. I don't want to."

"If you like, I can ask if we can keep the room for another hour."

"In an hour it'll be the same. I still won't want to go."

"So now we're just like all the other foreigners in Lisbon. Where we have to stay, we don't want to be. Where we want to be, we can't stay."

"If it were up to me—"

"It is up to you."

"Not entirely."

"For another hour it can be up to you."

"Half an hour?"

"Of course. What, in all of time, is half an hour?"

"But they add up."

"No, they don't. They really don't."

12

You were supposed to be for Iris, you know."

"Iris?"

Edward nodded. We were sitting at a back table in the British Bar, on Rua Bernardino Costa. On the famous clock, the hour hand was touching the four, the minute hand between the six and the seven. We had come here in order to put off, just a little longer, our inevitable reunion with our wives.

"It might have worked out that way, too, if it hadn't been for your glasses. Something about your glasses . . . They made me want you for myself."

"I don't understand," I said, though in retrospect I see that I did understand—that perhaps I had understood all along.

He told me the story. About a year after he and Iris married, she became pregnant. "And the pregnancy was terrible. She nearly died. So did the baby. Maybe it would have been better if she had."

"Iris?"

"No. The baby. Our daughter, you see, is what in olden times

people called feebleminded. An imbecile. I do so prefer these anti-
quated terms, don't you? They're so much more . . . bracing."

"I'm sorry."

"Well. She lives in California now, with my mother. But that's
another story. The point is, after she was born, Iris developed
this absolute terror of getting pregnant again. Because she was
convinced—absolutely convinced—that our daughter's condition,
as they say, owed to the circumstances of the birth. And so we just . . .
stopped. Sex, I mean. There was no treaty. It was more a matter of . . .
unspoken mutual consent. And then the other decision—to put the
child in the institution—it was Iris's to make. As the mother, she
had the right to make it. Not that she was ever easy about it. To be
honest, she felt rather guilty. She still does.

"We were living in New York then. The girl was three. She couldn't
speak, could barely walk. So we took her on the train to California—
she loved that trip. I really think those were the happiest days of her
life—and come to think of it, I walked the length of the train that
time, too. With her. And then we left her with my mother, and went
back to New York and sailed to France, where we began leading—
the good life, I believe it's called."

"And your daughter? Didn't you think about her?"

"Well, of course I *thought* about her. The trouble is, that's all I really could do, think about her . . . But I'm straying from the point,
which is to explain how you were supposed to be for Iris. You look so
surprised. As if the idea never occurred to you. Well, why do you
think I was talking about her underwear?"

"Are you saying that it was planned? That you planned it between you?"

"In a manner of speaking. It's a sort of . . . arrangement we have.
It goes back years. Le Touquet, that was the first time. As a matter of
fact, it was with Alec Tyndall, the fellow who bet me he could write a

murder novel faster than I could. Which just goes to show that there really is more to every story than meets the eye. Iris is right again."

"Wait—what happened with this Tyndall?"

"Well, we were in the bar at the hotel, and we were both very drunk. We'd been drinking for hours. And Iris had gone to bed, and Tyndall's wife was, as they say, indisposed, and we got to talking— trading dirty stories. He was really a very dirty-minded fellow, Tyndall. The British are, as a rule. He wanted to hear dirty stories, and of course I obliged him. I told him all sorts of things about Iris. Some of them were even true. And then, when I could see he was getting, oh, most excited, I slipped the key across the table to him. The key to our room. And I suggested he just . . . go up and let himself in."

"Did Iris know?"

"Oh, no. She didn't have a clue. I was acting entirely on impulse, taking—oh, yes—a tremendous risk . . . Only somehow I knew it wasn't really a risk. And I was right.

"He stayed with her all night. Did I mention that Daisy was with me in the bar? Daisy, my bosom companion of so many *madrugadas*. We walked up and down the promenade until dawn, didn't we, Daisy? Until we saw the lights go on in the room. Iris pulling open the curtains."

"What did she say?"

"She didn't say anything. She just . . . looked at me. The expression on her face . . . it was almost a smirk.

"Well, that was how it started. Mind you, it's never been a regular thing with us. Just a few times a year. Nor has it always worked out as smoothly as it did with Tyndall."

"And this was what was supposed to happen with me?"

"Well, why did you think she took Julia off to the vet like that?

Why do you think she told Julia to let us go off alone together to have a drink?"

"I don't believe what I'm hearing."

"No, it's not in the least believable, is it? Not, for instance, as believable as my being a con man."

"Is that why you're telling me this? Because you're upset that I thought you were a con man?"

"Upset! Why should I be upset? Why, with my bloodied shirt and my swollen lip and the world ending, should I be upset? I'm not being sarcastic, you realize."

"Yes."

"Besides, you need to know."

"Why?"

"Because Iris knows."

"You told her?"

"I didn't have to. She guessed."

Again I looked at the clock. I could make no sense of it. I could no longer make sense of time.

"But what is she going to do? My God, what if she tells Julia?"

"Oh, she won't do that. In fact it was the first thing she said— that Julia must never find out."

"You might have mentioned this earlier."

"Would it have made any difference?"

"No."

"Exactly. The trouble, my friend, is that this thing, this affair— let's call it by its name—it's serious. It matters. I mean, if it was just fun and games on the beach, a punch in the face, the occasional afternoon in a brothel, that would be one thing . . . But you see, I'm starting to have these mad notions about you. For instance, I want to dance with you. Isn't that mad?"

"No. I've thought the same thing."

"And not just any dance. An old-fashioned dance. A waltz."

"That would be quite a spectacle."

"Grown men dancing together . . . I know, it's ridiculous. Ridiculous—and yet sort of touching, when you think about it."

"Edward—has this ever happened to you before?"

"Strictly speaking . . . But how can one speak strictly of these things? There was the usual fooling around in boarding school, of course. And then once, when I was visiting my mother, we had a row, and I stormed out and and took the train to San Francisco and went to a bar. And even though I was underage, the barman served me. I met a sailor. He was dead drunk. That's how I got the scar on my chin."

"What happened?"

"It doesn't matter. Anyway, that's the sum total of it. My lifetime experience of buggery—until now. And you?"

"Me? Nothing. Never."

"You're joking."

"No."

"Not even in college?"

"Wabash was a very clean-minded place."

"Yet it seemed to come to you so naturally."

I didn't reply. I was embarrassed. Instinct embarrassed me, appearing this late in the game.

At last the hour had come when we could put off parting no longer, so we paid the bill and left. The rain had stopped. Mist rose from the pavement. Soon Rua Bernardino Costa gave way to Rua do Arsenal, which is famous for its shops that sell salted cod. On the sidewalks, warped strips of the stuff hung from hooks. They looked like dried-out sponges, smelled like ammonia. Back at the brothel, I had taken what my brother George called a "whore's bath," running a wet washcloth up between my legs. Now a gummy sweat coated the sides of my torso. When I got back to the hotel, the first hurdle would be to get into the bathroom before Julia caught a whiff of me.

Outside the Francfort's revolving door, Edward and I shook hands.

"Tomorrow?" he said.

"Where?" I said. "When?"

"How about four? No, three thirty. At the British Bar."

The prospect warmed me. I nodded.

He walked away, in the direction of the Elevator.

In the lobby, as I passed the front desk, I saw that the key to our room was on its peg.

"My wife is out?" I asked Senhor Costa.

"She has been out since two," he answered. "An English lady came and took her away."

"Was she tall, this English lady?"

"Very tall."

I thanked him and went upstairs. While I was gone, the room had been made up. The pillows were fluffed. Strangest of all, not a single item of Julia's clothing was to be seen.

Was it possible she had actually left? Taken her things?

No. On the dressing table, the requisite hand of solitaire was laid out. La Belle Lucie, in which the cards are arranged in fans.

She must have been in the middle of a game when Iris came for her.

I undressed, stuffed my clothes in a suitcase—later, when Julia wasn't looking, I would have them laundered—and locked myself in the bathroom. Much to my relief, the water in the tub ran hot. Down my arms and legs, a grayish residue slurried.

After I was dry, I put on clean shorts and an undershirt. Thinking I might rest for ten minutes, I lay down on the bed, atop the coverlet.

At midnight the sound of church bells woke me. The room was dark.

No sign of Julia.

I got under the covers and fell back asleep.

At one, there was a rapping on the door.

I let her in. She smelled of cigarettes, of gin, of a perfume not her own.

"I'm sorry to be so late," she said. "Were you worried? You must have been worried."

"I was, rather."

"I knew it. Iris said you wouldn't be, but I knew you would."

She kissed me on the nose.

"Your wife," she said, "has had a most extraordinary day."

13

From one night to the next, our roles had reversed. Such, at least, was Julia's view. Now it was she, not I, who had been out until all hours; she, not I, who was carrying the redolence of the public world into our private bed; she, not I, who, as she put it, had "some explaining to do."

And oh, how she longed to explain! Even as she washed up, I could hear her voice from behind the bathroom door, though I couldn't make out the words. Finally she eased herself into the bed, and it was as if a fiery ingot, fresh from the furnace, were pressing into my back. For she was always hot, my Julia. Sleeping with her was like sleeping with some fantastic tiny, overheated creature, one of those hairless dogs that in Mexico are used as hot-water bottles. Before Edward, this had excited me. Making love to Julia had been like a fever dream, in which I grew immense and she shrank to a fierce little Thumbelina, to whose supplications I had no choice but to yield . . . And now I wanted to push her away. At her touch I broke into a sweat. I feared flailing in the night and smashing her nose, rolling on top of her and crushing the life out of her in my sleep.

"Oh, Pete, what can I do to make it up to you?" she asked in the morning as we were waiting for our coffee at the Suiça.

"Make what up to me?" I said.

"Being so impossible these last weeks. So difficult. About rooms and so forth. And then last night, staying out so late . . . Were you terribly worried? Is that why you haven't asked me where I was?"

"I figured if you wanted to tell me, you would," I said, trying to affect a tone of woundedness.

She put her hands atop mine. "Oh, my poor darling, how petulant you're being. You really *must* have been worried."

Petulance seemed as convenient a screen as any other for what I was feeling. I shrugged.

"I must say, it touches my heart to see you like this. Why, yesterday I said to Iris—I really did—'Iris,' I said, 'the way I've been behaving, he'll probably be relieved that I'm not there. He'll probably hope I've gone for good.'"

"And what did Iris say?"

"That I was being silly. Self-dramatizing. And she was right. One thing you can say about Iris, she doesn't mince words. She can take you down a peg—but gently. Without hurting you."

"You mean she's bracing in her truthfulness?"

"Not exactly. It's more that she has a way of looking at things, a way you'd never consider if she didn't suggest it. But then, when you do look at things that way, they make a new kind of sense."

"And what's her new way of looking at you?"

"Well, that I'm angry at my family—and all these years I've been taking it out on you. Which is absurd and unfair, because you're the one who got me away from my family. Why, if it hadn't been for you, I don't know what would have become of me. And yet from the way

I've been acting . . . as if it was ever within your power to change things . . . But now I'm going to make it up to you, Pete. I promise. From now on you'll find me a changed woman."

She leaned back, almost rapturous in her contrition. Have you noticed how certain dogs, when you speak to them in a voice not your own, when you use a falsetto or meow like a cat, will become deeply agitated? I am like that. It bothers me when people don't sound like themselves. Cynicism, even outright hostility, I was used to from Julia. But earnestness—it made me shudder.

After that she told me the story. It seemed that no sooner had I left to fetch the car from Estoril than Iris had swooped down on her. "Swooped"—that was the word she used. "I mean, I was just tidying up a bit, thinking I might take a nap, when all of a sudden the telephone rings and it's Senhor Costa saying that there's a lady to see me. And so I went down and it was Iris. And she said, 'Get your hat—we're going on an expedition.' And I said, 'What sort of expedition?' And she said, 'Never mind that, just get your hat.' So I got my hat and we went out and she had a car waiting. She'd hired a car. And off we drove to Sintra. And, Pete, it's the loveliest town in the world! Like an Italian hill town, but greener. Not so stony or severe. And the air! You can *taste* how clean it is. And there are the most breathtaking views, and an old hotel—Byron stayed there— and a palace. So we had tea—outdoors, in the most beautiful garden, with climbing roses—and ate these delicious little cheese pastries that are a local specialty. And we talked. About Paris and New York and our childhoods and you and Edward. I told her about our drive from Paris, and it was then that she gave me the most exhilarating dressing-down, pointing out that whatever we might have gone through, it was far worse for other people, these poor people with no citizenship, no country, because unlike them, at least our passports are worth something."

"But that's exactly what I said at dinner. At dinner you argued with me."

"I know I did. Probably because—I have to admit it—it was you who was saying it. But this time, maybe because it was just Iris and me, and she'd pointed out how horrid I'd been, I could listen."

"A miracle worker, this woman."

"Don't make fun of her. It's not that she's a saint. It's that I'm an obstinate fool. And when you consider what she's had to cope with! Orphaned so young, and then the tragedy of the child."

"Oh yes, the child."

"You know, it breaks her heart that she couldn't raise her own daughter. Especially since, from what she tells me, the girl is absolutely beautiful. Just beautiful. But her mind . . . it isn't there. 'A blank slate,' Iris said . . . Well, it was getting on by then, and I said I really ought to be getting back, in case you should worry, but she said that in the long run you'd be glad that I was showing more independence, and in Portugal people keep late hours, so what was the rush? And so we had a walk around the town, and it was while we were walking . . . Now, Pete, promise you won't get angry."

"What?"

"Just promise that you won't lose your temper. Because once you've thought about it, I'm sure you'll see—"

"What, for God's sake?"

She drew in her breath. "I've rented a house."

"A house?"

"In Sintra. And, Pete, it's just marvelous! We passed it entirely by chance. There was a gate with ivy growing over it, and a TO LET sign. And so we stopped, and I was gazing through the gate, sort of dreaming, and Iris said, 'Why don't we ring the bell?' And I said, 'Pete will kill me.' And she said, 'It can't hurt to make inquiries.' So we did, and the housekeeper let us in. The owners are English.

They're in London now—the husband is doing some sort of war work—and they're letting the place month by month. Just until the war is over, you understand. A neighbor showed us around, a Portuguese lady, very cultured, she spoke perfect French. And, Pete, it's just exquisite! The architect is someone famous. I forget his name. Iris will remember. And not only did he design the house, he built all the furniture. Every piece. By hand. Beautiful things, oak and leather, no froufrou. Jean would love it. So I asked the price, and Pete, it was so *cheap* that . . . I took a leap of faith. I rented it."

"What do you mean you rented it?"

"Just that. I rented it."

"You're not saying you actually put down money—"

"Only the first month, since it was all I had on me. I said that this afternoon—"

"Did you sign anything?"

"Just a receipt."

"Not a lease?"

"No, not a lease."

"Are you sure it wasn't a lease?"

"Of course I'm sure it wasn't a lease. What do you take me for?"

"Come on. Get up." I threw some coins on the table.

"Why? Where are we going?"

"To get your money back."

"But I don't want my money back . . . Pete! You're hurting me! Oh, I knew it would be like this. I knew it. Iris said you'd come around, but I said . . . Stop! Where are we going? Pete, please!"

I didn't relent. I practically dragged her to Cais do Sodré. After a few minutes she gave up resisting, though intermittently she would make a noise—half cough, half moan—and pretend to be out of breath.

"Pete, if you'd just *listen* . . ."

We had reached the car. "Come on, get in."

"No! I won't get in."

She got in.

"Pete! You've no right to do this. No right whatsoever. And you haven't even given me the benefit of . . . You haven't even heard me out. I'm not an idiot. I've thought this through."

"You mean Iris thought it through for you?"

"No, I do *not* mean that. I have a mind of my own, though you seem to have forgotten that. The thing is, we talked it over with the neighbor and she's convinced that Portugal's a perfectly safe place to wait out the war . . . which in her estimation isn't going to last more than a few months . . . and she has that on inside authority. From the owner of the house. Who knows Churchill."

"Jesus!"

"What?"

"Julia, don't you realize that these people are taking you for a ride? Telling you what you want to hear?"

"It's not a question of what *I* want to hear, it's a question of what *you* want to hear. For some reason you absolutely will not listen— Slow down! You're driving like a maniac. It's you who absolutely refuses to consider the possibility—"

"What possibility? Have you taken a walk by the American consulate lately? If Portugal's such a paradise, why are all those poor people waiting hour after hour in the burning sun, hoping for a visa?"

"Yes, but there are other people . . . For instance, there's a Romanian, to whom this neighbor woman was on the very brink of renting the house when I came by. Which was why I had to act quickly—so that I could get it before he did."

"And you believed her?"

"Of course I believed her. Why shouldn't I have?"

"But it's the oldest trick in the book! Invent another customer to put pressure on the one you have."

"Don't be absurd. She's not some car salesman."

"Thank you."

"I didn't mean it that way. I mean, why should she lie?"

"And is he Jewish, this putative Romanian?"

"I don't know. I didn't ask."

"Because you are, in case you've forgotten."

"I'm American, too. And as Iris pointed out, if you're American or British—"

"And is *Iris* planning to stay in Portugal? Is *she* renting a house in Sintra?"

"No, she is not. But only because of the books. Pete! Will you slow down? You almost hit that woman."

"All right, this is what's going to happen. When we get to Sintra, you're going to get out of the car—"

"I won't get out of the car."

"You're going to get out of the car and you're going to put on your prettiest smile, and in your prettiest French you're going to tell this neighbor, whoever she is, that you made a mistake and you want your money back."

"I won't."

"You will."

"You do it if you're so determined. You do it."

"I didn't give her the money in the first place."

"I don't care. I don't care. I might as well just jump out into traffic right now. I might as well stand in the road and then you can hit *me*. Because that's what you want, isn't it? For me to be dead. Well, you'll have your wish soon, I promise you."

"If I wanted you dead, I'd leave you here, because that's what's going to happen if you stay here. You're going to end up dead. Or worse."

Julia groaned. Teary-eyed, hair amiss, she leaned her head against the window. And on the other side of that window . . . What beauty! For by now we had left Lisbon and were heading into the hills. The road curved as it rose. There were olive groves, and orchards, and a little girl in a bright dress carrying a basket of flowers, and now and then, through a chink in the hills, you could catch a glimpse of the Atlantic, the towers of Estoril, a villa with a patio on which a family was eating . . . And to think that, not so far away, whole cities lay shattered. Yet looking at these people on their patios, you would have thought that war was as remote as winter, as far-fetched as earmuffs or galoshes . . . Who can blame Julia for wanting to stay? Really, who can blame her?

And then we got to Sintra. Of the town itself, I have only the vaguest memory, for by then my rage had verged into a kind of euphoria. I was almost giddy with it. It was the kind of feeling you get when you drink too much coffee without eating anything. I recall thinking that Sintra was very much like all the other towns we'd visited where rich people go in the warm months. The surfaces had that sort of glossy sheen. Most of the cars were new, with Polish or Belgian plates.

"This house," I said. "Where is it?"

Julia's voice was listless. "Bear to the left. There."

I parked. There was a gate grown over with ivy, exactly as she had described. And a stone wall. And beyond the wall, a garden with citrus trees.

Instinctively she took a pocket mirror out of her purse, repaired her face, and patted down her hair.

"Pete," she said when I opened the door for her.

"No," I said.

She didn't persist. She followed me to the gate, stood behind me as I rang the bell.

The housekeeper answered. She smiled at Julia.

A conversation in three languages ensued, at the end of which the neighbor lady was fetched. She was imposing in the manner of Margaret Dumont in a Marx Brothers movie. She even had on ostrich feathers.

"Enchantée," she said, extending a bare arm, the fat of which wobbled a little in the breeze.

Before I could respond, we were being led through the gate, toward the house.

"Votre maison," Margaret Dumont said.

"No," I said.

"Comment?" she said, peering at me through her pince-nez.

I turned to Julia, who shrank back. As clearly as I could, I explained that my wife had acted rashly, without my consent. We could not stay on in Portugal. We were obliged to return to America. "À notre patrie." Therefore, if the lady would be so kind as to return the deposit . . .

"Comment?" she said again. "Qu'est-ce que vous dites?" Not as if she didn't understand; rather, as if she simply refused to accept my words, the way a shopkeeper might refuse to accept delivery on a shipment of bruised bananas.

I repeated what I had said.

"Mais ce n'est pas possible," she said. "Votre maison—"

"Ce n'est pas notre maison."

"Votre maison."

"Ce n'est pas notre maison."

But what was she to tell Monsieur in England? She had already wired him the news.

That we changed our minds.

But if the lady, my wife, had not been so insistent, she could have rented the house to the Romanian. And now it was too late. He had taken another property.

That is not my problem.

But she signed a receipt.

A receipt is not a legal document.

You are a judge, Monsieur?

I glared at her. She glared back. I tried to look menacing. She met my eyes fearlessly. She was implacable, this woman, in her armor of ostrich feathers. Not only that, she was right. It is never pleasant when someone reneges on what you assume to be a done deal. Had I been in her shoes, I too would have been worried about the gentleman in England. I too would have been thinking of my commission.

I am not ashamed that I was, for much of my life, a salesman. Indeed, it is because I was a salesman that I can refute with confidence the fallacy that the salesman is by nature a cheat. To succeed as a salesman, you have to believe not just in the product you are selling but in your own rectitude. To adopt a false position is a torture for you. Yet now I had no choice. For though the amount of money in question was not huge, neither was it negligible. We could not afford to walk away from it, as Edward and Iris could. More than that, it seemed to me imperative that I teach Julia a lesson. She had to face facts. It no longer mattered what she called herself. What mattered was what others called her.

So we stood in the garden, that woman and I, with Julia and the housekeeper hovering around us like bees. Several minutes passed. The question was which of us would blink first—or, more accurately, which would crack first: her pity or my resolve. For she must have seen that Julia was not well. Yet justice was on her side.

Then the bells of a church chimed twice. Once again, I had lost track of time. I was supposed to meet Edward at three thirty.

Despite myself I glanced downward—not at my watch, but toward it. And in that moment, the game was lost. I knew it, and so did the woman in the ostrich feathers. I could tell by the way she relaxed her shoulders, allowed herself to smile. For the ball was in her court now. She could be generous or not, merciful or not, as she chose.

"Voulez-vous du café?" she asked.

"Yes, please," Julia said.

An hour later we left with a third of our money.

"I am drained," Julia said as we got back into the car.

I said nothing. Back down the winding roads we hurried. This time I knew I was driving too fast. And of course, as is always the case when you are really in a hurry, obstacles of every variety appeared in my path. First I got stuck behind a horse-drawn carriage. Then, after the carriage turned off the road, I got stuck behind a bus. Then we reached a railroad crossing at the very moment the bar was being lowered. No longer was it a question of whether I would be late; it was a question of how late I would be. And would Edward wait for me? I had no idea. He might stay until I got there. Or he might leave after fifteen minutes.

At four we arrived at Cais do Sodré. Edward's parking gods must have been smiling on me still, for I found a space within a few minutes.

"I need to walk a little," I said to Julia outside the Francfort. "I'll be back."

She didn't protest. She slid into the revolving door and for a moment was multiplied and fragmented, as if the glass had absorbed her. I hurried over to the British Bar, in the murky depths of which—in fact, right under the famous clock—Iris was waiting for me.

14

I imagine you're surprised to find me here."

"Not as surprised as you might think."

"Well, you needn't worry, I won't stay long. Edward will be along as soon as I leave."

"He knows you're here?"

"My husband and I have no secrets from each other. Please sit down. What I have to say won't take more than a few minutes."

I sat. "Actually, I'm glad you're here," I said. "It gives me a chance to ask you just what the hell you thought you were doing, talking Julia into putting money down on that house."

"Talking her into it! I did nothing of the kind."

"Yet you didn't discourage her."

"Why should I have? There's no reason she shouldn't stay in Portugal if she likes."

"On the contrary, there's a very good reason. It's not safe."

"Is any place? Plenty of people have done plenty of guessing in the last few years—and look where it's got them."

"Yet *you're* not staying."

"I'm sure you'll understand, Mr. Winters, when I say that I don't think it would be in my best interest—or Julia's—for you and my husband to remain on the same continent."

"I see. So you're perfectly willing to throw Julia to the wolves—"

"How dare you accuse *me* of throwing Julia to the wolves, when it's you who's doing the thing that will surely kill her? Or should I put the matter more bluntly? Very well, I will. You are having sexual relations with Edward. I can endure it. Julia could not."

"And why does she have to find out?"

"Exactly. She mustn't find out. Not under any circumstances. Of course, there'd be less of a risk if you stayed in Portugal. But you've closed off that avenue of possibility, and now it seems that in a week or so, the four of us will be sailing off to New York. Won't that be grand? No doubt we'll sit together every night at dinner. And after dinner, every night, you and Edward will go off and—what lie shall we all agree upon?—have a cigar? That old ritual of the gentlemen and the ladies separating for a bit? Or do you prefer the afternoons? Teatime."

"Please! Not so loud."

"What, you're afraid of people hearing? Good. You should be."

She turned away and lit a cigarette. Her hands were shaking. There was something splendid about her, splendid and aristocratic and ungainly, what with the humped back and the disordered hair and the long, white neck poised for the guillotine.

"I know what you're thinking," she went on. "You're thinking I'm going to forbid you from seeing Edward. Well, I'm not. I'm not stupid. I know my own limits. And so instead I'm going to offer you what seems to me a quite reasonable proposition. You may do whatever you like with Edward, and I shall look the other way—so long as Julia remains in the dark."

"And why is it that all of a sudden you're so concerned about Julia?"

"Because she's vulnerable."

"And you're not?"

She blinked. "This may come as a shock to you, but I know my husband better than anyone alive. Trust me, none of this comes as a surprise."

"You're referring, I suppose, to your arrangement—"

"Is that what he calls it? How funny." She leaned across the table, until she was so close that I could smell her perfume, the perfume Julia had carried into our hotel room the night before. "Mr. Winters— Pete—please listen to me. You have no idea, no idea at all, what you're getting into with Edward."

"Don't I?"

"No, you do not. If you were a woman, I'd tell you the same thing. If you were me as I was twenty years ago, I'd tell you the same thing. He's not well, Edward . . . Oh, I know he comes across as charming and odd and clever. But that's only a screen. And yes, perhaps I've made it worse, coming to his rescue so many times, putting up with things no reasonable woman would tolerate . . . I don't know what he told you about the men. It's true that I slept with them. But not, as he seems to have convinced himself, because I wanted to. It was because *he* wanted me to. Which isn't to say there weren't a few times when I thought, Iris, you might as well enjoy yourself. You deserve to. In fact, there was one chap who was perfectly prepared to leave his wife if I left Edward. Now I wonder if I shouldn't have."

"Why didn't you?"

She leaned in close across the table. "Have you ever noticed that when we're walking down the street, the four of us, and it's too narrow to go two abreast, I always walk behind Edward? Well, do you know why? It's because if I went ahead of him, there'd be the chance that when I turned my head, he'd be gone. There, how's that for a confession? I love him—I can't bear the idea of losing him, no matter what it costs me. I'm not what I appear. I'm not indomitable. If anything, I'm weak. Embarrassingly weak. What Julia feels for you, I feel for Edward."

"Julia! I've always been a disappointment to Julia."

"It would be so much easier for you if that were true."

"I see, you're referring to the talk you gave her yesterday. 'Exhilarating,' she called it. An impressive feat."

"You speak as if I'm a mesmerist. If only I had that kind of power!"

"Well, whatever you did, the effect didn't last. She hates me again."

"Don't be foolish. When a certain kind of woman—I include Julia and myself in this category—when a certain kind of woman loves a man, she will do anything—anything—to hold on to him. Julia understands that as well as I do. It's why she's so determined to keep you in Portugal. Because she knows she has a better chance here than in New York. Even if she doesn't see *why*."

"And you? You're telling me that's the only reason you slept with all those men? To hold on to Edward?"

"I slept with them, yes. Just as I would have slept with you. So that afterward he could come and smell you on my body, on the bedsheets. So that I could answer his very *detailed* questions. So that he could take the nightgown I'd been wearing into the bathroom and . . . Don't look shocked. You've no right. Not after what you've done. That evening you went with him to Estoril, I'd prepared myself—I mean by that exactly what you think I mean. Only then the thing I've anticipated from the beginning, the thing I knew would happen eventually—it finally happened. The only surprise was that it was you. I'd always expected it would be some youth who slayed him, some stunningly handsome youth . . . Well, who can account for taste?"

"Thank you."

"I'm not deprecating you. In one sense I'm glad. You're less likely to drive him over the edge than a younger man would be. As for me, the whole business comes as something of a relief. Because at least now it's all out in the open. For you and Julia, on the other hand— honestly, I think it would be far better if you stayed here. Stayed away from us. We're poison. But I suppose it's too late for that now."

"If what you're asking is whether I still plan to take my wife back to New York, the answer is yes. Even kicking and screaming, I'll take her."

"Then there's only one other thing I have to say. Don't get it into your head that Edward will leave me. He won't. You can ask him yourself." She gathered up her things. "Well, I suppose I'd better be going. He's waiting across the street. He'll be in shortly."

"And what if Julia finds out—but not from me? From someone else?"

"The consequences will be yours to live with, won't they?"

I looked away, toward the baffling clock. She stood. "You probably think I've enjoyed this. Or at least that I've got some primitive satisfaction from it. Well, I haven't. For me this entire conversation has been extremely distasteful."

"Then why have it?"

"Because there are occasions when none of the choices are good. You simply have to calculate which is the least bad."

"Like going home."

"More or less."

I tried to laugh. She did not let down her guard. And how glorious she looked right then! Edward had been right to compare her to the *Madonna with the Long Neck.* There was something authentically Mannerist about Iris, a quality at once magisterial and freakish, as if her body had been laid out on a torture rack and stretched beyond endurance, and now the elongated splendor of her limbs, the erotic torque of her neck, testified to the indivisibility of suffering and grace.

A few minutes after she left, Edward came in, with Daisy.

"Are you all right?" he asked.

"*I'm* all right," I said. "What about you?"

He sat down. "What can I say, Pete? This is what happens when you get caught up with people like me. People who don't take precautions. If you never want to see me again, I'll understand."

"And what do you want?"

"I'm in no position to want anything."

"Fine. Let's go then."

"Where?"

"You know where."

He didn't even order a beer. Outside, the sun was at its most brutally bright, that brightness that precedes its setting. Daisy at our side, we walked toward Rua do Alecrim, toward the iron staircase and the unmarked door.

Nowhere

15

One afternoon—I think it was more or less in the middle of our stay in Lisbon—Edward and I took a ride on the Bica Elevator. This elevator, in case you do not know it, is actually a funicular. Its one car has three staggered compartments, rather like the treads of a stepladder. Well, that week we were always looking for places where we could be alone, Edward and I, even for a few minutes. And since the Bica Elevator was cheap, and it was relatively easy to get a compartment to ourselves, it became one of our haunts. I don't recall that we ever touched each other during those brief trips. For that was not the point. The point was to breathe, just for a moment, some air that no one else was breathing.

I have never much cared for funiculars. Chalk this up to the car salesman's native distrust of all vehicles that, in the fixity of their routes, deny the open road we cherish. And what is the funicular but a freak even among trains and trams and the like, humpbacked and fused to its precipitous track, from which it can never be parted and without which it cannot live? Edward used to say that the Bica

Elevator reminded him of Sisyphus pushing his boulder uphill. To me it was more like an invalid attached to an iron lung . . . Now it occurs to me that marriage itself is a kind of funicular, the regular operation of which it is the duty of certain spouses not just to oversee but to power. And the uphill portion, for all the effort it requires, is nothing compared with the downhill, during which there is the perpetual risk of free fall. Ask any bicyclist and he will tell you that descending is far more dangerous than ascending.

At any rate—and now this strikes me as apposite—it was aboard the Bica Elevator that Edward first told me that Iris was Roman Catholic. "I suspect that this was what her childhood felt like," he said as the climb began. "The nuns always giving her these little penances to perform. Yet no sooner had she completed one set than she'd commit another sin. And so on, forever and ever."

"Does she still practice?"

"Not anymore. She gave it up when she married me. The tenets of the faith, if not the terrors. The terrors—those are harder to get rid of." Years had passed since Iris had last gone to confession, and still she totted up her transgressions in a sort of spiritual account book, and tried to balance them with acts of contrition. The sin of which she considered herself guiltiest was pride, which is unique among the sins in being regarded by the secular world as a virtue. Pride in one's work, pride in one's success . . . These are good things, aren't they? And Iris was proud of her work, she was proud of her success, above all she was proud that for so many years she had kept the funicular from crashing to the ground. Indeed, there was only one thing of which she was not proud, and that was her love for her husband. Its very immoderacy shamed her. This was why she hated me so. For until she met me she had never once in her life let down her guard on this score, not even when she was at her most abject, not even on those dark nights of the soul when, having dismissed the lover Edward had sent to her, she turned to the wall and thought, "If only I had a mother . . ." For she could not imagine confiding such a thing in anyone but a mother. And now she had confided it in me, her worst enemy.

Mind you, she was not blundering. She was a skilled card player. She knew that when you are dealt a weak hand, the only thing is to play it as if it were strong. And the hand she had been dealt really was incredibly weak. For what cards did it hold? Habit—the habit of a long marriage. Loyalty—at least the hope of it. A daughter in exile. A dog nearing the end of its life. And these were the *strong* cards.

Well, she looked them over and she made a calculation. The best chance she stood of keeping Edward was not by forbidding the affair, but by managing it. To manage it, she had to manage me. To manage me, she had to persuade me that Julia, were she to catch so much as a whiff of Edward's scent on my clothes, would just crumble into a pile of dust. And here she had a lucky break. Our talk at the British Bar came right on the heels of that terrible episode in Sintra, indeed just minutes after I had left Julia at the Francfort's revolving door. And so the image that came into my mind as Iris made her case was not of my wife as I had first known her, that youngest child radiant in her willfulness, but my wife as I had last known her—frail and febrile, crossing through glass, crossing a river, crossing the Styx.

So that was that. Iris left the British Bar, and she saw that she had achieved her purpose. Never again would Edward and I be alone together. Wherever we went, she would be with us: Iris, and, through her, the specter of Julia, crumbling into pieces. Yet did Iris also see that, in ensuring my compliance, she had paid a higher price than she had to? For she had meant only to show me the depth of her pride. But instead she had broken down and shown me the depth of her passion. By comparison, sleeping with me would have been nothing.

Now I see her processing (that is the word for Iris) down Rua do
Arsenal. Not once turning her head. Along Rua do Ouro she makes
her way, past the Elevator and across the Rossio to the Francfort
Hotel, where, as she climbs the stairs, the clerk thinks, There is a
true English lady . . . She locks her door behind her—and it is only
then, in the darkness of that insalubrious bedroom where you had
to choose between suffocating from the heat or from the smell, that
she divests herself of the heavy armor with which she hid and pro-
tected her heart. For now she was utterly alone. She did not even
have Daisy for company. At the last moment, she could not resist
imposing a single condition on Edward: that when he went off with
me, he take the dog along. Probably she was hoping that Daisy would
prove an impediment to us—that because of Daisy we would be
turned away at doors or out of rooms—when really all she was doing
was depriving herself of the one creature from whose company she
might have derived some comfort in those terrible hours.

It must have felt to her as if she was being returned to her childhood. Once again she was making the sea journey from Malaysia;
once again she was being delivered into the cold, clean hands of the
nuns; once again she was peering down the path to the house of her
imposing relations. I suspect that it was in those years that she acquired her taste for penance, for even in the grimmest circumstances, you have to find some means of amusing yourself. Well, if
nothing else, it was good training for what was to come.

She met him in Cambridge, at one of those spring balls or
whatever they're called that they have there. He had then been in
England for eight months, studying philosophy under G. E. Moore.
From what I gather, Moore was considered a Great Force—and so
his endorsement of Edward carried great weight. Supposedly it was
all based on some papers Edward had written in Heidelberg.

Well, Edward asked Iris to dance—and at first she was suspicious.

She had never considered herself pretty in any way. More to the point, her relations had done their best to nip what self-confidence she had in the bud. For she stood to inherit a lot of money when she turned twenty-one, and if she married, these relations knew, their chance to manage that fortune would be spoiled. And so they made sure to remind her at every opportunity that she was not pretty, and that therefore any man who paid her the least attention should be regarded with distrust—a strategy that might have worked, had Edward not seemed so utterly guileless, which he was, and had he not compared her to the *Madonna with the Long Neck*, which he did. For until then her height had been her greatest embarrassment—and now he was telling her it was her greatest glory. Of course, far worse embarrassments were in store for her.

From what I am told, the first year of their marriage was a relatively happy one. In Cambridge they lived in some little hovel, some squalid nest, from which they would emerge once or twice a day to take a brisk walk around the green. A stranger observing them would have thought them, if not an attractive couple, then an interesting one—both so tall, and able to take such great strides. And they could talk to each other. In marriage this is no small thing. Julia and I could not talk to each other—and in retrospect I see what an impoverishment that was. Whereas Iris, despite her lack of education, had the sort of mind that Edward appreciated. Few people outside the rarefied circles of Cambridge could make sense of his papers—but she could. Nor did she begrudge him the effort they cost him. For when he was working, he was prone to a certain fanaticism, particularly regarding early drafts and pages with which he was dissatisfied. First he would tear the pages into shreds. Then he would burn the shreddings in the fireplace. Then he would bury the ashes in the back garden. All this Iris observed with a kind of erotic ravishment. What she could not bear were his disappearances.

These were sometimes figurative (he would hardly speak to her for a whole day) and sometimes literal (he would go for a walk—and not return until the next afternoon). They were sometimes accompanied by explanations (a sudden urge to see the Elgin Marbles) and sometimes not. And how Iris suffered during those long hours of his absence! It was, she said, as if the earth were trembling up under her feet, as if she might at any minute be sucked down into the abyss . . . Until he returned and the world regained its solidity. All this would have been tolerable had he given her some warning. But he never did. For Edward, his broad shoulders notwithstanding, was mercurial. You could reach for him, and sometimes you would grab hold of him. But sometimes all you would grab hold of was a reflection of a reflection in a revolving door.

Well, perhaps now you will understand why he lasted in Cambridge such a short time. For even in that haven of erratic temperaments, there were rules you had to follow. Granted, from an American perspective, they were strange rules, mostly having to do with dinners and teas at which it was obligatory to make an appearance. Especially if you were a junior fellow, your absence at these occasions was regarded with disfavor—not because the other fellows cared especially for your company, but because in not showing up you were flouting tradition. If you were a foreigner, it was worse. The infraction was then regarded as implying a national slight.

Anyway, Edward missed several of these teas and dinners—and in due course the master of his college sent him a note of chastisement. It was in the nature of a slap on the wrist. But Edward took it in deadly earnest and resigned.

The trouble, in my opinion, was that he had never had a real job—and so he had never been fired from a real job. Being fired is a signal experience for any man, one that he should have sooner rather than later if he is to get on in the world. For until he does, he will suffer under the delusion that employers are as forgiving as mothers. Well, all his life Edward had been told he was a genius, and cosseted accordingly; and so he failed to see that where the ego of a Great Institution is concerned, the whims of one little scholar are nugatory. And sometimes examples must be made.

So that was that. Far from begging him to change his mind, the master accepted his resignation coldly. Like most blows, Edward took this one without flinching. It was Iris who panicked. And who can blame her? In the course of a single day, her notion of her own future—as the charming wife of a charming don—had gone out the window. Of course, she had known that Edward could be capricious. What she had not guessed was that his caprice could carry him to such an extreme. And still she stood by him. She saw no alternative.

The next step was to decide where to settle. She had come into her inheritance, so money was not a problem. Edward said he wanted to go to New York, to see the great-aunt of whom he was so fond. Under her tutelage, he thought he could finish the book that was supposed to be his dissertation. It was during the crossing that the child was conceived.

Oh, the child! That really was the fatal blow. In Lisbon, Julia told me, Iris carried pictures of the girl in her pocketbook. She was very pretty—and, according to Iris, her lovely head was so empty it might have been made of porcelain. Iris was afraid to handle her—in case, in her clumsiness, she should drop her and that porcelain head should shatter. Whereas Edward adored his daughter without pity or guilt. He would talk to her for hours, undeterred by her failure to show even a glimmer of response. Or he would play with her, throwing her up into the air and catching her again. The spectacle of their capering disarmed his wife. She felt rebuked, rebuffed. Did he not realize that in being born, the child had nearly killed her? Not only that, since her arrival, he had not written a word of his book. And so when Iris conceived the notion of putting the girl in an institution—not an especially outrageous notion in those days—she was able to tell herself that it was for Edward's sake. The mistake she made was not giving him a chance to object.

It was then that they took that legendary trip to California—and as they trundled across the Midwest, poor Iris had no idea, no idea whatsoever, that she had just guaranteed what in the courts they call the alienation of her husband's affections. This was not entirely her fault. I don't believe Edward ever communicated to her the degree of his resentment over her decision to put the child away. I don't even know that he ever communicated it to himself.

So it was that the girl ended up in a gruesome state mental hospital that had the sole advantage of being a few hours' drive from Edward's mother—and from which his mother had the good sense, in a matter of days, to rescue her. And thank God she did. His mother—by all accounts a weird woman, a holder of séances and pursuer of psychical phenomena—was the silver lining on *that* cloud. For had it not been for her, the girl would have languished in that institution for the rest of her days, instead of which she grew up among the Theosophists, who regarded her as a kind of silent sibyl, through whom they hoped to make contact with their masters. Certainly a better life than the one to which the State of California would have sentenced her, and probably a better life than she would have led with her parents.

After that, Edward's book was abandoned, along with his child and the sexual side of his marriage—this last loss a double-edged sword for Iris, whose fear of conceiving another idiot exceeded her fear of losing her husband to another woman, though only by a hair.

They sailed to France, where they took up their vagabond life—that life of Daisy running up and down the corridors of first-class hotels—not because either of them especially craved itinerancy, but because neither had the disposition for settlement. For Iris, as Edward had observed, felt at home nowhere, whereas Edward had a habit of becoming besotted with a place until his infatuation soured into boredom, his boredom into depression, and he suffered what Iris called an "episode." The episode of the six bottles of champagne. The episode of the mixed-up pills. The episode of the train tracks. The episode of the fifth-floor balcony. And then, perhaps four years into their sojourn in the fairyland forlorn that was Jazz Age Europe, the episode of Alec Tyndall.

Now, Alec Tyndall—to hear Edward tell it, he was a bit player in the drama: the accidental instigator, first, of Xavier Legrand's accidental career and, second, of the "arrangement" by which he sent men to Iris in the night. My hunch, though, is that the role he played was far more crucial than that. For before Alec Tyndall, Edward had not realized that he could love another man.

Well, who can say what it was about Alec Tyndall that turned the tables for him? I certainly can't, never having met him. Probably to any eye other than Edward's, he was nothing special; a married businessman in his thirties; as unremarkable as . . . well, as I am.

And maybe that was the appeal. At the British Bar, Iris had told me that she assumed it would be some absurdly handsome youth who would "slay" Edward. Yet the truth is, no handsome youth could have slayed Edward. Edward was unslayable by handsome youth. Instead, what was fatal to him was the clumsy touch of a flawed and ordinary man.

Anyway, Tyndall—that was, for Iris, the beginning of her exile in the desert, her epoch of temptations and trials. When she opened her door to him that night, she could not at first believe her eyes.

Then his avid presence began to make a horrible kind of sense. For just that week Edward had had another episode, this one involving a borrowed revolver. Now she thought she understood why.

And so she allowed Tyndall into her bed—because she loved Edward. And yet what does that mean—that she loved Edward? I mean, if you put a drop of that vital fluid under a microscope, what would you see?

In Iris's case, I think what you would see would mostly be fear: fear of the earth opening up under her feet, fear of Edward's loss— which meant her own. She thought that she loved him as a saint loves God. Yet isn't the love of saints a kind of monstrosity? Saint Agatha with her breasts on a plate, Saint Lucy with her eyes on a plate . . . Wherever she turned, little red-tailed devils plagued her. Being devils, they knew exactly where to aim their pokers: at her pride. You might think they urged Iris into Tyndall's bed. No! They tried to keep her out of it. And what an ordeal it was, resisting their implorations, and submitting instead to the mortification of the flesh—her own flesh—that her love of Edward demanded. And not even Mrs. Tyndall cared. For this was France in, I believe, 1927. Infidelity was de rigueur. In sleeping with Tyndall, Iris was betraying no one but herself.

Now, let me return to Edward. I have mentioned the episode of the borrowed revolver. I have not mentioned the person from whom it was borrowed: an elderly Englishman, jovial and tipsy, who happened to be present when Edward pointed that revolver at his head, and who proved instrumental in convincing him to put it down. In fact, that Englishman might have been the most sensible person ever to stumble into their lives, for once the crisis was averted, he took Iris aside and said, "Your husband is a troubled chap. If I were you, I'd get him to a doctor." And at this advice she bristled—not just because she feared what a doctor, were one to be summoned,

might say; not just because she considered the Englishman impertinent; but because, in suggesting that Edward was "ill," the old man
had failed to appreciate her husband's genius—which, she was
certain, explained, even excused, his putting a revolver to his head.
Of course, in the long run it would have been better if she had
heeded the Englishman's advice. At the very least it would have
saved her some time. Instead she went up to her room and started
packing. Three hours later, they left—the first of many precipitous
departures, all before dawn, and all at Iris's instigation, as if by
fleeing to another hotel, another beach, another town, they could
leave Edward's difficulty behind. But it always followed them.

After that, things got worse. At the new hotel, Edward refused to
get out of bed. This impeded the maids in their efforts to make up
the room. The maids "talked." The talk led to speculation among the
other guests as to whether the odd American in 314 might have anything to do with certain rumors that had recently come in, as if by
carrier pigeon, from up the coast.

Alas, Iris took this gossip more seriously than she did her husband's condition. Now it was Edward who was asking for a doctor.
Every day, he said, he could feel himself sinking deeper into the
"slough of despond"—a phrase she could not place, but which, in
its very allusiveness, affirmed, to her ear, the vigor of his intelligence and the breadth of his learning and gave her the excuse she
needed to deprecate his ailment. For her notion of psychiatric ill-
ness, even by the standards of the times, was crude—another
benefit of her Catholic upbringing. What Edward needed wasn't a
doctor, she insisted; it was fresh air, wholesome food, sunlight—a
point she underscored by flinging open the curtains—at which he
groaned. Now, as much as she could, she stayed in his room with
him—until, one afternoon, the necessity to purchase certain items
too intimate to entrust to a servant impelled her to make a brief

foray into town. A mistake, as it turned out. For no sooner had she left than Edward, on his own, telephoned the hotel manager and asked for a doctor. It was, he said, an emergency. And so when Iris returned, it was to find the NE PAS DÉRANGER sign hanging from his door handle, and two old women loitering near the elevators. Not recognizing her as the wife, they informed her that the American in 314 had had "some kind of breakdown."

"Nonsense," Iris replied. "My husband has a cold. That is why he has been in bed these last few days." She then pushed past the two women and went into her own room, which adjoined his. Here she found Daisy whimpering by the connecting door. She gathered the dog to her breast and waited, braced for the worst, already planning their departure and anticipating their next port of call.

Twenty minutes later, the door opened. The doctor came in. "Are you Mrs. Freleng?" he asked.

She nodded.

"Well, I've examined your husband," he said, "and there's nothing wrong with him except that he's a garden-variety neurasthenic. You find them by the thousand in these places."

She was about to reply that her husband was not a garden-variety anything when Edward himself appeared. To her amazement, he had gotten dressed. He seemed immensely pleased—both by the doctor's diagnosis and by the proposed treatment: a month's stay at one of those *maisons de repos* in which the Swiss specialize, along with just about every other means of profiting from human misery and human greed. And this, to Iris, was the most confounding thing of all. For she had always taken it for granted that Edward was unique and special, and that therefore any malady from which he suffered would be a unique and special malady. And so the fact that Edward himself should welcome the news that he was just another idle, hotel-dwelling neurotic left her at a loss for words. She was, as the English say, gobsmacked.

The next day, they left for Switzerland, for the *maison de repos*, where Edward proved to be a model patient, submitting meekly to every order his nurses issued, no matter how arbitrary. And this was the man who, not so many years before, had renounced his Cambridge fellowship rather than knuckle under to afternoon tea!

Well, perhaps you see what I am getting at. At heart Edward was, I think, quite a modest person. The urges by which he was entranced and tortured were modest urges. He appreciated the doctor's diagnosis for the same reason that Iris disdained it: because it established his membership in the fraternity of ordinary men, even as it confirmed what he had suspected all along: He was no genius. He was no Great Force. His mind was sharp enough to perceive its own limits, not to transcend them. And this may have been why he was drawn to Alec Tyndall, and to me, and why he felt such fondness toward his daughter—because we did not require him to be remarkable.

And so Edward spent *three* months at the *maison de repos*. Loyal spouse that she was, Iris put up the whole time at a hotel down the road. Every day she brought Daisy to visit him. He would take her into the garden, where she would sniff at the edelweiss or whatever it is that grows in Swiss gardens. True to its name, the *maison de repos* put much stock in resting. Its inmates were required to rest something like twelve hours a day—and this suited Edward perfectly. So did the meals, which were ample and rich in the manner of nurseries: everything buttered and creamed and breaded, no bony fish to dismantle, no innards or brutish singed steaks. This is not to say that he received no treatment. There was a psychiatrist at the *maison*, with whom Edward talked every day. Mostly he talked

about Cambridge—about how, in the wake of his resignation, a
tranquillity unlike any he had ever known had suffused him. For
at last he was free from the vagaries of human endeavor. And yet
beyond the horizon of that great relief was great uncertainty. For
what was he to do with the rest of his life?

Inimical as I may be to all things Swiss, I must allow that the
maison de repos did Edward and Iris a world of good. Among other
things, it gave them Xavier Legrand. Like their daughter, the author
was conceived en route between two places—Montreux and Geneva,
I believe, as they were returning to France following Edward's
treatment. At first Monsieur Legrand was merely a way of passing
the time—and so they made the passing of time his raison d'être.
Bored in his retirement, he had taken to novel writing as other
pensioners take to watercolors. Of course, the fact that Tyndall had
put the idea into Edward's head lent the whole enterprise, for Iris, a
slightly sordid air. And still she went along with it, both because
Edward's psychiatrist thought writing would be good for him and
because, to her own surprise, she discovered that she rather enjoyed contriving plots. In Lisbon, Edward insisted that he had
never cared much about the novels, that they were "Iris's baby,"
that in their production he was at most a glorified amanuensis. I am
not at all sure, though, that this is true—for his fingerprints are all
over them. And of course, the first of them gave him the excuse he
needed to stay in touch with its inseminator and dedicatee, Alec
Tyndall.

So Xavier Legrand's accidental career was forged—in the oddest
crucible imaginable. In due course, the first novel came out. With
the copy he sent Tyndall, Edward included a note asking if Tyndall
wouldn't be a good chap and keep the secret of Monsieur Legrand's
identity to himself. Tyndall replied that he was more than happy to
do so. Indeed, he asked only that the next time Edward and Iris

found themselves back in England, they should give him and Muriel the pleasure of opening a bottle of champagne in their honor. But of course they never did find themselves back in England. Officially the reason was Daisy.

And that, for years, was their life. They wrote, and Daisy ran up and down the corridors of first-class hotels, and once or twice a year Edward had an episode that required him to return to the *maison de repos*. Increasingly these episodes involved men—Alec Tyndall giving way to a Greek, who gave way to an Austrian, who gave way to an Argentine—each, for Iris, unique, and uniquely harrowing, since in the erotic realm there is no predicting how a man will behave. One fellow hit Edward in the jaw, another fell madly in love with Iris, a third, having gotten in bed with her, suffered a fit of contrition and rushed back to his wife. Twice she thought she was pregnant. Long ago she had accepted the cessation of sexual intimacy between herself and Edward, in that spirit of penitential fervor that makes the sacrifice of pleasure in itself a kind of pleasure. Yet in comparison with what Edward demanded of her, even a life without sex of any kind would have been welcome . . .

Honestly, I don't know why she put up with it as long as she did—which is to say nothing of why he made her put up with it, when he could just as easily have done the sensible thing and gone looking for men to sleep with on his own. He had no excuse not to. He had done time at Cambridge, was sufficiently conversant with Krafft-Ebing and Havelock Ellis to see his own appetites for the commonplace things they were. Now I am convinced that Iris was as wrong to assume that Edward sought only to satisfy his own urges through her as Edward was dishonest to claim that he sent the men to her bed as a sort of recompense. He sent them to her bed for his own gratification—and to test how much she would tolerate. He did it to punish her and reward her, to draw her closer and drive her away.

And really, is it that uncommon to act out of mixed, even contra-
dictory, motives? If it had not been for Iris, Edward told me later,
he would likely have done himself in the day he tendered his resignation at Cambridge. Indeed, all that had kept him alive since was
her refusal to let go. He pushed her to the limits of human endurance, and still she would not let go. Instead she force-fed him. She
crammed the will to live down his throat just as sustenance was
crammed down the throats of the suffragettes. And so he was grateful to her—as the patient is grateful to the surgeon who saves his
life—and yet he despised her—as the prisoner despises his warden.

And that was how it went with them—for eighteen years. Privately, Iris worried lest a time should come when Edward would want
more than just words and smells; when he would want to watch the
other man in bed with her or (God forbid) try to get into bed with
them himself. But this never happened. They got older, and the
episodes came less frequently. These aside, you must understand,
their life was a relatively sedate one. They had the writing of the
novels to absorb them, and a wire fox terrier to amuse them, and
that companionability, that ease of understanding, that is the great
boon of marriage. In becalmed periods, Iris would consider the
other couples she knew. All of them had secrets: drinking, gambling, money troubles. She would listen to their stories and she
would think, Our problems are no worse than anyone else's. And
then Edward would send a man to her bed and she would think, I
am lying to myself. They *are* worse.

And in due course, they took the cottage in the Gironde, so that
Daisy could run about doggishly while she still had the wherewithal.
It was Edward who suggested the move. At first Iris was nonplussed.
Was this a trap laid by yet another devil, an infinitely more cunning
devil than the ones with which she had previously done business?
Apparently not—for Edward thrived in the Gironde. He did man-

nish things. He planted a vegetable garden and converted one of the outbuildings into a studio. In the mornings they would write. Then they would return to the house to eat whatever delicacies their cook, Celeste, had prepared for them. Then Edward would take Daisy for a gambol on the beach, and Iris would nap. And what a miracle that was, to be able to lie down on the sofa in the afternoon without worrying in case he should disappear, or threaten to jump off a balcony! For in the Gironde, it seemed impossible that he should disappear, and there was no balcony. True, he suffered one more episode, which necessitated one more visit to the *maison de repos*. Yet by and large these were for both of them years of ease, of pleasures that were all the keener for their plainness, and difficulties that were in their plainness close to pleasures.

One morning they stopped work early and took a walk on the beach. It was winter, and the wind was blowing the sand up into little eddies. Edward let Daisy off the leash, and she ran along the shore joyfully, darting in and out of waves that moistened her delicate paws, sniffing and marking and chasing the ball that he threw for her. She would catch it, carry it to him, and refuse to relinquish it, which pleased him to no end. For what, he asked, was a retriever if not a sort of sentient boomerang, a creature spellbound by its instinct to fetch and carry back, fetch and carry back? Whereas a terrier had grit. A terrier would be caught on the horns of a dilemma: whether to fight to hold on to the ball or let it go. A terrier understood the terrible predicament of being alive, the impossible choices it necessitated, the endless ceding and seizing and bargaining.

As Edward spoke, Iris pulled her shawl tighter around her neck. The wind was blowing behind them, billowing them forward. And then Edward did something he had not done in years: he took her hand.

She knew better than to speak. They kept on walking until Daisy returned with her ball. Only then did Edward let her hand go—and in that moment it was as if a great forgiveness, greater than anything she had dared hope for, descended upon them.

Six months later the Germans came—and then, in Lisbon, I came.

16

I wish we were in Bucharest," I said.

"Why Bucharest?" Edward said.

"Because from what I've read, if you're a foreigner—a civilian—
and you're in Bucharest, you're stuck there for the duration. God knows
you can't get a train, and to catch a boat you'd have to go to Greece."

"What about Iris and Julia?"

"Oh, they'd be somewhere else. Somewhere safe. It'd be just you
and me—and Daisy."

"I don't know about Bucharest, Pete. From what I've heard, it's
pretty grim. Maybe we could live outside the city. Aren't there enchanted forests in that part of the world?"

"And what would we do all day in an enchanted forest?"

"We'd fell some trees to build a cabin. In winter we'd sleep naked under a bear rug, in front of a log fire."

"And live off nuts and berries?"

"Are you kidding? Forget nuts and berries. We'd eat like kings.
Ragouts of wild boar and mushrooms, salads of dandelion greens,

grilled trout. There'd be a lake, of course. And when we were feeling especially carnivorous, you could slay a unicorn."

"There must be a penalty for that."

"Don't believe what you read about unicorns. They're vicious. Given half a chance, a unicorn will impale you on its horn and toss you about in the air like a toy."

"Did you hear that, Daisy? Don't mess with unicorns."

"Daisy will be too busy dealing with all the squirrels and chipmunks. And then in the afternoons I'll take her to the lake. She'll roll around on the dead trout. And so the days will pass."

"Until the war ends."

"How is it that I knew you were going to say that? You're a human alarm clock. All you think about is time."

"It's not as if ignoring time stops it."

"And it's not as if paying attention to it slows it down."

"I'm sorry. It's my nature."

"It doesn't matter. There is no forest. There is no Bucharest. It's half past six in Lisbon, and Pete and Edward have an appointment to meet Julia and Iris at eight."

"Damn."

"Why swear? It'll be fun. We'll paint the town red."

"I think I'm going to tell Julia myself. Get it out in the open."

"That's never as good an idea as it sounds. You might as well walk up to the unicorn and ask it to gore you."

"Did you know that in all the years of our marriage, Julia and I have never spent a single night apart?"

"How interesting. Needless to say, Iris and I have spent many nights apart."

"That wasn't what I meant. I mean, that wasn't why I said it."

"I know why you said it. It's the answer to your own question. It's why you must never tell her—and why you won't."

17

Suddenly we had a routine. Iris was its orchestrator, its architect. Each day, she allowed Edward and me four hours to ourselves, roughly the hours between four and eight, during which she would take Julia on expeditions—to keep her off the scent, I suppose. Then at eight we would reconnoiter at the Suiça—for drinks, and dinner, and more drinks. Aside from Edward taking Daisy along, this was the only condition Iris imposed—that we never fail to show up for this rendezvous. Well, we never did.

I must say, they made industrious use of their afternoons, our wives. They toured the Exposition and went to watch the Clipper land on the river ("like a water bug landing on a lake," Julia said) and had martinis at the Aviz, the swankest hotel in Lisbon, where they caught sight of Schiaparelli.

Edward and I, by comparison, were desultory. If we could, we would take a room at the brothel on Rua do Alecrim. More often than not, though, the brothel would be full, and we would be left to wander the city, aimless and fretful, constantly on the lookout for someplace we could be alone. And how difficult that turned out to be, for Lisbon was full to bursting that summer. Illicit lovers understand better than most the malaise of having to carry on private business in public. It is like trying to fit yourself into the last stripe of cool shade on a hot sidewalk. If we had no alternative, we would take refuge in men's toilets, our pants around our ankles and Edward holding Daisy under his left arm like a pocketbook. Or we would go for a drive in the Buick, hoping against hope to find some spot in the country where no passing bus or donkey cart would interrupt us. Once we actually found such a place—a grove of pines a few miles beyond Sintra. We got out of the car and, with characteristic economy of motion, Edward stripped us both naked, lay down on the hood, and pulled me atop him. And oh, the silence of that afternoon! There was no noise at all, not even birdsong. All I could hear was the squeaking of the tires. Through the canopy of leaves, strips of sunlight cut, so intense that afterward my back was red. "I've put my brand on you," Edward said later, touching the skin with a piece of ice.

Always in that last hour we fell behind schedule. "Hurry up, please, it's time," said the raging sun, brightest before it set. There was never a chance to bathe. By the time we met up with our wives at the Suiça, we would be soiled and stinking and invariably late. Yet if Julia found this strange, she never let on. I think her idea of what men did together was narrow, and rooted in memories of her brothers, who rowed and boxed. Well, perhaps she assumed we were rowing. Or boxing.

As we crossed the Rossio, and the Suiça came into view, Edward and I would stop talking. Instinctively we would step a little apart. Then Daisy would see Iris and pull at her leash, and Iris, as attuned to the chime of Daisy's tags as Pavlov's dog to the click of his metronome, would wave and cry out, "Daisy! Daisy!" Her hair in disarray, her stork's neck moist with sweat, she'd flail like a diva in a mad scene. Whereas Julia, pale and pallid, would be utterly still.

Then we'd sit down, Edward and I, and there would be a brief and terrible moment like the one when, your car stopped on a steep incline at a red light, you must simultaneously let the brake go and shift into gear. For a few helpless seconds, the wheels rolled backward, the asphalt seemed about to slip away under us—until the social engine kicked back into life. Someone asked how someone's day had gone. Iris lifted Daisy onto her lap. Drinking helped. We did a lot of drinking in Lisbon. Everyone did. For the fact was, the wheels *were* rolling backward, the asphalt *was* slipping away under us. Yet from the way people carried on, you'd have thought it was a joyride.

One evening we ran into the Fischbeins. "Ah, the Americans!" Monsieur Fischbein said, raising his glass of beer in a toast. "Do you know what I have learned in these days? The American passport, it is the *sésame ouvre-toi*. At the sight of mine, all doors shut."

He laughed—and this time his wife, knitting what appeared to be a noose, did not bother to be embarrassed for him. He went on to explain that, having been turned down by the Americans for a visa, they had tried the Argentines, the Brazilians, the Mexicans, and the Cubans, before finally turning to the Cambodians, from whom one could in a pinch purchase a visa at a price that varied according to demand, "as in the bourse." Of course, Monsieur Fischbein added, such a visa had no practical value. They were not so foolish as to imagine they could ever get to Cambodia. "But it is very pretty to look at"—he opened his passport to show us—"and sufficient to allow us to renew our residency permits for one month more."

"And in a month?" Edward asked.

"In a month, who knows? We will have obtained another visa, from another country impossible to reach. Or we will be abroad. Or we will be dead."

I think this was three or four days into that last week—three or four days, that is, since Iris and I had had our little chat at the British Bar. A factitious jollity carried us through those evenings, the pretense that we were just two couples out on the town together and not what we really were, which was a little commedia dell'arte troupe of three, performing its pantomime for an unwitting audience of one . . . Yes, I'm sure if you'd seen us those evenings, you'd have thought us the best of friends, eating lobster and drinking *vinho verde* and talking about . . . what? Politics. Books. (Mostly Edward and Iris's books.) And questions of such grave import as, Did Salazar have a German mistress? Was Wallis Simpson a hermaphrodite? Was the woman at the next table the Grand Duchess of Luxembourg? We thought she might be. We weren't sure. For when it came to it, none of us had the remotest idea what the Grand Duchess of Luxembourg looked like, and wasn't that hilarious? Everything was hilarious, hilarity was our means of keeping at bay the coarse instincts rooting around under the table, lust and envy and enmity and the desire to kill . . . Nor was the performance all that difficult to sustain, for what roles were we required to play but the roles of ourselves—Iris jittery and chattery, Edward glum and acerbic, me anxiously attentive to Julia? And how ironic! Of the four of us, Julia was the only one who failed to conform to type—and she was the only one who was not acting. It had been like that since Sintra. She was—how else to put it?—tight-lipped. Not surly, not short-tempered or petulant. Just tight-lipped. In public she maintained a posture of irreproachable civility. No matter how uncomfortable the chair, she kept her back straight. No matter how peculiar the food put before her, she ate an acceptable portion of it. Even Daisy's habitual licking of her ankles she tolerated without protest. I found it uncanny. For me, a change of temperament is always more frightening than a change of mind.

I wondered if Iris had anything to do with it. Beyond the details of their sightseeing, Julia never spoke of the afternoons they spent together. Yet Iris had to be saying something to her in the course of those afternoons. She had to. For she was determined to remind me, at every opportunity, of my wife's dependency on me, and so how could she resist doing whatever she could to foster that dependency? What bothered me most was that Julia thought that Iris cared about her. But Iris did not care about her. She cared only about herself, and holding on to Edward. And so, as I sat at the dinner table those evenings, I would find myself thinking that here was yet something else I had to protect Julia against: I had to protect her against Iris. Which might have been exactly what Iris intended—that I should feel the cords of conjugal duty tightening around my neck. Yes, we were all double agents . . .

18

⁓

B ack at the Francfort, alone with me in our room, Julia was, if anything, more reticent than she had been at dinner. Briskly she performed her complex toilet, rubbing one kind of cream onto her cheeks, and another onto her hands, and a third under her eyes, before settling down to play the ritual last game of solitaire that she played every night before going to bed, as if to propitiate some god of slumber. Only now she played it in silence.

I tried to make her talk. I asked her questions. I asked her what she and Iris talked about when they were alone.

"The usual things."

"Such as?"

"This and that."

"And me? Do you talk about me?"

"Why do men always assume that women talk about them?"

"Well, don't they?"

She shook her head derisively. Her game spent itself. She reshuffled. Time and again we came up against conversational brick walls like this. It drove me mad. The trouble was not that she had never given me the cold shoulder before. She had. Once she had given it to me for a full ten minutes—before breaking down, with no prodding from me, and telling me what was wrong. For the Julia I knew, though she could be impassioned, was never systematic. She could initiate but she could never sustain. And so this regimen of silence that she had been keeping up for days—without wavering, without flinching—baffled me. And yet I dared not say anything, for fear of what I might unleash.

Now it is clearer to me what was happening. The double life was beginning to tell. It was putting me at cross-purposes with myself. On the one hand, I still saw it as my duty to protect Julia. On the other . . . But that was the trouble, the other hand. It reached always, and only, for Edward. And Edward, for his part, was becoming, every day, more remote. Exactly how I couldn't quite put my finger on. It was more of an instinctive perception—that he was making a gradual retreat or withdrawal from the fervency that had marked the early stage of our affair. For we had now known each other more than a week, and by the standards of the summer of 1940, a week was a year, five years, an eternity.

Then I lost my patience.

It was during one of our afternoon outings. For the second day in a row Señora Inés had no rooms, and it seemed to me that Edward was not sufficiently disappointed. Not only that, when I asked him where he wanted to go instead, he temporized. "You decide," he said.

"I suppose we could take a drive," I said.

"Yes, why not?" he said. "Why not take a drive?"

I took the Estoril road. As we passed the docks, he held Daisy up to the open window so that she could sniff the briny air.

"Why is it that whenever we go out of the city, we go north?" he asked.

"Do we?" I said. "I hadn't realized . . . Well, I suppose it's because this was the route we took that first night, when we went to the casino."

"But there are so many other ways we could go. For instance, we could go south."

"You want to go south? Fine. I'll turn around."

"Oh, don't turn around on my account. It makes no difference to me."

"Then why did you bring it up?"

"No reason."

I held my tongue.

"In a sense, it might be said that our failure is to form habits."

"What? What failure?"

"Pater. I'm quoting from *The Renaissance*. 'Not to discriminate every moment some passionate attitude in those about us is, on this short day of frost and sun, to sleep before evening.' I think that's how it goes. Sorry, Daisy, my lap's falling asleep." He lifted her up, uncrossed his legs, recrossed them in the other direction. "It's the bourgeois way to fall into a routine, to eat always at the same restaurants, to always take the same walks. Then you get to a new place and you think you can break free. You feel the freshness of the unknown, you tell yourself that this time you're really going to explore. Only it never lasts."

"But that's not true in our case. We've been all over Lisbon."

"At first. Then the ambit narrowed. Rua do Alecrim, the British Bar, the road to Estoril."

"All right, then, how about this? We'll take the next turn. Wherever the next turn leads us, we'll go."

But the next turn, as it happened, led us to the very grove of pine trees where we had stopped a few days before. Now a Cadillac with Polish plates was parked there. While the chauffeur smoked, two couples picnicked on the sand.

"How dare they?" I said. "Don't they realize we have the prior claim?"

"I don't see what you're making such a fuss about," Edward said. "They have as much right to be here as we do."

"I was kidding."

"Were you?"

I put the car in reverse. Determined to get us lost, I took the first turn I came to, then the first turn after that, then the first turn after that. But the turns kept turning in on themselves, bringing us inevitably back to the original road, the one I wanted to escape. There were people everywhere. Even when we stopped to relieve ourselves— the three of us pissing in a row, Edward and I on foot and Daisy in a placid squat—a cadre of nuns interrupted us, their parasols as black as their habits. A little further on, three skinny children were trying to make a cat smoke a cigarette. We got back on the road, only to find ourselves stuck behind an ancient truck carrying a vast quantity of cork, the bark in rolls, like giant cinnamon sticks. There was no room to pass. After about twenty minutes we came to a fork.

"Whichever way that truck turns, I'm turning the other way," I said.

The truck went right. I went left. A parked car came into view. The Cadillac. The Polish picnickers.

"We're going in circles," I said. "All day we've just been going in circles."

"Like Francesca da Rimini," Edward said.

"Yet another allusion I'm too ignorant to grasp," I said.

"Oh? I assumed they would have taught Dante at Wabash," Edward said.

I pulled to the side of the road. "Get out," I said. "You can walk back to Lisbon."

"Fine." He stepped out limberly, put Daisy on her lead. I slammed the door and floored the accelerator. I wanted the tires to squeal.

Two hundred feet down the road, I stopped. In a fury I backed up, to stir up dust. The cloud settled, revealing Edward and a panting Daisy. They had not moved.

I pushed open the passenger door. The expression Edward wore as he got in was not one I had seen before. There was no humor in it, only grit and ennui.

"Look at her," he said, holding Daisy up. "She's got dust in her coat, dust in her eyes. She hates it when she gets dust in her eyes."

By now my anger had dissipated, leaving in its wake a nauseated remorse. "Edward, I'm sorry," I said. "But you drove me to it."

"*I* drove you to it? You're the one who's doing the driving."

"Look, at least I didn't leave you there. I could have. The way you left me in that room."

"If you had, at least it would have been interesting."

"Oh, so in addition to being ignorant, I'm not interesting? It's second nature to you, isn't it? Showing people up, reminding them at every opportunity how disappointing you find them, how much more you know than they'll ever begin to—"

"Stay still, Daisy!" He was wiping at her snout with his shirttail, which he had wet with spit. "Look, I really don't see what you're getting so worked up about. If you don't understand something I say, you need only ask me to explain."

"I get tired of asking you to explain."

"But how could anyone get tired of asking someone to explain? I ask you to explain things all the time. Such as what's that thing-amajig called."

"The choke."

"Yes, the choke." He made as if to strangle himself.

"But it's not the same. It's the professor asking the maid what she uses to clean the toilet, as opposed to the maid asking the professor—I don't know—who Aristotle was."

"If I was the professor, I'd be delighted if the maid asked me who Aristotle was."

"And if I was the maid . . . Look, let's just drop it, all right? Let's just agree that you're smarter than I am and leave it at that."

"God, this really is like Francesca da Rimini. Exactly like Francesca da Rimini."

"You're determined to tell me who she is, aren't you? All right, go ahead."

He cleared his throat. "Francesca fell in love with her husband's brother," he said. "Her husband was a dwarf or a hunchback or something, and the brother was noble and handsome and played the lute. And they would sit together in a bower, Francesca and the brother, and he would play his lute and read aloud to her the tale of Lancelot and Guinevere—until the dwarf-husband got wind of what was happening and had them killed. For that they were consigned to the Second Circle of Hell, to spin forever in a furious whirlwind—the fate, if Dante is to be believed, of all illicit lovers."

"And is that where we are? In the Second Circle of Hell?"

"Maybe. Or maybe it's the Tenth Bolgia of the Eighth Circle, the zone reserved for alchemists, counterfeiters, impostors, and perjurers. I'd say that's a fair description of Lisbon, wouldn't you? Georgina Kendall is a counterfeiter. You're an alchemist. I'm an impostor. We're all perjurers—except Daisy. No lie has ever passed her sweet black lips."

As if in response, Daisy issued a noise partway between a groan and a howl. I glanced over to make sure she was all right. Edward had his eyes closed. With his right hand he was stroking her ears.

"You know, you're wrong to think I'm so smart," he said. "The truth is, I'm just a junk heap. All these allusions and references, these little associations I draw—they're junk. And all I do all day is sift through them, line them up, move them around."

"I don't mind your allusions. I mean, that's not really why I threw you out of the car. At first I thought it was. But it wasn't."

"Then why was it?"

"I just wish I understood what you want. From me. From this."

"This?"

"This."

"What I want," Edward said ruminatively. "Everyone always asks me that, when the truth is, I'm not sure I ever really *want* anything. No, that's not true. I want not to make others unhappy. And somehow I always do."

Quietly, without our noticing, Lisbon had overtaken us. I looked at the clock on the dashboard. Quarter past eight.

"We'll be late again," I said.

"It doesn't matter," Edward said. Nonetheless, when we got out of the car he picked Daisy up and carried her, presumably to hasten the walk. His shirt, I saw, really was filthy. And how on earth would he explain that to Iris when the time came, when they were alone in their room at the Francfort Hotel, and all the other guests were sleeping, and the dawn light was leaking into the sky? Yet another scene to which poor Daisy would bear mute witness. Yet Edward was right: no lie would ever pass her lips, nor, were she granted the gift of speech, would she ever say a word against her masters. Not even to me.

Daisy, you were a good girl. May you caper forever in that paradise where good dogs are sent. May there be a plenitude of fish carcasses for you to roll in. And if it is not too much to ask, may you forgive me for getting dust in your eyes.

19

It was almost eight thirty when we got to the Rossio. As soon as she saw Daisy, Iris stood and waved, as always, while Julia, as always, remained in her chair, smoking and gazing into the distance. In her quietude she resembled one of those sleepy settecento Madonnas whose smiles belie the horror and the apotheosis to come.

"Sorry we're late," Edward said as we sat down.

"What happened to your shirt?" Iris said.

"What happened to it? Dirt happened to it," Edward said.

"And Daisy—she's all dusty."

"Dogs get dusty. Especially white dogs. It's an occupational hazard."

Iris lifted Daisy onto her lap and began picking through her coat. "I wish you'd take more care with her," she said to Edward, tweezing a nugget of something from Daisy's fur and holding it between her fingers to examine.

"My dear, if I could control the weather, I would, but it's not within my power," he said. "When it doesn't rain, the soil gets dry. When the soil gets dry, dogs get dusty."

"I'll have to give her a bath tonight." In one motion, Iris put Daisy down and pulled herself up. "Well, we'd better be going. We have a reservation at Negresco."

"But I haven't had a drink yet."

"If you wanted a drink, you should have been on time. You can have a drink when we get there."

With exaggerated, even comical, weariness, Edward hauled himself out of his chair. Iris handed him Daisy's leash. Once again, there was that mysterious decoupling and recoupling, as at a train depot— only now it was Iris and I who were moving ahead, Julia and Edward who were falling behind.

"I thought you preferred to walk behind your husband," I said to her, once we were far enough away that they couldn't hear us.

She smiled cryptically. "Hasn't it occurred to you that I must have a reason for wanting the four of us to have dinner together every night?" she said. "It's because when we're together, I know he won't disappear. It's the *cavalier servente* in him, he'd never do anything ungentlemanly in front of a woman. Well, besides me. And you have to admit, it's only fair that I should get something out of the arrangement."

"Such as?"

"Sleep. Since you came on the scene, I've been sleeping better than I have in years. I know that when I wake up, he'll be there."

I didn't answer. I thrust my hands into my pockets, gripping the keys in my fist. Somehow the weight of them, at that moment, was a comfort.

"And while we're on the subject of marriage, how are things with Julia?" Iris said.

"Funny, I was hoping you'd tell me."

"How should I know?"

"Just a feeling I have."

She laughed archly. "As usual, you overestimate my powers of clairvoyance."

"It's not your clairvoyance I'm worried about. It's your influence."

"Influence! What do you think I am, a Svengali?"

"I don't know. That's the trouble. Since she met you, Julia's been acting . . . well, in a way she's never acted before."

"And you think that's my doing?" Iris clicked her tongue. "This tendency men have to blame everyone but themselves for things! It's almost funny . . . Hasn't it occurred to you that it might be since she met *Edward* that she's been acting differently? After all, it's him you're sleeping with."

I glanced over my shoulder to make sure they couldn't hear us. "On your advice, I've made sure she doesn't know that—"

"Oh, it's true, you haven't rubbed her nose in it. But that doesn't mean she doesn't *know*. She knows something's up even if she doesn't know what it is. Which only makes it worse."

"Then why not tell her?"

"Well, why not break it off with Edward, if it comes to that?"

"I think you're wrong. I don't think Julia has the slightest clue what's going on . . . Anyway, if I was the bastard you think I am, I could just say to her, 'Fine, you stay in Sintra, I'll go. When I get home, I'll wire you money.' Then there'd be no obstacle to my going on with Edward. But I haven't done that, you'll have noticed. I refuse to abandon my wife."

"How noble of you."

"My point is that I care enough about Julia to protect her. That's what you want, isn't it?"

"Or are you afraid of how guilty you'd feel? Not that it matters, because you've got the wrong end of the stick. There's more on Julia's mind than going home."

"Such as?"

Iris touched her hand to her forehead. "Oh dear, how do I put it? . . . I gather it's been rather a long spell since you and she last had—what is it the courts call them? Conjugal relations?"

"Did she tell you that?"

"Of course, if it was par for the course, it would be one thing. But given that you've been such an amorous pair until now—twice a week on average, isn't it?"

"Shut up. I can't believe she told you that."

"You really don't know much about women, do you? Not that *that* comes as any surprise." She stopped in her tracks, turned to look me in the eye. "All right, here's some education for you. Women aren't like men. They'll talk about anything with each other. Anything . . . Why, Pete, you look positively stricken! Poor thing, you're such an innocent in some ways. Such a *novice.* You think there's a protocol to all this—that if you make love to your wife, it'll be tantamount to cheating on your lover. But there are no rules here. We're beyond rules . . . Anyway, if you're worried what Edward will think, you can relax. I promise not to breathe a word. It'll be our little secret."

"And why should I trust you—about anything?"

"You shouldn't. But you should believe me."

Our spouses had now caught up with us. "Sorry about that," Edward said, a little breathlessly. "Daisy slowed us down."

"You shouldn't let her stop to lick everything," Iris said. "God knows what's been spilled on the pavements around here."

"It's not just that she stops to lick at everything. It's that she's old. She can't move the way she used to."

"She moves just fine with me." Iris made a sound like a gear shifting. "Oh, Pete, I meant to tell you—this afternoon Julia showed me the pictures of your apartment in *Vogue*. It turned out we'd already seen it—only we hadn't realized it was yours."

"I'm not surprised, since our name wasn't given."

"I thought the couple in question was called Client," Edward said.

"They're rather *dramatic* rooms," Iris said. "So . . . uncluttered."

"It's true," I said. "Whenever I was in them, I always felt as if I was spoiling an effect."

"Out of curiosity, why *didn't* you give your name?" Edward said.

"It was Julia's decision. I remember at the time I said, 'But, darling, if we don't give our name, how will your family know it's our apartment?' And she said, 'My family would consider it the height of vulgarity to give our name.' In so many more ways than she cares to admit, my wife is her mother's daughter."

"Your memory is off," Julia said. "We made the decision jointly. We didn't want to seem to be showing off."

"Well, but why have an apartment in *Vogue* in the first place if not to show off?" I said.

"Don't be facetious."

"Actually, I think Pete has a point," Iris said. "I mean, one *would* want to show off an apartment like that. Certainly I would."

"In any case, I don't see why you're kicking up such a fuss about it now," I said. "It's not as if you were ever happy there."

"Of course I was happy there."

"Really? As I recall, you were always worried about spilling something on the carpet, or knocking over a lamp, or scratching something. It was why we never had people over."

"That's not true. We did have people over."

"And then that leather desk you wouldn't let me use—"

"One doesn't *use* a desk like that—"

"Then what's the point of having it?"

"Living among beautiful things is its own reward."

"I agree," Iris said. "Beautiful things lead to beautiful thoughts."

"No beautiful thoughts were ever thought in that apartment," I said bitterly. "At least by any of its inhabitants."

"Is there a reason you're being so horrid?" Julia said.

"I wish your decorator could have had a go at our house," Iris said. "So much clutter! Eddie's one of those people who'll never throw anything away."

"As if it makes any difference now," I said.

"What do you mean?" Julia said.

"Well, how likely is it that any of us are ever coming back to France?"

"Iris, will you excuse me?" Julia said. "I'm not feeling terribly well. I don't think I'm up to dinner."

"Julia," Iris said.

But she was gone. It was remarkable how fast my wife could move when she wanted to. She was like Daisy in that regard.

Suddenly Iris turned to me. "Good God, what were you thinking?" she said.

"What do you mean? If she doesn't feel well—"

"Are you mad? Go after her. She might *do* something."

"Yes," Edward repeated, almost hissing. "Go after her."

I looked at him. His face was contorted with something like rage. And I thought: Of course. He cannot bear other people's scenes— only his own.

20

When I got back to the Francfort, the key was not on the peg. Seeing this, my heart rose and sank at once, if that is possible.

Slowly I climbed the stairs . . . I have not, in these pages, written much about the sexual side of my marriage to Julia. Given the story I am telling, you might think that this is because our marriage was a sexual failure. In fact, though, it was a sexual success. By this I mean that in the bedroom my wife and I were happy together in a way that we rarely were in the living room or the dining room, much less in restaurants and cafés and cars. Yet such were Julia's innate if peculiar notions of discretion that, when she was alive, I would no more have spoken of these matters with strangers than I would have forced her to have her name appear in the pages of *Vogue*. This was why it mystified me to learn that she had confided in Iris. To confide in *anyone* went against her nature. It suggested that she was in extremis. And while it was true that our sexual habits had changed since leaving Paris, so had our eating habits, our sleeping habits, our digestions. It had never occurred to me that Julia might see the cessation of conjugal relations between us (to quote Iris's charming phrase) as significant above and beyond the other disruptions we had suffered—or, for that matter, that it might *be* significant above and beyond the other disruptions we had suffered. As Edward had observed, I was not used to the double life.

I found her at the dressing table, playing solitaire with more than her usual vehemence.

"What are you doing back so soon?" she asked.

"I wanted to make sure you were all right," I said.

"Well, as you can see, I'm fine," she said. "So you might as well go back to the restaurant."

"No point," I said. "The dinner's off."

"Why?"

"What, did you think the three of us would just go ahead and eat without you?"

"Yes, as a matter of fact."

"Well, we didn't."

She resumed her game. The sound her cards made as they hit the table was like the swatting of flies. Beleaguered Castle, this variety of solitaire was called.

I undid my tie. I lay down on the bed and put my arms behind my head. On her bedside table, *The Noble Way Out* lay splayed open. To judge from the placement of the bookmark, she had read about half of it.

"What do you think so far?" I said, picking it up.

"About what?"

"Their novel."

"It's all right, I suppose. Of course, you can see how it's going to end from a mile away."

"So you read ahead?"

"Of course I didn't read ahead."

"Then how do you know how it's going to end?"

"I don't. I could be wrong. I probably am."

She threw down another card. I replaced the book on the table.

"Julia . . ."

"What?"

"Why did you storm off like that?"

"I didn't storm off. I just didn't feel like eating."

"It upset the Frelengs. They're worried about you."

"They'll get over it."

"I realize that what I said about the apartment must have annoyed you."

"Why should I care what you think about the apartment?"

"Then that I said it in front of them."

"If you want to make me look like a fool in front of other people, there's nothing I can do about it—except hope that they'll see through to your real motives."

"Which are?"

"I have absolutely no idea. Nothing you do makes sense anymore."

"But, Julia, you must realize, since Sintra you've hardly spoken a word to me. It's why . . . Well, perhaps I wanted to hit a nerve."

"Oh, so that's what this is about. Sintra. Well, you needn't worry about that. I've given up on that."

"But that's just my point. It's not like you to give up on things."

"So what are you saying, that you want me to fight you just so you can beat me down again? Humiliate me again? No, thank you."

"Iris told you to say that, didn't she?"

"Iris? What has she got to do with any of this?"

"It's just been my impression that you're—I don't know—in thrall to her."

"Me! If anyone's in thrall to her, it's you. You're obsessed with her. Sometimes I wonder if you're not in love with her."

"With Iris? Good God!"

"Well, for your sake, I hope not, because you'll never get anywhere with it. I mean, she doesn't even think of you as a *man*. She just goes on about how sweet you are, and how devoted you are, and how I should be grateful to you for treating me like dirt because you're only doing it for my own good. Hardly the way a woman talks about a man she wants."

"Is that supposed to be wounding? A blow to my ego?"

"Take it however you like . . . You mock the apartment, but I dream about it every night. That I'm back there. And some other woman—some German woman—is sitting at my table. Using my things. I wish I'd stayed. Then I could have defended it. I might have ended up dead, but so what? Everything I care about I've lost . . . And now, as if things aren't bad enough, I've seen Aunt Rosalie."

Suddenly she threw down her cards. Her voice was tremulous. I sat up in the bed.

"Aunt who?"

"Aunt Rosalie. From Cannes."

"You mean the black sheep?"

She nodded. "It was at the Aviz. I was with Iris, and suddenly there she was, asking for a table. Rosalie. And I panicked. I pretended I was sick. I asked Iris to take care of the bill and I ran to the bathroom. I don't think she spotted me."

I laughed. I couldn't help it. An unseemly relief had flooded me.

"What's so funny?"

"Nothing."

"Then why are you laughing? Oh, this is so typical . . . You pummel me into telling you things, I tell you, and then you treat it as if it's a joke."

"No, it's not that. It's just—well, if Aunt Rosalie's in Lisbon, so what?"

"Isn't it obvious? It means she'll be sailing on the *Manhattan*. She'll descend on me, she'll cling to me, the way she used to when she visited us in New York. My mother didn't even want her in the house, and still she showed up. And she'd come up to me in the front hall or the living room—once she even came into my bedroom— and put her face close to mine so I could smell the wine on her breath and say, 'We're just alike, you and I. Two peas in a pod.'" Julia shuddered.

"Well, but aren't you?"

"Aren't we what?"

"Two peas in a pod."

"Pete!"

"I just mean that your lives took the same course. Both of you left New York, both of you settled in France."

"How dare you compare me to that woman? She's a parasite. Living the high life all these years, doing God knows what with God knows who—and all of it on Edgar's money. Loewi money."

"But, Julia, are you even sure it's her?"

"Of course I'm sure it's her. There's nothing wrong with my eyes."

"But sometimes in Paris you saw people you thought were your relations—and then it turned out they weren't—"

She dropped her head on the table. "Now do you see why I haven't said anything about it? I knew you wouldn't take me seriously. I knew it. All these years, I thought I'd escaped—for good. But you never escape. Not really."

"What? What don't you escape?"

She shook her head. She did not weep. Instead she took a deep breath, straightened her back, and tucked her cards into their box.

She went into the bathroom. When she came out a few minutes later, she had her pajamas on.

I undressed and put on my own pajamas. We got in bed. I had forgotten to close the shutters. They strained the moonlight, as cheesecloth strains broth.

"It's the streetlamps," I said. "They're still on. We've never gone to bed this early, so I never knew when they were switched off."

"It doesn't matter."

"And you're sure you don't want me to close them?"

"It doesn't matter." As usual she had her back turned toward me. She was keeping as much distance between us as the narrow bed allowed. And still I could hear her heartbeat, the thrum of that hot little engine, her heart; and who was I but the mechanic charged with the maintenance of that engine—for life? It was not indentured servitude. It was the path I had chosen. Only I had never considered that a day might come when my wife would want something I could not or would not give her—for her sake, or for my own.

I pressed my hand against her back. She shivered—but did not flinch.

"Shall I scratch your back a little?"

She almost nodded. Lightly I ran my nails along her spine, and she sighed.

"You never scratch my back anymore. You used to. All the time."

"I'm sorry. I've been tired."

"It's since we met the Frelengs."

"Oh, but Julia, it's not because of Iris—"

"I didn't say it was."

"No, I mean, it's not because of you. It's just that the days here are so long, and by the time they're over—"

"It's all that tromping around you do with Edward. It would wear anyone out."

"Yes."

"Iris says we should count ourselves lucky, since as long as you two are off together, at least you're not succumbing to the wiles of foreign seductresses. I find I weary of Iris . . . Oh yes, there. Lower. To the left. Up a bit. Is that a mosquito bite?"

"I don't think so."

My wrist was going numb. Julia's breathing deepened, and as it did, I slowed the motion of my fingers to match it. What relief I had experienced earlier was quickly dissipating, giving way to worry and grief. For something must have gotten through to Julia, some cognizance of love felt or voiced where it should not have been, or else she would never have thought I was in love with anyone. I never had been, after all. Not with anyone but her.

I had a terrible headache. The moonlight, though dull, held intimations of sharpness, as if shards of the noonday sun were embedded in it. All I had to do was get up and close the shutters—yet if I was to get up and close the shutters, I would have to let her go—and this I dared not do.

"When they get back to the States, they're going on a lecture tour," she said a moment later, a little drowsily. "Forty cities."

I kept scratching. I tried not to scratch too hard.

"Funny—Edward never mentioned it."

"Really? Iris won't shut up about it. Apparently she got a clause put in the contract that they mustn't travel and perform on the same day. Someone told her that's how it is for opera singers, and so she said, 'What goes for opera singers should go for authors.'"

"Clever of her."

"Pete . . . Do you ever wish we hadn't met them? The Frelengs?"

"Do you?"

"I don't know . . . Sometimes it just seems that things were simpler before. When it was just us. I mean . . . I have no idea what I mean."

"Don't worry," I said. "It's been a long day. For both of us." And I moved my hand lower, to the cleft above her lean buttocks—at which she let out a little high-pitched sigh, almost a whinny.

Another minute passed and she turned to me. "Forgive me for how I've been behaving," she said. "I'm falling all to pieces these days."

"Nonsense," I said. "I'm the one who should be apologizing."

"It's all right," she said. "Oh, Pete . . . My Pete . . ."

Then she took my hand and pressed it between her legs, held it in the grip of her strong thighs.

"I love you," I said, not sure if I was lying—for I hadn't spoken her name.

21

Later that night I woke suddenly. For a few seconds I had no idea where I was or whom I was with. I was naked, as was this person sleeping next to me. Julia never slept naked, so how could this be Julia? I never slept naked, so how could this be me? I sat up—and that was when I saw her pajamas and mine tangled together on the floor. Wan moonlight filled the room. It made the furniture look as if it were phosphorescing.

I had no idea what time it was. I thought it must be very late, but when I checked my watch I found that it was only two in the morning. Ordinarily at two in the morning we would have just been getting back to the hotel, brushing our teeth. Then I remembered how early we had gone to bed the night before, and with that memory came a sensation of sinking, of being dragged down into a disturbed wakefulness deeper than sleep, stranger than dreams. As quietly as I could, I got out of bed. I dressed in the dark and went out. The light in the corridor hurt my eyes. All the doors were shut, even the one belonging to the woman Julia had dubbed Messalina, the woman who stood all day in her doorway, smoking, waiting for someone who never arrived . . . The lift was broken, so I took the stairs. I had to tip the night porter to be sure that he would let me back in. There was no one in the street. All I could hear was the distant rumble of taxis, the sleep-cooing of pigeons. I walked to the Rossio, where for a while I stood in front of the Francfort Hotel, looking up at the moon. A few lit windows studded the dark facade. None of these, I knew, belonged to Edward, for his and Iris's room, he had told me, faced in the other direction, onto the market. And in that room—what was happening now? Were they naked? Was Daisy in the bed with them? There was so much more about them that I didn't know than that I did.

How long ago had it been that I had taken the train to Estoril, and hoped that when I got there I would find Edward waiting for me, and then, when I had gotten there, he had been waiting for me? A week at most. So why did it now seem too much to wish for that if I stared hard enough at the door to the Francfort Hotel, it would open and he would step through it? And still I gave it a try. I focused all my attention on that door, willed it to open, willed him to step through it . . . But he didn't. Considering the hour, the Rossio was tranquil. A beggar cried for alms, an old man sang a fado, from the Chave d'Ouro a couple emerged—the man in black tie, the woman in an evening gown—and made their way to the fountain near the statue of Dom Pedro, where they took off their shoes and stepped gingerly up over the rim and into the water. But then a policeman appeared, and they got out and skittered away. I saw that I had two choices—I could stay here all night or I could go back to my room— so I decided to go back. Despite the tip, the porter answered the door grumpily, and when I asked him if he could make me a sandwich, either he did not understand me or he pretended not to understand me. Back in the room, I tiptoed so as not to wake Julia. I took off my clothes and was about to put on my pajamas when I remembered that I had not had them on before I went out. Naked again, I climbed over Julia into the bed. She flopped around onto her back. It was only when I had the sheets pulled over my chest that I realized I had once again forgotten to close the shutters.

22

For the rest of the night I didn't sleep. Is there really such a thing as a sleepless night? Much later, a psychiatrist would tell me that people who complain of sleepless nights actually do sleep—but dream they are awake. To me this is one of those fine distinctions that mean nothing.

In any case, my memory of that night is less of anxious inertia than of ceaseless and exhaustive labor. I was in our Paris apartment—not the apartment as I had lived in it, but as it had been photographed for *Vogue*: bleached of color, bereft of human presence, expensive, cold, magnificent, and austere. All night I walked the corridors and paced the rooms, trying to commit them to memory, a surveyor without tools. I have a poor sense of direction—though there might be an alarm clock in my head, there is no compass—and so I have never quite accepted that the apartment faced south on one side and north on the other, because to me it felt as if it faced east on one side and west on the other. That was something else I did during that night: try to situate the apartment in space, correct my perspective, align myself.

Obviously I felt guilty—for how I had talked about the apartment, for my cavalier treatment of Julia. "Beautiful things are their own reward," she had said—words at which I had scoffed. Yet who was I to doubt their authenticity, I whose aesthetic sense was no more sophisticated than Daisy's? Most people are exactly what they appear to be, I have found. To imagine otherwise—to think that in our absence our loved ones lead secret lives, sleep with the concierge's son, shoplift diamonds—is just self-amusement. I wish Julia hadn't spent so much time playing solitaire, but she did, and so it made sense that she should have wanted an expensive, cold, magnificent, austere apartment to play it in. Nor was the woman who stayed home and played cards all that remote from the girl who had defied her family and run off with me to Paris. For the signal quality of Julia's character was immobility of purpose—and is it such a long journey from immobility of purpose to immobility? Too often, what looks like change is really just a hardening of the spirit.

In any case, *she* slept that night. Her breathing slowed, her skin cooled. The engine idled. The resumption of sexual relations, I am told, often has a soporific effect on women. For me it was unsettling. I was now so habituated to Edward's body, its hardness and hairiness and seeming indestructibility, that I found myself treating Julia with an excess of caution, as if I were Gulliver and she some Lilliputian bride . . . Not that my wife was delicate. Far from it. Though small, she was sturdy—as sturdy as Edward. My fear of crushing her physically, I knew, was really a fear of crushing her morally . . . I wondered if this was how my father had felt, returning from his mistress to find my mother passed out at the kitchen table: regretful, guilty, sorry—and wanting nothing more than to get the hell out of there. And, at the same time, glad to be home. For there is always something comforting about returning home, especially when you have been tramping about in the wilderness, rowing and boxing. It is like meeting someone with whom you share a native language after weeks of stumbling about in a foreign one. The fluency comes as a relief, even if the things you need to say most you cannot say.

At long last, the sun rose. Julia got out of bed. I kept my eyes shut until I heard the bathroom door click shut. Then I jumped up and got dressed.

"Oh," she said when she came out. "I thought you were asleep." She too was dressed. She had dressed on the sly, where I couldn't watch her.

"No, I'm up." I felt my pocket for the keys. "Well, are you ready?"

"I'm ready," she said. "But, Pete . . . couldn't we have breakfast here this morning? At the hotel?"

"Why? What's wrong with the Suiça?"

"Nothing's *wrong* with it. I've just been thinking, why waste the money when breakfast here is included in the price? And since we've been in Lisbon, we've been spending money right and left."

"A cup of coffee's not going to make any difference."

"Restaurants, drinks, gasoline for all those excursions you make with Edward. Things add up. Do we even have enough cash to pay the hotel bill? Have you checked?"

"We will when I sell the car."

"But you haven't sold the car."

"Don't worry, I'll sell it."

"I can't see why you haven't sold it already, given how eager you claim to be to get away."

It was this last remark that took the wind out of my sails. We went downstairs. The dining room was crowded with our fellow guests, none of whom I had bothered to get to know and few of whom I recognized. There was only one free table. It abutted, on one side, the door to the kitchen, and on the other a woman so fat that I could barely squeeze past her to get into my chair.

"God forbid she should get up to make room," I said.

"Not so loud," Julia said. "She's speaking English."

The woman was indeed speaking English—that schoolroom English that is the lingua franca of exile. "Me, I have a visa, I have money," she was telling a companion whose back was turned toward us, "and now they say me I cannot sail on the *Manhattan*—the *Manhattan* is only for Americans."

"Did you hear that?"

"What?"

"They're only letting Americans on the *Manhattan*."

"I know. Iris told me. What of it?"

"But there can't possibly be more than six or seven hundred Americans in Portugal. The ship will sail half-empty."

"What a pity. It means I can't give her my ticket."

"The Liberty statue, she turns her back on me and spits," the woman said.

A waiter in a stained uniform approached our table, poured us coffee from a dented silver pot, and was gone again. I took one sip of the coffee and spit it out.

"This coffee is terrible. It's even worse than at French hotels."

"Really? I don't see what's wrong with it."

"Then why are you putting in sugar? You never put in sugar."

"I'm allowed to put sugar in if I want. Anyway, you're putting it in."

"Yes, but I always put it in. And why hasn't he brought us anything to eat? Garçon!"

"Just relax. You're not going to starve."

197

"At the Suiça we'd have been served by now."

"Oh, for God's sake, if you're so keen to go to the Suiça, just go."

"I'm only pointing out that if the purpose of this exercise is to get our money's worth, the least we can expect is something to eat. Or is this really about the Frelengs?"

"What about them?"

"That we're more likely to run into them at the Suiça."

"*I'm* not afraid of running into them."

Unceremoniously, the waiter dropped a basket of croissants onto our table. I bit into one. "These are stale," I said. "They're not even proper croissants. Only the French know how to make proper croissants. Italian ones are bad enough, and these are—Julia?"

But she was gone. Vanished. It was as if a portrait had run out of its frame.

I found her in the room, furiously rubbing lotion into her hands.

"What happened? Why did you leave?"

"It was her. Aunt Rosalie."

"Where?"

"In the dining room. I don't think she saw me. I think I got out in time. Go down and see if she's still there."

"Why?"

"Because otherwise I'll have to stay in the room all day."

"All right. But Julia—how will I know her?"

"She was sitting two tables away from us. Alone. Wearing a cap—a sort of sailor cap."

I returned downstairs. Sure enough, two tables from ours sat a woman in a sailor cap. She was not Aunt Rosalie. She was Georgina Kendall.

"Ahoy!" she called, waving with nautical gusto. "Eddie's friend, isn't it?"

"That's right."

"I'm so bad with faces, I wasn't sure. Join me for coffee, won't you? Was that your wife? She left in rather a hurry."

"She wasn't feeling well."

"Too much absinthe, I'll bet." She winked. In the glare of the dining room I saw how spotted her skin was, like the endpapers of a book. "Now, I'm sure you're wondering what I'm doing here, and I'll tell you. We got thrown out of our hotel in Estoril. It was Lucy's fault. That girl! She had too much champagne and tipped over a vase. One of those big Chinese vases. Ten to one it was a fake, but try convincing a hotel manager of that. Luckily, our driver took pity on us and brought us here. Not the Aviz, but, as I told Lucy, it's only for a few days, until the *Manhattan* sails. She wanted to take the Clipper, but one has to draw the line somewhere. I'm not made of money! And what about you? Will you be sailing on the *Manhattan*?"

"Us? Yes."

She leaned in confidentially. "You've heard, of course, that they've decided not to let foreigners on board. Such a lot of griping about that, though if you ask me, it's the only way. Especially after what happened last month, when the *Manhattan* went to Genoa. The idea was the same as here, to pick up stranded Americans, only they didn't bother to control the sales of the tickets, and foreigners bought them all up. Jews. A friend of mine was on board, she wrote to me about it. The ship was packed to the gills with 'em! They were camped out on the floor of the Palm Room, the Grand Salon, even the post office. So many babies, the laundry couldn't cope with the diapers. Now, I hope you believe me when I tell you that I have all the sympathy in the world for those people—all the sympathy in the world— but when we reach the point where an American citizen can't get his laundry done on an American ship . . . Well, the line has to be drawn somewhere, don't you agree?"

"And how is your book going?"

"Oh, like a dream. You know, I really don't understand what Eddie was carrying on about that night. All I can think is that he's planning a book of his own and he's mad that I've beat him to the punch. And are he and Violet sailing on the *Manhattan*, too?"

"Yes, they are."

"Oh, good. We'll have loads of fun, the five of us. The six of us. And really, you must admit"—here her voice downshifted into seriousness—"it'll be a far more pleasant journey, *far* more pleasant, if it's just our sort."

The waiter arrived with coffee—which gave me the chance I had been looking for to make my excuses and return to the room.

Julia was standing by the window, peering out at the street.

"What took you so long? Was she there?"

"No. I mean, yes. But it wasn't her. That's why I was so long. I knew her. I'd met her with Edward."

"Who?"

"That woman. The one who isn't your aunt."

"But it *was* my aunt. You must have been talking to the wrong person."

"Julia, how many women in sailor caps do you think there are in that dining room?" I touched her on the shoulder and she flinched. "Really, darling, you shouldn't be so nervous—"

"Stop it. It was her. I saw her."

"I'm sure you think you saw her. But you were mistaken. It's probably because you're so nervous—"

"Don't believe anything she tells you. Promise me you won't. She's a liar."

"Julia—"

"My mother thinks she killed Uncle Edgar. Very convenient that he was buried at sea. It meant there couldn't be an autopsy."

"But I thought he died of a diabetic coma."

"We only have *her* word for that. Hers and the ship doctor's—and God knows they can't be trusted . . . And to think that she actually had the nerve to come back to New York every winter, and take a suite at the St. Regis—the St. Regis, of all places!—and throw tea parties. Of course, we always refused her invitations. Well, I went once. Just out of curiosity. And God, what a disappointment that was. I'd expected her at least to be glamorous. Instead of which, here was this lumpy little thing in Dior. And she couldn't even see that she was being snubbed. That was the irony of it. She thought she was having her cake and eating it too, that she could live it up in France and come home and be welcomed with open arms."

"How sad."

"And then, after we moved to Paris, she started sending me these letters, insisting I should visit her in Cannes, repeating all that nonsense about how we were just alike, how I was the daughter she'd never had. Once she even showed up at our apartment, the way she used to show up at my mother's."

"Really? When was this?"

"Six, seven years ago. I didn't want to tell you. I had the maid say I was out. But I could hear their conversation. Rosalie didn't believe it for a second—she knew I was there. Which must have just sharpened her determination to find me. To show me up."

"But Julia, isn't it possible she doesn't want to show you up? That she's just looking for—I don't know—a kindred spirit?"

"Oh, God!" Julia turned away. "Thank you for confirming my worst fears. Thank you for confirming that my own husband thinks what everyone else in my family does. That I'm just like her."

"That's not what I'm saying. Listen to me. I'm saying that when you look at it objectively, the circumstances of your lives do bear a certain surface similarity—"

"And therefore we're the same on the inside? Is that it? Two peas in a pod? And now we're going to arrive in New York on the same ship. When we get off, she'll be clinging to me . . . Oh, I can't bear it."

"But Julia, none of this is going to happen. Please, darling, none of this is even real. That woman you saw in the dining room isn't your aunt. Your aunt's not here. Look, shall I take you downstairs and introduce you to her so that you can see for yourself?"

"No! God, no . . . All these years I thought I was free, but it was a lie. Paris was only a reprieve, a stay of execution. I'll never be free."

"Julia—"

She held up her hand. "Please. Stop talking."

"But you don't even know what I'm going to say."

"I don't need to. Whatever you say will be wrong. It always is. Even when you think you're saying the right thing. Especially when you think you're saying the right thing."

Suddenly she was very quiet.

"Lie down," I said. "Maybe you should take a pill."

"I don't want one."

"It'll calm you." I fetched the Seconals from the bathroom, shook one onto my palm, and handed it to her. She swallowed it. I closed the shutters and laid her atop the coverlet. "Just rest," I said, removing the tiny shoes from her feet. "I'll be back in a few hours."

"Where are you going?"

"To see about selling the car."

This wasn't true. I was going to the Suiça. I was going to look for Edward.

As I was crossing the lobby, Senhor Costa waved me over to his desk. He was holding the telephone, covering the mouthpiece with his hand. "Sir, for you. Madame Freleng."

"*Madame* Freleng?"

He nodded. I took the phone.

"Pete, is that you? It's Iris. Look, are you alone? Is Julia there?"

"No."

"Good, because I need to talk to you privately. First of all, how is she?"

"How is she? How should she be?"

"That's why I'm calling. The way you were behaving last night—it was very . . . well, worrisome. Perhaps you don't see it so clearly, just how close to the edge she is. Edward's terribly upset about it."

"Edward is?"

"He was up all night. And so I'm calling to ask you, please, to be gentler with her."

"I want to speak to Edward. Pass me to Edward."

"I can't. He's out. But it was he who asked me to call. I'm sure you don't believe that. I'm sure you think this is some machination on my part, some scheme, but it isn't. I am genuinely afraid for Julia's life, Pete. We both are."

Right then Georgina came out of the dining room. Her cap was askew on her head. Halfway to the elevator, she stopped in her tracks and began rooting through her pocketbook. Perhaps she was looking for her key.

"Anything Edward has to tell me, he can tell me himself," I said to Iris and hung up the phone—at which Senhor Costa, in that time-honored manner of eavesdroppers, got very busy with his ledger.

"Sir," he called as I was heading for the door.

"Yes?"

"As you may know, the *Manhattan* is to sail in a few days."

"Yes."

"May I assume that you and your wife—"

"Yes."

"Then perhaps we could speak of settling the bill—not right at this moment—"

"Of course. If you get it ready, I'll pick it up when I get back."

"Thank you, sir."

Whatever Georgina was trying to find in her pocketbook she still hadn't found. I walked right past her, through the revolving door and into the bright morning. A few pigeons smudged the sky. Otherwise it was blamelessly blue. And I thought: She is afraid of me. Iris. She is more afraid of me than I am of her.

23

E dward was not at the Suiça when I got there. However, he had
left me a note with the maître d'. In it he proposed that instead
of meeting at the British Bar, as we usually did, we meet at the
entrance to the castle. This was clear on the other side of Lisbon
from the British Bar—which made me wonder if he was trying
deliberately to steer us clear of Señora Inés's place. And why had
he left the note at the Suiça, where there was the chance I might
not get it, instead of the Francfort?

Most of that day I walked. Every half hour or so, I would pass by
the Suiça on the off chance that Edward might show up, but he
never did. Then I would return to the Francfort to check on Julia,
but she was still asleep. Then I would go out again. It occurred to
me that since arriving in Lisbon I had hardly spent a minute by myself. I had always had one or the other of them to guide me. Now, in
their absence, I found myself noticing things I hadn't before. For
instance, the cars. Along with the usual assortment of Citroëns and

Fiats, their lawnmower engines sputtering, there were Studebakers, Chevrolets, Cadillacs. Most of them were new or newish. Doubtless some had been purchased—for a song, as they say—from refugees like me. And of course, I had told Julia that I would try to sell the car this morning, and of course I was not trying to sell the car . . . As I walked, I thrust my hands into my pockets. I fondled the keys. I squeezed them. They left red welts on my palm, an acrid metallic smell on my fingers. They had worn a hole in my pocket through which, now and then, centavo coins spilled. And still I could no more imagine not having them there than I could imagine not wearing a watch, not wearing a tie.

An idea came to me. What if I didn't sell the car? What if, instead, Edward and I got our wives aboard the *Manhattan*, settled them in their cabins, and snuck off? Then we could drive . . . anywhere. If it came to it, we could stay in Portugal. For somehow Portugal with Edward was not the dire and dismal prospect that it was with Julia. Instead it was an adventure. Why, if we wanted, we could offer our services to our government, become the spies for whom, I felt sure, we were already mistaken. And though it was true that Julia would suffer, at least for the duration of the crossing she would have Iris to console her. With any luck, she might even have a shipboard romance, arrive in New York engaged to a diplomat or a journalist . . . a better man than me. Now that I have had more experience of infidelity, I can identify the particular delusion into which, that afternoon, I was falling—the delusion that if the spouse you are betraying also has an affair, your own betrayal will somehow be canceled out in the exchange. And yes, such things do happen, especially among the French. Only we were not French. Nor was Julia the sort of wife to go off and find herself another man, either to make me jealous or to satisfy herself . . . None of which stopped me from spending the rest of that long day playing with my plan;

tipping it up into the air and bouncing it off the end of my nose; clapping my flippers as an unseen audience applauded, an unseen circus master threw a fish for me to catch in my mouth and swallow whole . . .

Then something happened.

It was around two in the afternoon. I was returning to the Francfort to change clothes before meeting Edward. As I neared the Elevator, two boys ran past me. They might have been eight or nine. They were trailing lottery tickets like the tails of kites. That, however, was not what caught my attention. What caught my attention was that each boy was wearing one shoe. So far as I could see, the shoes belonged to the same pair. One boy was wearing the left, the other the right.

They tumbled across the street in the direction of the line that had formed at the entrance to the Elevator. Probably they intended to try to sell their tickets to the men and women in the line, but before they could get there, they were stopped by two police officers. In those years, the Lisbon police wore helmets like those of London bobbies, which gave them a deceptively benign look. An argument ensued. At first I assumed that it was about the lottery tickets. Then I saw that the officers were pointing at the boys' feet. They were shouting. Nearby, the elevator operator stood in his usual spot, smoking, presumably awaiting the exact minute when his schedule would permit him to open his doors. Suddenly one of the officers laughed and in the same instant slapped the boy wearing the left shoe hard across the face. The boy cried out. The officer slapped him again, harder. The boy fell to his knees. The other boy broke into a run, but the second officer caught him by the collar. He held him up in the air, as a mother dog does her puppy. The boy's one shoe fell off. His legs were like sticks, his feet smaller than Julia's. After a moment, the elevator operator looked at his watch, stubbed out his cigarette, and pulled open the gate. Silently the good citizens in the line filed through.

A woman was standing next to me. She was about my age, with a no-nonsense look. "Terrible, this," she said in a Midwestern accent. "You see, Salazar's made it against the law not to wear shoes— part of his effort to bring the country up to snuff for the Exposition. But these people are poor. They can hardly afford to buy shoes for their children, much less themselves, so they split a pair between every two. And it's not as if the boys know any better. They've gone shoeless all their lives."

"What will happen to them? Will they be arrested?"

"Who knows? Anyway, it's not the boys that matter. It's the people who are watching. All this is for their benefit—a little reminder of what's in store if they cause any sort of trouble. Remember this the next time some twit starts holding forth about what a wonderful thing Salazar is for Portugal. Well, good day."

She strode off. The boy who had been slapped had not risen. The other dangled like a corpse from a gibbet. Then I must have caught the eye of one of the policemen, for he yelled something at me and signaled me to cross the street. Immediately I started walking in the direction of the Hotel Francfort. I didn't look back. If he put his hand on my shoulder, I decided, I would plead ignorance of the language. But he did not put his hand on my shoulder. I plunged through the Francfort's revolving door, nearly knocking over the bellhop. "Excuse me," I said, hurrying up the stairs—only to realize, when I got to my door, that I didn't have a key.

I knocked. No answer.

"Julia, it's me."

Had she gone out? Was she in the bathroom?

There was nothing to do but return to the lobby. As usual, Messalina was standing in her doorway, smoking. She nodded to me, and I nodded back. Briefly I considered asking her if she would get the key for me, but she was in her dressing gown, and I had no idea if she spoke English, so I went on myself. In the lobby, the scene was tranquil. No police were waiting for me. No officer was interrogating Senhor Costa. I got the key, went back upstairs, and let myself in.

Julia was in bed. She was still asleep.

I looked at my watch. By my calculation, she had been sleeping for five hours.

"Julia," I said. Again, no answer. I lifted her by the shoulders. Her head lolled. "Julia, wake up."

But she didn't wake up. I felt her wrist. She had a pulse. The bottle of pills was where I had left it, on the edge of the bathroom sink. Eight pills were left in it. How many had there been this morning? There couldn't have been so few or I would have noticed. For it was my duty as a husband to make sure that the supply of pills never ran low, much less ran out. And so if there had been fewer than a dozen, I would have made a mental note to get some more before the *Manhattan* sailed.

I went back into the bedroom. I opened the curtains, the window, the shutters. Sunlight fell on Julia's face, exposing faint freckles that she usually covered with powder. She didn't open her eyes.

"Julia," I said. "How many pills did you take?"

She muttered something unintelligible.

"Hold on," I said. "I'll get a doctor. Just hold on."

I hurried out into the corridor. From her doorway Messalina gazed at me in curiosity. "Doctor," I said, tumbling back down the stairs to the lobby. "Doctor," I said to Senhor Costa.

"Sir?"

"It's my wife. She won't wake up. I need a doctor."

From behind me a voice said, "I'm a doctor. How can I help?"

209

I turned around. It was the woman in whose company I had just witnessed the harassment of the half-shod boys. She was sitting on one of the armchairs, a pot of tea and a plate of biscuits laid out before her.

"Oh, hello, it's you. I'm Dr. Cornelia Gray." She stood, brushed crumbs from her skirt. "Whatever is the matter?"

"My wife—I think she might have taken too many pills."

"What pills?"

"Seconal."

"Barbiturates. I'd better see her." She headed for the stairs. "Well, come on."

I looked at Senhor Costa. He shrugged. With her prim skirt and flat shoes and fair skin, Dr. Gray might have come out of Hollywood central casting—the small-town ingenue who loses her way amid sophisticated New Yorkers or Europeans and is inevitably upstaged by a more famous actress in a supporting role. In such a film, she would have been a nurse. Here she was a doctor. Nor had I any reason to doubt that she was a doctor. And so I followed her up the stairs, which she took two at a time. "Excuse me," she said, elbowing past a couple on the landing. "Excuse me," she said to Messalina, who got out of her way fast.

I opened the door to our room. "Julia?"

The bed was empty. Water was running in the bathroom.

"Julia!"

"What is it?" she asked, coming out.

She had on her dressing gown. The tub was filling.

Dr. Gray looked at Julia. Julia looked at Dr. Gray. They both looked at me.

"Pete?"

"I'm sorry. I thought—"

I sat down on the bed.

"Pete, are you all right?"

"He's fine," Dr. Gray said. "He's just had a bit of a shock. He thought you were dead."

"Dead! I was asleep."

"Yes, I'm sure you were," Dr. Gray said, putting a hand on Julia's forehead. "No fever. Look at me. Pupils not dilated." She touched Julia's wrist. As the seconds passed, I held my breath. Over her shoulder Julia gazed at me in confusion.

"Sixty-two," Dr. Gray said. "The low side of normal. You haven't overdosed at all, have you?"

"No," Julia said.

"Open your mouth. Say *aah*. Throat normal." Dr. Gray took off her jacket. "Well, as long as I'm here, I might as well examine you. May I wash my hands? I'll see you downstairs."

It took me a moment to realize that this last remark was addressed to me.

"Downstairs?"

"After I finish."

"Oh, of course."

I left. In the lobby, Senhor Costa trundled up to me. "Is everything well, sir?" he asked—and in his voice I heard a note of pleading, as if he was urging me to answer him in the affirmative.

"It's all right. The doctor's examining her now."

"You mean she is not—"

"No. She's awake."

Senhor Costa's waist expanded visibly. He went back to his desk.

For lack of anything better to do, I sat in the chair opposite Dr. Gray's. The tea was getting cold. Without thinking, I reached for one of the biscuits. Only as I was biting into it did I realize that I was committing a faux pas. For I hadn't paid for those biscuits. They were Dr. Gray's biscuits. Yet, having taken the bite, I could see no good in putting the biscuit back down. So I ate it. I ate all the biscuits. I licked the crumbs off my fingers. I didn't touch the tea.

Twenty minutes later, Dr. Gray emerged from the stairwell. I stood up again. "Your wife is fine," she said, taking my hand in hers. "Well, fine. What I mean is she hasn't tried to kill herself. She *is* dehydrated. Possibly anemic. If I were you, I'd get some fluids into her right away. And tell her to stay off the Seconal."

"Thank you," I said. "I'm sorry for the false alarm."

"Oh, it's no trouble. The truth is, I've been itching to do a little doctoring since I got here. Those are awfully thick glasses you're wearing. Myopia, is it? Astigmatism?"

"Not that I know of."

"Glaucoma? Cataracts? Watch my hand. Move your eyes, not your head. How many fingers am I holding up?"

"Two."

"Good. Other than being blind, you seem to be in good health. Sit down, why don't you?"

"I think I should be getting back—"

"Not yet. She's having a bath. Give her a little time to collect herself . . . I take it you're on your way back home?"

I nodded. "We're sailing on the *Manhattan*. How about you?"

"Us? Oh, we're coming, not going. My husband and I arrived a week ago. On the Clipper. We're with the Unitarian Universalist Service Committee—and if you've never heard of it, don't worry, because it was only formed last month. We're trying to organize something for the refugees who are stuck in France. To help them get to Lisbon, and from Lisbon to the States. If we can. Only it's a bureaucratic hornet's nest. Even worse than Prague, where we were last spring. Luckily Don, my husband, handles that side of things. Right now he's meeting with the consul, trying to work out something in the way of visas. And in the meantime we've somehow been dragged into this entirely quixotic but most worthy effort to get a freight car's worth of powdered milk to Marseille. There's a terrible milk shortage in France. It's not like here, where you can get everything. Speaking of which, would you like some tea? Oh, it's steeped too long. Never mind, I'll order another pot."

She summoned the waiter. He arrived on the spot. You had the feeling he wouldn't have dared to make Dr. Gray wait. For there was something about her that commanded respect, even though she was the very opposite of what you would call glamorous, with her neat brown hair, her pared nails, her authoritative, unfussy voice.

Fresh tea arrived in record time. "Awful little episode that was, over by the Elevator," Dr. Gray said as she poured. "It makes you remember you're in a dictatorship. Of course, we don't feel it so much—certainly not the way one did in Prague. I mean, when the newsstands carry every newspaper from home, why check if the local ones are censored? Which, by the way, they are. It drives me mad, this hands-off attitude toward Salazar, when really he's no better than Musso. The difference is he's only interested in maintaining his dominion, not taking over the whole world. We foreigners, we're a distraction to him, a circus come through town. As soon as we're gone, he'll return to the business at hand, which is bludgeoning the Portuguese citizenry into submission."

"I see that now. I didn't before today."

"And why would you have? I only know it myself because—well, I'm in the business, I suppose you might say. And it's not like it's obvious, the way it was in Prague. Or Berlin, God forbid. I mean, here the worst we can really complain of is boredom, of having to spend too much time in the cafés on the Rossio. Yet we shouldn't forget, the Rossio used to be the site of the most monstrous public executions. Thousands cheering. That was what passed for entertainment during the Inquisition. And it could come to that again.

Have you seen those boys parading around in their ridiculous uni-
forms? You know why Salazar chose green, don't you? Because black
and brown were already taken."

"I take it you're planning to stay then?"

"Not for long, I hope. Once Don's cut through the red tape, the
plan is to drive to Marseille, set up the main office there, and then
just maintain a satellite operation here in Lisbon. Of course, in
this business there are always unexpected obstacles. For instance,
who would have guessed it would be such an ordeal to get an international driver's license?"

"Do you have a car?"

"Not yet. Why, do you know of one?"

"I do, actually. A Buick. Nearly new."

"Then you should speak to Don. He'll be back this evening. Oh,
I never even asked your name."

"Winters. Pete Winters."

"Pleased to meet you, Pete Winters."

We shook hands. And did that handshake last just a few seconds
longer than it might have? I wasn't sure. For suddenly it was as if
my hand were no longer mine, as if the voice speaking through my
mouth were a ventriloquist's. I was there, in the lobby, and at the
same time I was far away, in the back row of a cinema, watching the
film.

"Well, I'd better be off," I said, pulling my wallet from my pocket.
"How much do I owe you?"

"For what?"

"The house call."

"Don't make me laugh. You've given me something to do. Since
we got here, I've been bored stiff. I loathe bureaucracy. I can't wait
to get out of this godforsaken city and start doing something again."

"In that case, I can but thank you." I got up. "Oh—but I ate your biscuits. At least let me pay for the biscuits."

"I can always get more if I want them. Well, goodbye. And if you need anything, don't hesitate to call on me."

"I won't."

"Just knock on my door. Room 111. Easy to remember."

"Yes."

"Any hour of the night or day."

For the second time we shook hands. I went upstairs. While I'd been with Dr. Gray, Julia had gotten dressed.

"What was that all about?" she asked. "Whatever made you think I'd taken too many pills?"

"There were only eight in the bottle."

"Yes, and when you left there were nine."

"But there can't have been that few. I'd have noticed."

"Clearly not."

"But why didn't you wake up? I shook you and still you didn't wake up."

She began brushing her hair. "I didn't *want* to wake up. What's there to wake up for? This grim little room, that woman downstairs."

"You mean Dr. Gray?"

"No, not Dr. Gray. You know who I mean."

"Aunt Rosalie."

"So you admit it's her."

"No. I mean the woman you think is Aunt Rosalie. Whose name, by the way, is Georgina. Georgina Kendall. What time is it? I've got to run. I'll be late."

"For what? Where are you going?"

"To meet Edward."

"Oh, Pete—must you go out this afternoon? Couldn't you skip it?"

"Not on such short notice."

"But I'm afraid to be alone."

"You won't be alone. Iris will be along any minute."

"Oh, God, Iris! I can't face Iris today. She makes me so uncomfortable. And I'm not well, Pete. That doctor said so. She says I'm dehydrated. Anemic. And don't they say you should never go on a sea journey when you're ill?"

"But you're not ill. You just need to drink more water. Anyway, there'll be a doctor on the ship."

"Yes, just like there was a doctor on the ship when Uncle Edgar died."

"Don't be silly."

She was now pulling hairs out of the brush. "Sometimes I feel like I don't know you anymore," she said. "The man I married—he'd never leave me like this." Suddenly she turned to face me. "Where are you really going when you quote-unquote meet Edward?"

" 'Quote-unquote?' I do meet Edward."

"And it's this important to you to meet up with him? Important enough that you'd abandon your wife when she needs you? Or is he just your cover? Who are you really meeting, Pete?"

"I told you. Edward."

"You're having an affair, aren't you? It's why you haven't touched me. Not until yesterday."

"Julia, this is absurd. This whole conversation. Why you should think I'm having an affair—"

"Which you haven't denied. It's that doctor, isn't it? I could see it in her eyes, the way she looked at me . . ."

I took a deep breath. "All right, I'm only going to say this once. I have not been lying to you. The only person I ever see in the afternoons is Edward. It's Edward I saw yesterday, and Edward I saw the day before that, and Edward I'm seeing today. Or who I'm supposed to see today, if I ever get there . . . I don't know where you get these wild ideas. Is it from Iris?"

"You don't give me much credit, do you? You think I'm stupid or blind. But I'm not. I have eyes."

"I don't know what to say to you anymore. You don't believe that woman downstairs is Georgina Kendall, you don't believe I'm meeting Edward. And you say *I've* changed?"

She sat down at the dressing table and rested her head in her hands. "Look, just forget it. Just go."

"No. I'm staying."

"But I don't want you to stay. I need to be alone."

"You didn't five minutes ago."

"That was five minutes ago."

I took off my jacket. "I don't care. I'm staying."

"Oh, for the love of Christ, Pete, just leave! Look, I promise I'll be a good girl, all right? I'll play a nice game of solitaire, and then I'll go sightseeing with Iris, and then tonight we'll all meet up at the Suiça and it'll be just like old times. We'll paint the town red."

"But it isn't like old times—"

"*Shh.* Don't say another word. This is your out, don't you see? So wherever you're going, whoever you're seeing, just . . . go. Put on your jacket and go."

For a few seconds I didn't move. And how I wish I had a photograph of Julia then! She looked, well, radiant. Her cheeks were flushed. The glow in her eyes was of an intensity the likes of which I hadn't seen since New York, when I'd promised to rescue her from her family and bring her to France. And now the thing I had given her I was taking away from her—and that thing was nothing less than her freedom. Yet in defeat—this was the surprise—she was even more splendid than she had been in victory, that victory of

217

which I had assured her fifteen years ago as we sailed out of New York Harbor, presumably never to return.

I put on my jacket. I left. I shut the door behind me. From her perch, Messalina smiled at me with what I could only call compassion. I never learned who she was, this woman we called Messalina. I never learned where she came from, or what she was waiting for. And yet at that instant it seemed to me that she knew me better than anyone in the world, and that with her smile she was giving me some kind of permission . . .

In the lobby, Dr. Gray had left her armchair. A book lay open on the table she had been using. Though the title was printed in letters too small to make out, there was no mistaking the author's name: Xavier Legrand.

24

Edward was waiting for me at the castle gates, with Daisy at his feet.

"Thanks for meeting me here," he said, taking my hand. "I've been wanting to see these peacocks. And now we've only got a few days."

"Not just to see the peacocks," I said.

He opened his mouth; seemed, for a moment, to make a mental calculation; said nothing. We entered the castle grounds. I am told that they have since been restored. In 1940, tree roots pushed up the paving stones. The ramparts were crumbling. Leggy rose bushes blossomed amid ragged cypresses and jacarandas. Along dusty pathways and across patios the peacocks ambled, at least a dozen of them. But for the occasional blue or green streaks on their breasts, they were brilliantly, almost ostentatiously, white. They wore little plumed white shakos and dragged their white feathers behind them like bridal trains. Other than the birds, the only thing to admire was the view, which would have impressed me more had I not been to the top of the Elevator. The castle itself had a moldy quality, as if centuries of rain had washed it clean of any lingering human presence.

The peacocks captivated Daisy. Motionless, tail and ears erect, she gazed at them. "Easy, girl," Edward said, getting down on his knees and stroking her neck. "Strange, this sudden interest she's taken in birds. Terriers aren't usually birders."

"I guess she's not the only one who's changed direction since coming to Lisbon," I said.

This time I got a response out of him—a laugh, if a halfhearted one. We sat on a stray bench. "You've got the devil in you": that was what my mother used to say when, as a child, I would get into the sort of mood I was in now, where nothing would satisfy me short of needling her into slapping my face. Nor was I sure why I had the devil in me, given that at last the moment had arrived toward which I'd been counting down since morning—the moment when I could be alone with Edward. Yet I did. I wished it wasn't so, but it was. I was angry that he had insisted that we meet here, so far from Rua do Alecrim, and that he had left the note for me at the Suiça rather than the Francfort, and that Julia had made me late by not swallowing too many Seconals . . . One of the peacocks strolled over to us. Head turned sideways, it half-unfurled its fan, then retracted it again. Daisy's leash tautened. She was all tension, attention—whereas Edward's posture was laconic, legs stretched out in front of him, left arm resting behind, but not touching, my neck.

"You're awfully quiet today. What's on your mind?"

I balled my hands into fists. I tried to push the devil down.

"What's on my mind?" I said. "Well, let's see. I still haven't sold my car. The Nazis are in Paris. I'm cheating on my wife. What else? Oh, of course! I've just been told—not by you—that when you get back, you and Iris will be heading off on some lecture tour."

Edward closed his eyes, raised his face toward the sun.

"Forty cities, isn't it?"

"So I am informed."

"So you are informed?"

"It's a cabinet-level decision."

"And do you always go along with cabinet-level decisions?"

"I find it's simplest."

"So if Iris told you never to speak to me again, you'd never speak to me again?"

"But she hasn't. She wouldn't."

Again the peacock approached. Again it did its little striptease move, the tantalizing glimpse no sooner offered than withdrawn.

"What do you say when she asks about me?"

"Nothing. She never asks about you."

"Not even at the beginning? Not even when you were working out the terms of— what shall we call it —this arrangement? That we'd get the afternoons and nothing else?"

"All that was her idea."

"But at some point she must have insisted that you stop seeing me. She must have."

"No. Never."

"And if she did?"

"I told you. She wouldn't."

"And if I did?"

"What?"

"Asked you to leave her?"

"Please don't ask me that, Pete."

"Why? Because for once you'd have to answer? You'd have to say no—or yes?"

Right then the peacock bloomed. I don't know how else to describe it. The effect was astonishing—as if, from its feathers, a thousand tiny white birds were being set free, a thousand tiny white birds casting off into the sky. Pigeons groaned as if in pain. A breeze rose up, against which the fan held like a sail. Only the peahens remained equable, as women so often are when confronted with the spectacle of male vanity.

Then the show was over. Daisy let out a series of barks like a klaxon. The feathers infolded, like masterfully shuffled cards.

I turned to Edward. He had tears in his eyes.

"I'm sorry," he said. "I wish I could tell you what you want to hear. But I can't. I'm not brave, Pete. The heroic life, the life of adventure—I'm not cut out for it."

"And you think I am?"

"Yes. As you're only now discovering."

"I don't believe you."

"You must. I'm only alive because of Iris."

"Then be alive because of me."

"No. There are worthier objects."

"Isn't that for me to decide?"

"All these years, it's just been Iris dragging me up from Hades, over and over. And she never turns around. And now you won't turn around, either. I wish, just for once, that one of you would turn around, that one of you would look me in the eye and let me go. I never asked for any of this."

"But you did. You did. You came to my room, you took me to Guincho—"

"What I started, you kept going."

"We both kept it going."

He wiped his eyes. "You're right. You're right. I let you down, Pete. But you see, I never guessed it would go this far. Or that you'd ever think . . . I mean, I assumed Julia was the safeguard. That, so long as there was Julia, there was a line we couldn't cross. And so when Iris said that Julia mustn't find out, that she wouldn't survive finding out, I went along with it, yes, to placate her . . . but also because it suited me. Do you see now? I'm a coward. It's yet another reason you should want to be rid of me."

"Isn't that a backhanded way of saying you want to be rid of me?"

"No. I wish it were that simple. But no."

I was silent. The peacocks dispersed. Somewhere there had to be young. Nests. Chicks. What did you call them? Peachicks?

"So what happens now?" I asked.

"Beats me. We board the ship. We cross the Atlantic. Assuming a U-boat doesn't sink us, we land in New York—"

"And Julia and I go off to Detroit, and you and Iris go off on your lecture tour, and maybe, in a few years, if we happen to be in the same town, we all have dinner together? No. It's not possible."

"And this is? Lisbon? This war? Ask the people around here if any of this is possible, and they'll tell you no. None of it is. Yet it's real."

"I refuse to accept that. We have more choices than they do. For instance, we could stay. Other people are. Some are even *coming*. I mean, those Clipper flights that arrive each week—they don't arrive empty."

"Stop, Pete. This isn't real."

"Maybe not. But it's possible."

"Not for me. And certainly not for Julia."

"I'm not her first husband, you know. There's no reason to think I'll be her last."

"Yes, there is. I'm sorry, but there is. If you don't believe Iris, believe me. We're so much alike, Julia and I. We're two peas in a pod."

I laughed.

"What's so funny?"

"Just that you chose that phrase. Of all the phrases in the world."

All through this exchange, Daisy had been watching the peacocks. Now she lunged. "Daisy, no!" Edward commanded and jumped
up to reel her in.

When he sat down again, it was a little further down the bench.
Nor, this time, did he rest his arm behind my neck.

I put my face in my palms. I could feel my heart beating. In
Paris, Julia and I would sometimes go to a cinema that the Métro
passed under. And sometimes the Métro would rumble in a way
that took us out of the film—during a love scene or a song—but
sometimes it would rumble just at the moment when, on the screen,
a train was surging into a tunnel, or a plane was crashing into the
sea, or guns were firing into the air . . . And now my heartbeat was
that rumbling, and on the screen, two men and a dog were sitting
on a bench before a ruined castle, and peacocks were strutting
in the sun. None of it had anything to do with me. I was neither of
the men, nor was I the dog or even one of the peacocks. I was just the
rumble that might have been the traffic on the boulevards, or the
war raging hundreds of miles away, but was really only my heartbeat. I wasn't crying. I wished I could. I shut my eyes tight, tried to
make myself cry. But I could no more cry than Julia could, earlier
that afternoon, after she had disappointed me by not killing herself.

Then I felt something wet on my cheek. I opened my eyes. Daisy
had climbed onto my lap. She was licking my face.

"Oh, Daisy," I said, stroking her neck. "When all is said and done,
you're the one I'll miss most of all."

"She's the one we'll all miss most of all," Edward said.

Everywhere

25

In the spring of 1941, two books set in Lisbon were published:
Xavier Legrand's *Inspector Voss at the Hotel Francfort* and Georgina
Kendall's *Flight from France*. I appear in both of them, though it is
unlikely that you would recognize me. In the first, I am "Mr. Hand,"
an American salesman on his way back home after several years
living in France. In the second, I am "Bill," the husband of the author's niece "Alice," whom she has not seen for many years.

Inspector Voss at the Hotel Francfort opens with the following, I
think rather clever, paragraph:

"At the British Bar in Lisbon, on a June afternoon in 1940, two
gentlemen, one American and one English, were playing cards.
Their names were Hand and Foote. Both, as it happened, were
salesmen—the former of cutlery, the latter of vacuum cleaners."

Two pages on, Hand wins the hand. Foote accuses him of cheating. An altercation ensues, at the end of which they are asked to
leave the bar. The next morning, Hand is found hanging from
the ceiling of his room at the Hotel Francfort, while Foote has

disappeared from Lisbon, a fact that—combined with the coincidence of their names—leads the novel's narrator, Fred Gentry of the American consulate, to suspect that they are spies. In the hope of exposing an espionage ring and thereby furthering his career, Gentry asks the famous Inspector Voss of the Paris *sûreté*—in Lisbon because his name has appeared on a Gestapo hit list—if he will assist in the investigation. Voss is reluctant, but he agrees when Gentry hints that the fate of his American visa hinges on his cooperation. The two now proceed to delve into the lives of Hand and Foote—and the deeper they delve, the more the evidence confounds them. Among other things, they find a diary written apparently in code; a dog-eared copy of *Clarissa* ("the last book you would expect a cutlery salesman to be reading"); a letter from a Fräulein Lipschitz offering Hand money to marry her and take her with him to New York; and some solitaire cards, one of which, the Queen of Diamonds, has a folded-back corner. But none of the pieces fit. The resolution of one mystery only opens up another. Most resist resolution altogether. "When everything might mean something else," Gentry remarks near the end, "how can one know if anything means anything?"

I take it for granted that Edward was responsible for that line. I also take it for granted that he was responsible for the solution to the crime, which, in the last pages, Inspector Voss reveals with stunning sangfroid. Hand and Foote are not spies. Instead they are exactly what they appear to be: salesmen. Not only that, the murder is exactly what it appears to be. Angry because Hand cheated him at cards, Foote strangled Hand—then tried to make the killing look like a suicide. In the end it is Gentry himself who is exposed as a fool: "Everything I thought I had discovered—the codebook, the book code, the letter, the card with the folded corner—was dust on a dry road, churned up by my own impatient feet." Nonetheless, he remains true to his word and obtains a visa for Inspector Voss, who, as the novel ends, is standing on the deck of the *Excambion*, watching the Portuguese coastline recede and wondering what the future holds—for him and for Europe . . .

Rather than offer a summary of Georgina's "memoir," which is unsummarizable, I think I will just copy out the pertinent chapter:

"Since leaving Paris, I had got used to running into the most unlikely people in the most unlikely places. I had seen the Grand Duchess of Luxembourg eating a sandwich whilst sitting cross-legged on a railway siding in Vilar Formoso and I had seen Elsa Schiaparelli washing her hair in the WC on the Sud Express. I had seen Julien Green praying in the old Cathedral in Lisbon and I had seen Madeleine Carroll pumping petrol in Spain. Old friends and new popped up again and again—now at the Portuguese consulate in Bayonne, now at the customs house in Fuentes d'Oñoro, now at the craps table in Estoril. Yet of all of them, the one I was most surprised to see was a niece of mine from New York with whom I had not spoken in many years. To protect what little remains of her reputation, I shall call her Alice.

"She was the youngest daughter of my first husband's sister, a girl of great beauty, but raised in the most old-fashioned household imaginable. Long before her birth, her parents had mapped out her future for her—that she would marry an eligible young man and bear him children. Yet from when she was a tiny child, it was evident that Alice had other intentions. It was evident in all she did: in the way she tore the bows from her hair and refused to eat her soup, in her preference for roughhousing with her brothers to playing dolls with her sisters, in her proud carriage and penchant for talking back. Even more distressing than these traits, for her mother, was the fondness the child showed toward *me*, that young lady of dubious provenance whom her brother had, in her view, shown such poor judgment in marrying! Nor was I indifferent to this niece who doted on my every word. On the contrary, I saw in Alice many aspects of myself at that age, and determined to provide for her what was never provided for me: the encouragement of an adult who truly understood her!

"Elsewhere I have told the story of how I came to Europe, that fatal voyage across the Atlantic for what I imagined would be a stay of six months—and turned out to be a stay of thirty years. I have not until now spoken of the effect that the news of my imminent departure had upon little Alice. To say that it propelled her into a condition of anguish would be an understatement. Distraught, she came to me and begged me to bring her along. As patiently as I could, I explained why this could not be, no matter how much I might wish it. And still she would not be placated—not until she had extracted from me a promise that I would arrange for her to visit me on her next school holiday. Together, I assured her, we would tour the great capitals, see the sights of Europe. Alas, little did we know what fate had in store for us—first my husband's untimely demise, and then the war . . .

"I can but imagine in what a condition of grief the discovery, a few months later, that our separation was to be prolonged, perhaps indefinitely, left my poor niece; the many tears of woe that she must have shed, even as her mother shed tears of joy. For there is no doubt that my sister-in-law, upon learning that—for a few years, at least—her child was to be freed from my malignant influence, could hardly contain her glee. Now, she must have thought, she would have *her* turn! At last she would set the girl on the proper course from which I had diverted her! Of course, what she failed to count on was the very thing on which all mothers, including my own, fail to count—namely, a resolute female's determination to have her own way.

"All through those years of the war, Alice and I remained in touch. In my letters to her I wrote of my busy life in Cannes and the war work I was doing. In hers she described her childish hopes, the French nobleman who, in her dreams, came trotting up to her on his white horse and swept her off her feet, to live with him happily ever after in his fairyland castle *en France*. And in these innocent fancies—unwisely, as it turned out—I encouraged her. For often it is from such girlish whimsies that the ambitions of bold women—journalists and writers and artistes—are stirred into being. Luckily I still had accounts at all the New York shops, and so was able, even from abroad, to keep Alice supplied with *petits cadeaux*: hats and gloves and all of Colette's Claudine novels in translation and a charming little set of Patience cards in an alligator-skin box . . .

"At last the war drew to its end. At the first opportunity, I sailed to New York, where to my dismay I discovered that, in my absence, Alice had grown into a young lady of great charm but little sense. For it seemed that, at her mother's urging, she had foolishly gone ahead and married the 'suitable' young man selected for her. Now, let me make it clear that there was absolutely nothing wrong with this young man—other than that he was deadly dull! If anything, the poor fellow appeared rather shell-shocked to have on his hands such a temperamental bride, when he had expected a girl like her sisters, drearily domestic creatures all. That said, he was a gallant, and willing to do what he could to win his wife's love. My own advice to Alice was to make the best of her lot. As I reminded her, my own first husband, her uncle—he, too, had begun life as a rather dull young man, and look what I had made of him! Under a clever woman's tutelage, even the least promising male can have a great career. Patience and cultivation are all that is required. But alas, patience was not one of my niece's virtues.

"From there, I am sorry to report, things only went downhill.

Through trusted friends I learned that, far from heeding my coun-
sel, Alice had flouted it. Casting her husband aside, she had entered
into an affair with a Frenchman of noble birth but ignoble character,
whose reputation for idleness and vice had yet to follow him across
the Atlantic. As soon as I heard this grim report, I summoned Alice
to my suite and warned her in no uncertain terms that she was making a grave error, that she must end the affair at once or risk being
engulfed in scandal. But she would hear none of it. For she was in
love, she declared, and intended shortly to leave her dull husband,
marry the wastrel, and return with him to Paris, there to commence
the *grand vie* for which, since her childhood, she had believed herself destined . . .

"O illusions! I wish I could have done something for Alice—but
it was too late. Willfulness, when not tempered by intelligence, is a
force that it is beyond the capacities of even the most persuasive
woman to suppress. No sooner had she left my suite than Alice hied
herself to her lover's rooms, where she threw herself at his feet
and declared her undying love for him. Now, if you are a French
nobleman with a bad reputation at home, it is one thing to amuse
yourself with a pretty young American girl, another to be pounced
upon by a vixen determined to trap you in matrimony. And so this
jeune homme did what any *jeune homme* in such circumstances would
do: contriving a specious family emergency, he hopped aboard
the first boat sailing out of New York Harbor. Only once he was
safely back in France did he write to inform poor Alice that, being
already engaged to a wealthy girl of the merchant classes whose
family wished to buy their way into the aristocracy, he could not
marry her, now or ever. To make matters worse, Alice had lately discovered she was 'in the family way.' Nor was her dull husband so dull
as not to realize that the child could not be his own. Enraged, he
demanded a divorce.

"And so the waves of scandal broke over my niece—and oh, how I felt for my poor sister-in-law at that moment! Yet when I paid a call on her to offer my companionship and to assure her of my eagerness to help her in any way I could, far from accepting my proffered sympathy, she pointed the finger of blame *at me*! Yes, *I* was responsible for Alice's rash actions! I had put 'ideas in her head'! Such an unjust accusation, coming from such a stupid creature, neither surprised nor shocked me, for by then I was already inured to that vilification that is the inevitable lot of any truly independent-minded woman. No, what really disappointed me was the discovery that Alice herself had taken up her mother's line, joining the legion of slanderers now accusing me of having led her astray. Insult I can tolerate with equanimity. Disloyalty wounds me to the quick.

"A few days later, wiser and sadder, I returned to France. Of Alice's subsequent fate I learned only secondhand, from trusted friends in New York. No sooner had her condition become visible than she was hustled off to the countryside, to one of those institutions where, for a dear price, dear girls such as Alice are unburdened of their unwanted cargo with maximum discretion. Meanwhile in New York, one of her sisters began going about with a pillow stuffed under her skirt. When the infant, a boy, was born, passing it off as the son of its aunt proved relatively easy, especially since Alice herself had no wish to lay claim to or even know the child, much less to publicize its origins. For a few years after her divorce, she cast about aimlessly, until at last she met a gullible if well-intentioned young man, a clerk, who fell in love with her and took her off to Paris, where until the second war she led some simulacrum of that life she had dreamed of since childhood.

"During the years that followed, only a few hundred miles separated me from my niece. Even so, I never once saw or spoke to her, though on numerous occasions she attempted to revive our old intimacy, sending me letters that I did not answer, or, when I was in Paris, leaving me messages at my hotel, which I did not return. This was not cruelty on my part so much as self-preservation. Much as I might wish the best for Alice, I could not tolerate her . . . My mistake, I see now, was to think that she had the goods to lead the life I longed for her to lead—that exciting life of the aviatrix, the brave lady lawyer, the *saloniste*—when really, like her mother, she was mediocrity through and through. In my own eagerness to nurture a young version of myself, I had given Alice more credit than she deserved.

"And then, in Lisbon, I stumbled upon her. It was at the very end of my sojourn there. Having had our fill of Estoril, Lucy and I had decamped to town, to the Hotel Berlino. One afternoon as I was crossing the lobby, I happened to observe two ladies in the early autumn of their lives sitting together near the bar. One I recognized immediately as Fleur, that scribbler of inconsequential murder novels whom I had befriended, along with her husband and *petit chien*, on the Sud Express. The face of the other was in shadow. While Fleur talked, this other played patience. Spurred on by that curiosity that is the writer's prerogative and bane, I took a step closer—and saw that the set of cards with which this game of patience was being played resided in an alligator-skin box. Could it be? Yes! The woman laying those cards out on the table was none other than Alice!

"I crept a few steps closer. Though time had stolen much of her freshness, as well as the charm that only hope for the future can keep alive, there was no mistaking that face that I had once cherished with maternal fondness. And at the realization that through all these long years, impatient Alice had held on to those patience cards, that gift I had sent her so casually, my heart skipped a beat. On impulse I spoke her name. She turned. I opened my arms to her—at which she uttered a little cry, leapt to her feet (in the process upending the table), and ran off up the stairs. 'Alice,' I cried again—at which Fleur, too, leapt up. On the carpet, along with glasses and cigarette ends, the little cards lay scattered. No words passed between Fleur and me. Instead, as if by instinct, we got on our knees and began gathering up the cards. Now, of course, I wonder why we chose to busy ourselves with this trifling task rather than chase after Alice. Was it because we both understood that the cards could be collected—as her wits never could be?

"Shortly thereafter Alice's husband, Bill, appeared on the scene. I had met him, too—with Fleur's husband, by coincidence. We explained to him quickly what had transpired, at which he expressed confusion: how could I be his wife's aunt, he asked, given my name?

"Not being inclined, right then, to share the elaborate tale of how I had come to acquire my *nom de plume*, I informed him that his wife had gone upstairs in something of a rush, and handed him the alligator-skin box, into which I had stuffed the cards willy-nilly . . . He took it from me, thanked me, and hurried off.

"Fleur and I talked for a few moments. Though she pressed me for details of my relations with Alice, however, I refused to divulge any but the most superficial information. (The first thing a scribbler learns is never to trust a member of his own tribe!) Subsequently she went off, looking vexed and bewildered. Lucy came down.

" 'Whatever is the matter?' she asked when she saw my crestfallen expression.

"I merely shook my head. 'A face from the past,' I said. 'Just another face from the past.'

"The next evening I returned from dinner to hear the news that a young lady, also a guest at my hotel, had thrown herself off the roof of the Santa Justa Elevator. I did not need to ask her name. I already knew."

26

I am not, I gather, a very good storyteller. At least that would be
the prognosis of Georgina Kendall. A few years ago, while sift-
ing through the old magazines that inevitably pile up in every doctor's waiting room, my wife came upon an issue of *Good Housekeeping*
in which there appeared an article by Georgina entitled "Ten Rules
the Novice Writer Should Follow." Being of an accommodating nature, and knowing that, since my retirement from Ford, I had been
contemplating writing a book of my own, my wife clipped the article
and gave it to me. If she recognized the author's name, or realized
the role that she had played in my life, she didn't say—though of
course not saying so would be just like her.

I didn't read the article. Instead I put it away in the drawer where
I kept all the other ephemera of my European past: the few photographs I had of Julia and the few letters Edward had written to me
over the years; my copies of *Flight from France* and the Legrand novels; the issue of *Vogue* in which our apartment was featured; and
then a miscellany of random objects, buttons and pencils and keys

and tie pins, the significance of which I could no longer recall, and that were somehow all the more poignant for their elusiveness. The book I had told my wife I wanted to write was to be an account of those few weeks I'd spent in Lisbon in the summer of 1940. For nearly a year I had been preparing myself to write it. I had virgin pads at the ready, sharpened pencils, a new portable typewriter. Yet until that evening, I hadn't put down so much as a word. Now I see that it was Georgina's article—not its contents so much as its sheer talismanic presence—that gave me the impetus to begin. For, starting on the evening that my wife presented it to me, I wrote steadily for six months, until I reached the chapter describing the visit I had made to the castle with Edward. And then I could not go on, though I didn't know why. I put the manuscript away in the drawer with the old letters and photographs and books and buttons and so on . . . for six months. And then, just the other day, on impulse, I opened the drawer again and took out—not the manuscript, but the article: "Ten Rules the Novice Writer Should Follow."

Georgina, I have you to thank for this work. It was the discovery that I had broken every one of your rules that impelled me to complete it.

To wit:

1. Never set scenes of dialogue in cafés. They provide insufficient business for the characters.
   (But where did we spend all our time in Lisbon if not cafés?)
2. Never leave loose plot threads.
   (But what of the way war tears stories into shreds?)
3. Never introduce a character whom you don't plan to bring back later.
   (I never did learn what became of the Fischbeins.)

4. Keep the competition in mind.
   (Following a brief surge of popularity in the mid-forties, Xavier Legrand's novels lapsed into desuetude.)
5. Remember that an unhappy ending is more likely to lead to big sales than a happy one.
   (But my story did have a happy ending.)
6. Make sure that the motive for a character's action is clear enough that a reader can explain it easily to a friend.
   (I still don't know why Julia killed herself.)
7. Don't strain credulity.
   (The majority of the crew members aboard the *Manhattan* were German-born, anti-Semitic, and supporters of the Axis. The ship's newsletter could have been written by Ribbentrop himself.)
8. Never allow a first-person narrator to step outside his range of observation.
   (Where does one draw the line between observation and dream?)
9. Don't rely on coincidence.
   (Who would have believed it, Georgina? You really were Aunt Rosalie.)
10. Never let facts get in the way.
    (How the facts got in the way—that is the story I am trying to tell.)

27

S till, I suppose I am duty-bound to report what happened to everyone.

Three weeks after the *Manhattan* docked, Daisy died. Iris and Edward embarked on their lecture tour, but halfway through—in Terre Haute, I believe—Iris left him. Eventually she married a French-born jeweler and launched a literary career on her own. In this she has earned some distinction.

To this day, Edward lives—alone, so far as I am aware—on the Upper West Side of Manhattan. I have no idea what he does or how he earns his keep.

Julia's son—again, so far as I am aware—still believes himself to be his late mother's nephew. He is a lawyer with an office on Wall Street. He is married. He has three children.

Edward and Iris's daughter continues to reside in the Theosophist community that her grandmother founded. She is not feeble-minded. She is autistic. (When she was a small child, the syndrome had not yet been identified.)

Last year, Georgina Kendall published her fifty-seventh book. Salazar remains prime minister of Portugal.

Two months ago, in the window of a shop on Madison Avenue, I caught sight of the leather desk from our apartment in Paris. The asking price was four thousand dollars.

28

Exactly why so many Europeans showed up at Alcântara that day, when they knew perfectly well that they would never be let on board the ship, I could not fathom. Hope born out of desperation, I suppose. In any case, those of us with tickets had no choice but to push our way through the crowd that had massed on the dock, the men and women and children clustered amid piles of luggage that in a few hours they would just have to haul back to the station, or to the pensions at which they were putting up. Three porters led our group. Each carried four suitcases tied to the ends of a cord strung around his neck. More suitcases and trunks were piled on wooden carts, which they maneuvered with surprising agility, considering how encumbered they were and how much resistance they met. Without those porters, I don't know that we ever would have made it aboard.

"Whatever has become of Lucy?" Georgina asked. "I hope that stupid girl hasn't forgotten what time we sail."

"I'm sure she'll be along," Edward said. He held Daisy in his arms. Through clouded eyes, she gazed over his shoulder at the city she was leaving forever, her expression impassive, as if not even the stench of all those close-packed bodies was enough to stimulate her curiosity. And this from a dog whose entire life had been devoted to the most vigilant attention! For over the course of the previous few days, the senescence Daisy had warded off for years seemed to have ambushed her, and with a suddenness that would have been terrifying had fear not been one of the many forces it had blunted. How much she understood—how much she had ever understood—was a mystery. But I think she understood more than Edward and Iris gave her credit for.

Nearer to the ship, the crowd grew denser. I thought I caught a glimpse of Messalina's face. Then it was gone. We kept pushing, until at last we reached the rope barrier that the police had erected. A hundred feet on, the *Manhattan*'s hull loomed, black and gleaming like a whale's skin.

"It was two years ago that I last sailed on the *Manhattan*," Georgina said, as if into a tape recorder. "Not a bad ship, though if you ask me, the Colonial American theme is laid on rather thick. Those murals in the dining room! Frightful." She handed her passport to the inspector, who waved her through. He waved us all through— except for Iris, since her passport was British and the inspector wanted proof that she and Edward were married, which led to a long argument that Edward eventually won by asking the inspector if he made it his habit to carry his marriage certificate in his pocket. "The scrutiny to which our English friend was subjected eliminated any doubts I harbored about the seriousness of my government's policy," Georgina said into her interior tape recorder, leading me to reflect that one of the easier things about her company was that she didn't really care if you listened to her or not. Since Julia's suicide, she had attached herself to us with an avidity that was all the more puzzling for its apparent guilelessness. Every morning at breakfast, there she was at my table. Every evening at dinner, there she was at the restaurant. We never invited her. She just showed up. Nor did we really mind her garrulous presence, since it relieved us of the necessity to talk to one another . . . Entirely on her own initiative, and in her capacity as Julia's aunt, Georgina had taken charge of the business side of the suicide, dealing efficiently with the police and the consulate and the various other governmental bodies by which my poor wife's death had to be certified, notarized, validated, verified, and generally officialized. Thanks to her, this process, which might have dragged on for months, was wrapped up in forty-eight hours.

A strange listlessness marked our last days in Lisbon, as if, after weeks of swimming against the current, we had suddenly been dropped into one of those warm saltwater pools that speckle the Portuguese coast, and to which invalids repair for therapeutic purposes. What was this city to us, after all? A landing stage, a holding pattern, a way station. All we had done here was wait. At first we had fought the waiting. Then we had gotten used to it. And now it was coming to an end—and I didn't want it to. Each morning I woke wishing for bad weather, a storm—anything that might delay the *Manhattan*'s departure. For with Julia's death, the tension had drained out of the days, leaving behind a malaise that was almost pleasant. No longer did I feel any urge to reach under the table to touch Edward's leg, though curiously he was forever reaching under the table to touch mine, kneading my knee with a relentless and clumsy persistence that elicited in me only weariness and numbness. Nor did Iris stare daggers at him when his hand disappeared under the table. Instead she sat slack-jawed, her chin in her hand, listening as Georgina went on about everything under the sun, since now no subject was verboten—not Julia's early life, not the child she had

had before she met me, not even the mystery of the suicide itself, which in Georgina's view was no mystery at all. "My niece couldn't bear the thought of your finding out she'd lied to you about the boy," she said in the matter-of-fact voice of a detective wrapping up a case. "That was why she was so adamant about not going back to New York—because in New York you might run into someone who'd let something slip." At the time, I didn't have the wherewithal to do more than absorb this theory. Since then, I have thought about it quite a bit, and come to the conclusion that it doesn't hold water. For Julia knew me better than anyone in the world—and so she would have known that, upon learning that she had a son, I would not have threatened to divorce her or kill her. Rather, I would have taken her in my arms, wiped away her tears, perhaps encouraged her to seek the boy out, to try to establish some sort of relations with him—which, for her, would have been far more terrible than any threat. For so long as an ocean separated Julia from her child, her guilt was just barely endurable. But if she were to find herself in a position to hear news, see pictures—God forbid be introduced to him—some unsuspected maternal impulse might arise in her, and her own remorse would flay her alive.

I don't recall, in those last days, feeling much in the way of grief over Julia's death. I really don't recall feeling much in the way of anything—except self-reproach. For she had told me, time and again, that she would sooner die than return to New York—and I had never taken her at her word. Yet was even her word sufficient explanation? I don't believe you can ever really explain a suicide. Had Julia done it to hurt me or her family? To spare herself humiliation? To bring an end to unendurable pain? Or was she taking, to borrow Xavier Legrand's title, "the noble way out," removing herself from the picture for my sake, or for her son's? I still don't know. Nor, in those last days in Lisbon, was I in any condition to reflect.

There was too much to do. Among other things, the hotel bill still had to be paid. To raise the cash, I sold some of Julia's jewelry. I didn't sell the car. I had an idea that I might give it to Dr. Gray and her husband. But the one time I ran into Dr. Gray, in the lobby of the Francfort, she yanked me aside and interrogated me about my own condition with such an intensity of concern that I didn't even have the chance to broach the subject of the car. "You must take care of yourself," she said, holding my hand in hers. "Are you remembering to eat? Try not to drink if you can. The relief will only be temporary and you'll feel worse afterward. The same with the Seconal. Flush it down the toilet."

"How funny. I'd completely forgotten about the Seconal."

"Forgive me for asking, but did she leave a note? Your wife?"

I shook my head. "She never said a word. If anything, that last day she was unusually quiet."

"Then there was nothing you could have done. Her mind was made up." Dr. Gray squeezed my hand. "Well, if you need anything, you know where to find me. Room 111. Any hour of the night or day."

29

As soon as we crossed the rope barrier, the temperature dropped five degrees. The concrete was no longer so hard under my feet. It made me remember Edward's story about the walk into Portugal from Spain, how the rain stopped the instant he and Iris stepped over the frontier. And just as, at that instant, Spain and all its privations seemed to evaporate, so now the crowd behind us, its fear and frustration, seemed to recede into some impossibly remote distance. Silently our little group processed up the gangplank, at the top of which the purser awaited us with a clipboard. His German accent was unmistakable.

"The kennel is on B deck," he said to Edward as he checked off our names on the manifest.

"What?" Edward said. "Oh, you mean Daisy? That's all right, we'd just as soon keep her in the cabin with us."

"I'm sorry, sir, but ship regulations require all dogs to be housed in the kennel."

"But she's fifteen years old," Iris said. "She's never been in a kennel in her life. Surely you can make an exception."

"No exceptions will be made, Madame."

"But that's outrageous! I won't accept it!" As if to prove her point, Iris grabbed Daisy out of Edward's arms and clutched her to her breast. "I can't believe that on an American ship, an American citizen can't keep his dog in his own cabin. I want to speak to the captain. And I'd like your name, sir."

"You may speak to the captain if you wish. But he will tell you the same."

"I'm not about to be told what to do by a German—"

"I am an American citizen, Madame. Unlike you."

Georgina pulled us aside. "I've just been speaking to that lady over there—she understands German—and she tells me the whole crew is German. Well, German-born. She says she overheard some of the stewards talking just now, and one of them was saying that in a year we'd be watching the Führer march down Fifth Avenue in a ticker-tape parade. Can you believe it?"

"I don't care what anyone says," Iris said. "I haven't abandoned Daisy yet and I'm not about to abandon her now. If it comes to it, I'll sleep in the kennel."

"Please," I said, and touched her shoulder—at which she jerked away. "Just hold on a minute. Let me see if I can do something."

With that I went off, and found a steward who did not have a German accent, and got from him directions to the kennel. "You catch more flies with honey than with vinegar": this advice—from my grandmother, of all people—has served me in good stead throughout my business career. Certainly it did on this occasion. For as it turned out, the kennel master was a fellow Hoosier, a kindly old gent with a face like a blancmange, from whom I was able to obtain in about five minutes the exception to the rule that the Frelengs could never have obtained for themselves in a million years. And this was simply because they were the sort that believes that the way to get results is to go over people's heads. Yet I ask you, how many heads can you go over before you reach the head over which there are no other heads? Any salesman will tell you that in threatening to go over someone's head, all you do is raise the price on yourself. What we lose in dignity we make up for in commission.

Ten minutes later it was done. "It's all arranged," I said to Edward. "You can keep her in the cabin."

He smiled. "And how did you manage that?"

"It doesn't matter," I said. For I was in no mood to gloat, nor did I much care that my success had brought this glow of admiration to Edward's eyes and, to Iris's, this look of unalloyed hatred—as if, in doing her a kindness, I was thrusting the knife one last time into her back. After all, I was the last person in the world to whom she wanted to be beholden. The truth, in any case, was that I hadn't done it for her, much less for Edward. I had done it for Daisy.

Iris turned away from me. "I'm going to the cabin," she said to Edward.

"I'll be along in a few minutes," he replied.

Without even a nod, she left. Georgina had wandered over to the railing to watch for Lucy. For the first time since the castle, Edward and I were alone.

He came and stood close to me. "I told you that you were brave."

"Brave? All I did was bribe an old man."

"I don't mean that. I mean the way you've conducted yourself these last few days."

"I don't see that I had many alternatives, other than to do myself in too."

"But you'd never have done that. You said so."

"So I did."

"You know, in some ways I hold myself responsible for Julia's death."

"Why? As it turned out, it had nothing to do with you."

"I realize that. But you see, she and I were so similar. And so I wonder if I should have recognized how desperate her situation was. Then I might have stopped her."

"But Iris stopped you—and you only resented her for it . . . Anyway, it wouldn't have made a difference. Julia didn't like you. She said you were a know-it-all."

"You see? She did understand me."

"And she was dead-set on doing it—if you'll pardon the pun. Do you know what the Elevator operator told us? That she dove. Head first. So that was one piece of advice from Iris she took to heart."

A foghorn blew. "How many minutes until we sail?" Edward asked.

"I have no idea," I said. "I don't know what those foghorn signals mean."

He edged closer. "Pete . . . I hope that—well, that it's not all over between us. That we can be friends." Now he was standing so close to me that I could feel his breath on my cheek. "Friends—an ambiguous word, I know . . ." And I thought, For the next week I'll have a cabin to myself. At last we'll have the chance to do what we've wanted from the beginning: to spend a whole night together—and not have to get up in the morning. Only now I wasn't sure that I wanted to spend a whole night with Edward, much less sleep in with him. For the fact was, I was tired of sleeping in. I was ready to start waking up early.

I stepped away and looked at my watch. "I'd better be going," I said.

"Of course . . . We'll see you at dinner, I trust?"

"I don't know. I'm tired. I might eat in my cabin."

"Oh, don't do that. Not the first night out."

"We'll see."

"Pete . . . I hope . . . No, never mind." Yet even as he said "never mind," I knew that what he hoped was that I would ask him what he hoped. And I didn't. Once he had told me that he didn't fear the future, only the past. Whereas what I feared, I saw now, was the present, its endless prolongation, hour to hour, week to week, year to year. A landing stage, a holding pattern, a way station.

We shook hands then, and he left. I watched his broad back disappear from view. I never saw him again.

30

What happened next—that, I suppose, is the story Georgina would tell me to tell: how on the spur of the moment, I asked a steward to gather together my luggage; how without looking over my shoulder, I descended the gangplank of the *Manhattan*; how I returned to the Hotel Francfort, and knocked on the door to room 111, and offered Dr. Gray not just my car but my services as a driver . . . And then how, for the next two years, with the Grays as my partners and Marseille as my base, I ferried refugees over the Pyrenees, in my faithful Buick, in the middle of the night . . . until the Germans occupied the unoccupied zone and we had to flee, once again, to Lisbon. But I'm not going to tell that story, because it's already been told many times, and anyway I didn't do anything that someone else couldn't have done. Besides, I despise books in which all the interest lies in the fame of the people the narrator runs into, or serves, or saves. Leave that crap to Georgina. I don't have the patience for it anymore.

What I do want to write about is this: what the Grays' room

looked like that afternoon, with the curtains filtering the late-afternoon sunlight so that it softened the harsh geometry of the floor. On the dressing table, bottles of gin and vermouth, not jars of unguents and creams, were ranged. Where solitaire cards should have been spread, newspapers rested in neat piles. Quietly Cornelia—she now insisted that I call her Cornelia—did a cross-word. "Why don't you take off your shoes and lie down?" she said, and I said that, yes, that sounded like a good idea; and I did lie down, atop that bed that she shared with her husband, and fell more deeply asleep than I had in weeks, waking only around six in the evening to realize that the *Manhattan* was now at sea. Then I looked up at Cornelia, and she was still sitting in the chair in front of the dressing table, doing her crossword, and for an instant it was as if the future were casting its shadow over the present, or a train had arrived at its destination, though it hadn't yet left; and in that moment, I swear, I could see everything that was going to happen next: that in my future there would be more infidelity, another marriage broken up, though not my own; and I regretted that Julia, with the intuition of the betrayed, should have seen what was com-ing even before I did. And I wished that her last weeks on earth could have been happier ones.

"How are you feeling?" Cornelia said.

"Better, thanks." I sat up, touched my feet to the floor. "Oh, I forgot to tell you—when I took the taxi here, something funny happened. I said 'Hotel Francfort,' and the driver took me to the Francfort Hotel."

"What? I thought this was the Francfort Hotel."

"You mean you don't know?"

"Know what?" My wife has always been a woman who dislikes not knowing things. And so I told her what Edward had told me the morning I met him, the story of how the hotels had come to have the same name—but I told it as if I had come upon it all firsthand, as if he had played no part in any of it, not even the witticism that he attributed to the refugees themselves, though in fact I had never heard it out of any mouth but his: "Just think, here we are fleeing the Germans, and we end up at a hotel called Francfort!"

Acknowledgments and Sources

In researching *The Two Hotel Francforts*, I drew on many sources and benefited from the help of many friends, scholars, and experts. In particular I am indebted to Mitchell Owens, Irene Flunser Pimentel, and the late Sally Broido for their generosity of wisdom and knowledge. I am also indebted to Jill Ciment and Mark Mitchell for their astute readings of the manuscript.

Some of the scholarly works that I read—and learned much from—were Hanna Diamond's *Fleeing Hitler: France 1940* (Oxford University Press, 2007); Ghanda diFiglia's *Roots and Visions: The First Fifty Years of the Unitarian Universalist Service Committee* (UUSC, 1990); Neill Lochery's *Lisbon: War in the Shadows of the City of Light, 1939–1945* (PublicAffairs, 2011); Jeffrey Mehlman's *Émigré New York: French Intellectuals in Wartime Manhattan, 1940–1944* (Johns Hopkins University Press, 2000); Ellen W. Sapega's *Consensus and Debate in Salazar's Portugal* (Penn State University Press, 2008); Frederic Spotts's *The Shameful Peace: How French Artists and Intellectuals Survived the Nazi Occupation* (Yale University Press, 2008); Susan Elisabeth Subak's *Rescue and Flight: American Relief Workers Who Defied the Nazis* (University of Nebraska Press, 2010); Ronald Weber's *The Lisbon Route: Entry and Escape in Nazi Europe* (Ivan R. Dee, 2011); and, most important, Irene Flunser Pimentel's *Judeus em Portugal durante a II Guerra Mundial* (A Esfera dos Livros, 2006).

It was, in many cases, the books mentioned above that led me to the primary sources—memoirs, diaries, articles, letters, and novels—from which I gleaned much of what I know about Lisbon in the summer of 1940. These included Jack Alexander's "The Nazi Offensive in Lisbon" (*The Saturday Evening Post*, March 6, 1943); Eugene Bagger's *For the Heathen Are Wrong* (Little, Brown, 1941) (like Edward and Iris Freleng, Bagger and his wife traveled to New York via Lisbon in the company of an elderly wire fox terrier; their book is also the source for the story of the woman trapped on the International Bridge); Suzanne Blum's *Vivre sans la patrie: 1940–1945* (Plon, 1975) (though Blum was in Lisbon at the same time as the Duchess of Windsor, with whom her life would become inextricably and scandalously bound, they did not meet there); Ronald Bodley's *Flight into Portugal* (Jarrolds, 1941); Sylvain Bromberger's "Memoirs of a 1940 Family Flight from Antwerp, Belgium" (*Portuguese Studies Review*, Volume 4, Issue 1, 1995); Suzanne Chantal's *Dieu ne dort pas* (Plon, 1946); Alfred Döblin's *Destiny's Journey: Flight from the Nazis* (Paragon House, 1992); Rupert Downing's *If I Laugh* (Harrap, 1943); Julien Green's *La fin d'un monde: Juin 1940* (Editions du Seuil, 1992) (it is to Jean-Michel Frank that Green attributes the bon mot with which this novel concludes); Peggy Guggenheim's *Out of This Century* (Dial Press, 1946); A. J. Liebling's *World War II Writings* (Library of America, 2008); Harvey Klemmer's "Lisbon—Gateway to Warring Europe" (*National Geographic*, August 1941); Lucie Matuzewitz's *Le cactus et l'ombrelle* (Guy Authier, 1977); Alice-Leone Moats's *No Passport for Paris* (Putnam, 1945); Lars Moen's *Under the Iron Heel* (Lippincott, 1941); Hugh Muir's *European Junction* (Harrap, 1942); Polly Peabody's *Occupied Territory* (Cresset, 1941); Denis de Rougemont's *Journal d'une époque: 1926–1946* (Gallimard, 1968) (Rougemont is the source for the joke about the Four Aces carrying ex-Europeans into exile); Maurice Sachs's *The Hunt* (Stein and Day, 1965); Antoine de

Saint-Exupéry's *Wartime Writings: 1939–1944* (Harcourt, 1986); Elsa Schiaparelli's *Shocking Life* (Dent, 1954); Joseph Shadur's *A Drive to Survival: Belgium, France, Spain, Portugal 1940* (Kenneth Schoan, 1999); Sir Edward Spears's *Assignment to Catastrophe* (A. A. Wyn, 1954 and 1955); Tom Treanor's "Lisbon Fiddles . . ." (*Vogue*, October 1940) and "What Comes After War," a series of dispatches filed for the *Los Angeles Times* in August and September 1940; and Alexander Werth's *The Last Days of Paris* (Hamish Hamilton, 1940).

I am grateful to the University of Florida for providing me with a sabbatical leave and research support during the writing of this novel; to Michael Fishwick and Anton Mueller of Bloomsbury; to Jin Auh, Tracy Bohan, Jacqueline Ko, and Andrew Wylie of the Wylie Agency; to Jamie Fisher for giving me the line about the water bug landing on a lake; to Will Palmer for his excellent editing; and to the staffs of the Biblioteca Central de Marinha (Lisbon), the Bibliothèque National de France, the Condé Nast Library, the Hemeroteca Municipal de Lisboa, the New York Historical Society, the New York Public Library, the Rockefeller Archive Center, and the University of Florida, in particular the extraordinary John Van Hook.

Unlike Pete Winters, I have occasionally, in these pages, followed Georgina Kendall's advice and ignored facts that interfered with the story. For instance, it is not certain that in 1940 there were as yet peacocks roaming the grounds of the Castelo de São Jorge in Lisbon. For this and any other betrayals of history, local color, and common sense, I take full credit and blame.

A Note on the Author

David Leavitt's books include the story collection *Family Dancing* (finalist for the PEN/Faulkner Award and the National Book Critics Circle Award) and the novels *The Lost Language of Cranes*, *While England Sleeps* (finalist for the Los Angeles Times Fiction Award), *The Body of Jonah Boyd*, and *The Indian Clerk* (finalist for the PEN/Faulkner Award and shortlisted for the IMPAC Dublin Literary Award). He is also the author of two nonfiction works, *The Man Who Knew Too Much: Alan Turing and the Invention of the Computer* and *Florence, A Delicate Case*. His writing has appeared in the *New Yorker*, the *New York Times*, the *Washington Post*, *Harper's*, *Vogue*, and *The Paris Review*, among other publications. He lives in Gainesville, Florida, where he is professor of English at the University of Florida and edits the literary magazine *Subtropics*.